Storms in the Cotswolds

THE BRITISH BOOK TOUR MYSTERIES | BOOK 6

EMMA DAKIN

CAMEL
PRESS

Seattle, WA

A Camel Press book published by Epicenter Press

Epicenter Press
6524 NE 181st St. Suite 2
Kenmore, WA 98028.
For more information go to:
www.Camelpress.com
www.Coffeetownpress.com
www.Epicenterpress.com

Author website: www.emmadakinauthor.com

This is a work of fiction. Names, characters, places,
brands, media, and incidents are the product of the
author's imagination or are used fictitiously.

Cover art by Teresa Hanson
Design by Rudy Ramos

Storms in the Cotswolds
Copyright © 2024 by Marion Crook

ISBN: 9781684921812 (trade paper)
ISBN: 9781684921829 (ebook)

LOC: 2023951889

Printed in the United States of America

DEDICATION

To Jill and Janice, my Beta readers. You give me good advice.
And to the enthusiastic readers of the previous books who
anticipate the next in the series. You keep me writing.

ACKNOWLEDGEMENTS

My thanks Chris Reid formerly of the Metropolitan police for his advice and his vast knowledge of the Cotswolds. As well, I was warmed by the encouragement of Ann and Tom Hatley and to the kind people of Cirencester who helped with my research and showed me what it was like to live there: Belinda Bertie, the two singers at Cirencester Cathedral, Joelle at Abby Park, Willie and Margaret McIvor, and Margaret and Caroline on the bus. I am indebted to the many helpful people who trundled my suitcase up stairs, held open doors for me and stopped to say "Do you need a hand, mother?" You allowed me to travel, research and write in comfort.

CHAPTER ONE

"You have days off?" I asked Mark. He was happily ensconced in the wing chair in front of the flickering fire, the newspaper spread wide over his lap. The paper was open to the rugger results. Gulliver, my spaniel, peered at the print as if taking an intelligent interest in the scores. You'd think Mark had been deprived of oxygen for all those months during the pandemic when the Cardiff Blues couldn't compete.

"You have to understand, Claire. They can't travel. They're going to miss the South African match!" he'd told me, looking shattered. He'd lived in England for over twenty years, but Wales held his heart.

It's a game, I'd wanted to remind him but had more sense than to say that aloud.

He was breathing deeply of sport news now, with England versus Wales engrossing him. He even managed to pick up a daily dose of football news. Apparently, Tottenham was going to make an offer to a Swansea City team. Mark wasn't vitally interested in football; rugby was his passion. I was beginning to accept his avid interest in sports and enjoyed watching some games, but I was unlikely to work out the complicated twelve-tiered football league system sports fans seemed to learn at birth or even the comparatively simple rugby organization. *Face it, Claire. You're not interested.* I was fascinated by my new husband, but not his sports interests.

"Two completely free days," Mark said with satisfaction, just as his mobile rang.

Gulliver lifted his head and looked at Mark's mobile. I raised my eyebrows. I was sure the gods had been listening—and laughing. I expected those "two free days" were going to disappear like a comforting dream. We juggled our lives, sometimes with complicated arrangements to find time together. Mark was assigned to what he called "police boards" which were a rotation of scheduled work days, but he seldom followed the schedule. Interruptions were usual. It made for an unpredictable life

He frowned at the number then hit the 'connect' icon. "D.I. Evans here."

It would be his boss Superintendent Marjorie Addison, an efficient manager, but in my opinion a failed human being. No sense of humor.

"Yes, ma'am. What's the address?" He picked up a pen from the table beside him and jotted the directions on the newspaper. "How many? What's the charge?"

He was silent as he waited for her instructions.

I glanced over the lounge. The Georgian fireplace added an elegance to a comfortable but ordinary square room you might find in any nineteenth century modest house. I stretched out my legs and wiggled my toes, giving a sigh of satisfaction. Me, Claire Barclay, living in a centuries-old house? Marvelous. The slate floor beneath my feet was a treasure, old and dark. The garnet rug covering the area in front of the fireplace added a warm ambiance to the room. A picture of the San Juan Islands hung on the wall behind Mark's chair. I contemplated the lush scenery and wandered in my mind to my days working in Seattle where everything seemed big, wild and energetic. Washington State was beautiful, but I didn't belong there. It was good to be back in England, and in Hampshire.

My tour business had been going well before the pandemic and was starting to pick up now that foreigners could travel. I could again take tourists to sites of mystery novels. I loved my work and was surprised to find I was happy being married as well. I thought Mark was happy, too, but at the moment, he was scowling. After he had disengaged, he checked the time on his mobile.

"Superintendent Addison?" I diagnosed.

He grunted. "I have to go to Southampton."

"When?"

"Soon."

"Oh." I sighed, but I was resigned. Responsible response was expected in Mark's job as a Detective Inspector assigned to the Major Crimes Investigation Team. He had three degrees of that response: instant, soon and later.

Mark hit a speed dial number and spoke firmly. "Sorry, Andy. We're scheduled at the docks in Southampton at 1600." Andy Forsyth, his detective sergeant, had planned a few days off to play with his two young sons. Now, he'd have a couple of hours before leaving.

Mark listened for a moment, then said. "I know. Illegal immigrants. Packed in a crate…Yes, bring the kit."

The regulation kit assigned to detectives contained a first aid box, pepper spray, a taser, handcuffs, recorder, collapsible baton and camera. Mark had added a naloxone kit, paper towels, plastic gloves, face masks, spare pens and likely more since I'd last looked at it. Andy had a similar kit. I also had a kit for emergencies—minus the baton, handcuffs and taser.

Mark ended the call. He ripped his notes from the newspaper and stuffed them into his back pocket. He'd transcribe them onto his tablet eventually. He folded the newspaper and put it on the table beside him, giving it a regretful look. Gulliver stirred, then settled back beside him.

"Sounds ugly," I said.

"Customs found a load of fifty people in a large packing crate smuggled in from Turkey."

"Isn't Turkey an EU partner, or was an EU partner? Couldn't the people come across without a visa?" I thought about Brexit and the changes leaving the EU might have caused.

"I don't suppose it's a government sponsored tour. Probably some private, greedy, nameless bloke running a business. Probably starving himself. It's *digywilydd*."

"In English?" Most Welsh is still unintelligible to me.

He hesitated, then translated, "Shameless."

"So, not political."

"Everything's political these days!" Twenty-five years of working in the constabulary had given Mark a decidedly cynical view of the decision-making process in our justice system.

"And why do they want you? It's not murder."

"It *is* murder. Two people in that crate are dead. There's going to be an investigation. There was a baby in that crate."

A baby! Why bring a baby? Then I felt foolish. When fleeing from a wretched situation, people brought the things that mattered most to them, including their children. What were they supposed to do? Abandon them on the beach while they sailed away?

"Did it die?" I wanted to know the terrible details first, so I wasn't looking for another horror down the road. I could process it, imagine it as I always did, then set it aside as a problem for Mark.

"No, but two other poor sods did."

I was sorry for the adults, but the thought of the baby tugged at my heart. A baby? Her parents must have thought she'd have a better chance in a crate to England than where she was. I don't why I thought the baby was a girl, but I did, seeing pink onesies and a head band in my mind. "Horrible."

"Right." His face flushed. I knew he hated facing the despair he was going to see on the faces of those illegal immigrants. They would have to go back.

We stared at each other. I was often surprised at how much he cared about justice. After all these years in the police force where he often saw injustice, he still cared. There wasn't much I could do for him on that score. Justice was a slippery concept and an imperfect practice. This case stirred him deeply. I thought aloud. "People are so desperate. They'll take chances and those traffickers exploit them."

He nodded. "Bloody wicked."

He carefully dislodged Gulliver who looked surprised at being dumped on the floor and trotted over to me to complain.

"What are your plans for today?" Mark asked, changing the subject. Her couldn't do anything for the immigrants until he had more information. He was used to his life being disrupted and I admired the way he dealt with his chaotic work life, but I wanted to keep my own life predictable.

I petted Gulliver. "I'm picking up overseas guests from Heathrow: a couple from Montana, three Canadians—one from Vancouver, two from Nova Scotia—and a couple from Cornwall. Most of them will be at Heathrow, but I'll get the Cornwall tourists from the train station in Basingstoke." My tour business with guests who were usually well-read, polite and looking for pleasure was the antithesis of the people in Mark's working world.

"After that, you're busy for a fortnight?" Mark smiled at me. His smile is rare. It isn't the quick grin of a handsome man who wants to share a moment with you. It's the slow smile of a good man who has honest feelings that seep into that smile. It warms my heart every time. Not that he's placid. Those snapping dark eyes can convey an edginess when he's on high alert, which wasn't now. Now, he was relaxed and wanted to know where I was going and when I'd be back. He said he liked to think about what I was seeing and doing while we were apart.

"Yes. Two days here in Ashton then the rest of the time in Cirencester. I'll leave an itinerary for you."

"Sorry about abandoning Gulliver." He'd planned to stay home and care for Gulliver. I always had a back-up strategy, though. His job made him an unreliable dog sitter.

I shrugged. I was used to it. "Did you get your letter?"

"What letter?"

"I put it on hall table. It came in today's post."

He fetched the letter and settled back in his chair. He had a little more time before he had to leave. Gulliver immediately jumped up beside him. I studied my tour itinerary and left him to his reading.

He smiled. "Uncle Lionel." Uncle Lionel was his mother's sister's husband. His aunt, Addie, had died two years ago, only a year after Lionel had retired from the Truro constabulary. They had bought a sea side house with a cottage in St. Mawes years ago with the view of living there in their senior years. Aunt Addie had retired from her nursing position first and had spent a great deal of time renovating and decorating the new house. They'd even repaired and renovated the small cottage on the property they were going to let as an income stream when Uncle Lionel retired. Mark and I had stayed there for a weekend once. It was beautiful.

"He's been lonely down there, I think," Mark said.

"Didn't he rent out the big house and move into the cottage?"

"Yes. He said he didn't want to keep up all the garden and let it to people who would look after the front half. It's a good setup for him. He can walk to restaurants or chip shops if he wants. He's taken up birding."

I smiled, thinking of that stocky, tough old sergeant tracking birds.

Mark returned to his letter. "He's asking for something. That's rare."

"What does he want?"

"He is, at the moment, at a hotel in Cirencester. That's where you're going, isn't it?"

I'd just told him that. "Which hotel is Lionel visiting?"

"The Queen Bess."

"That *is* where we're going."

"He says he has a friend, Bran..... I can't read the last name who is on your tour to the Cotswolds."

"Bligh," I said. "Bran and Eseld Bligh."

"The fellow's also retired from the local station and taken up birding. Uncle Lionel wants to know if he can join your tour. He'll pay the fee. He says he has already stayed for a week at the Queen Bess Hotel and would be glad of new company."

I pictured the van I'd be driving. I had one empty space. "I can do it," I said. "He's already booked the hotel, so he can just join us when we get there."

"He'd like to pay you something. He has his pension and the proceeds of the sale of their house in Truro and some insurance from Auntie Addie, so he can afford it."

"All right. I'll charge him a little then, to cover the cost of any meals or admissions to events." A tour guide was used to changes. The odd thing was that, although I quickly changed plans for my guests, I didn't like change in my personal life. There, I wanted predictability.

Mark smiled at me." Thanks."

I thought about Uncle Lionel's old-fashioned approach. He wrote Mark to ask me if he could join my tour. It would be pushy to ask me outright, at least in Uncle Lionel's eyes. This way, if I didn't want him on the tour, I could tell Mark and Mark could tell him of my refusal— diplomatically. It seemed convoluted to me, but the Cornish have their own social rules.

I mentally reviewed the coming itinerary. "He's already at the Queen Bess?"

"Yes. I think he's dealing with the loneliness by staying someplace new for a time, A few weeks at a hotel gives him some meals and some company. It is in the center of a town where he can easily walk to the restaurants. I think he misses Aunt Addie—and her cooking."

He petted Gulliver then carefully decanted him onto the floor. "I'm sorry I can't look after the mutt."

Gulliver, who is no mutt but a pedigreed Cavalier King Charles Spaniel, looked his reproach at Mark and ambled over to me. I patted my knee. He jumped up and curled onto my lap, all silky hair and warm love.

Mark headed for the stairs. He would pack a bag with enough clothes for a couple of nights in case he couldn't leave the job. Southampton wasn't far, about forty-five minutes, so he might come home. I heard his feet thumping up the stairs.

Gulliver cocked his head. I explained.

"Face facts, my charmer. You're being abandoned. Mark won't be home to look after you. Who can take you?" His huge brown eyes stared at me as if he understood the question. I would probably love Gulliver if he were ugly, but he isn't. He's beautiful with the sable coat of a true Cavalier with enough white interspersed through the browns and blacks to make him distinguished and distinctive. "Who will take you, my sweetie?"

"Rose!" shouted Mark, answering for Gulliver. My sister Deirdre and her family were Gulliver's usual sitters but they were off visiting her in-laws and wouldn't be back to their home in Guilford for four days. This was going to get complicated.

"Right." I'd already asked Rose if she could keep Gulliver until Deirdre could pick him up. With Mark's erratic work hours I thought I might need her.

A tour guide is supposed to be an expert at adjusting to change. After all, people make demands I can't always anticipate, and I have to make sure they're happy. I was accustomed to chopping and changing, sorting and getting sorted and accommodating fussy and sometimes eccentric tourists. For the most part, Mark and I managed a fairly regulated life, but neither the criminals nor his boss considered our home life. I explained the plan to Gulliver.

"Rose will look after you, luv. At least, you know her and she likes you. Her kids might spoil you. But there are worse things. Then you'll spend a week with Deirdre and her family, including the dogs. You'll be fine." Deirdre's two Labs were more energetic than Gulliver, but they were gentle with him. Between Rose and Deirdre, he'd be well cared for.

Rose cleaned the house for me once a week, brought in all the village gossip and fed Gulliver liver treats when she thought I wasn't looking. She'd be good to Gulliver, but I'd miss him. Now to make it happen. First, I rang Deirdre. She was cooperative.

"Michael will come for Gulliver on Saturday. He'll drop Josh off at his football game and loop around and pick up Gulliver. What's Rose's address?"

I gave it to her.

"I hope your guests are a calm bunch this time. No murderers."

You'd think from Deirdre's tone I advertised for killers. "That was just once."

"Once is enough."

It pays to keep my temper with Deirdre. She was going to look after Gulliver, after all. I disconnected my mobile and called up the stairs to Mark. "Gulliver's sorted."

My tour to the sites of mystery novels was not starting out as planned. In fact, the world was not turning as planned. The corona virus had decimated not just our population but many businesses. My tour company simply folded while the virus raged over the world. Mark's work had continued. There were still murders to solve and he was designated "essential". I was not essential, although the absence of tourists contributed to the recession. The Cotswold district alone usually got thirty-five million visitors a year—that's the population of Canada. From thirty-five million to zero was a huge economic loss. Still, no one wanted me to take tourists around the country in the middle of the pandemic. That would be tantamount to transporting Typhoid Mary. It was amazing how quickly we understood what we had to do individually to stop the spread of the virus and how willing most people were to cooperate. It took the politicians longer. The consequence of all public awareness of the transmission of the disease and the edicts that finally came from the governments on restricting travel, effectively shut down the tourist business all over the world.

When I had gone out during those plague days, I only walked down the path, across the green and to the grocery store or took Gulliver down to the river. The birds were, as usual, fascinating. I even saw a rare red kite. I saw the courting, nesting and the raising of many chicks. Life slowed down. There were interesting moments but it was immensely frustrating.

The virus finally swallowed itself, mitigating it's ferocity until we could tolerate it. Gradually, reservations for tours trickled in. I took mini tours—four people for three days—for the first few months. Tourist confidence grew, and finally, I had a full tour.

We were going to the beautiful Cotswolds, the setting for M.C. Beaton's Agatha Raisin stories, Ann Granger's Michell and Markby series, the new Cherringham series, and all those luscious Miss Read books that are not mysteries but essential reading, nevertheless.

Mark left after lunch, expecting to stay in Southampton. The staff at the Alton police station where Mark was based had arranged a hotel room there for him and his sergeant. He had an assigned car, so he would pick up Andy on the way. Superintendent Addison had agreed to let him leave the district whenever the Major Crimes Investigation Team asked for him—but she didn't like it. At least he was away from her nagging in Southampton.

Rose agreed to take Gulliver.

"He's a foxy one. Gets what he wants with those big brown eyes." She straightened and dusted her hands on her jeans. She was an energetic, wiry young woman, mother of two, and constantly busy. "I have a fenced garden, and I won't let him out without someone with him. The kids can brush his coat every day, but they aren't old enough to be responsible for walking him. So I'll do that. Or Frank will."

She'd come over for her regular cleaning day, and we'd finalized the arrangements. We agreed on her dog sitting fee, and I promised to have everything ready for her. I was bringing my guests to Ashton for the first two days of the tour, so I could look after Gulliver until Day Three. I hoped her children would remember to brush his coat. It got dirty quickly. Rose was inclined to feed him too many treats; she might make him sick. He could pine for me. I clamped down on my anxieties. He would be fine!

"I'll send you a daily picture while he's with us," she promised.

"Oh, thanks?" I felt a little obsessive, but I would like to know he was happy.

I drove from Ashton-on-Tinch to Heathrow the next morning, thinking what a good decision it had been to quit my job as a teacher at *Executive English and Etiquette* in Seattle, return to England and purchase a house in this village. The unexpected legacy left to me by my step-father allowed me to buy my house and start this new life. I'd settled into the village and the work of a tour guide much more easily than I'd expected. This was home.

Of course, just when I thought I had all aspects of my life in control, Mark dropped into the mix, creating an emotional earthquake. I was adjusting to sharing my life with Mark when the fates slammed humanity with the virus, tossing all my plans to the wind. When it was over, I did my best to organize my work, gradually coming to trust my plans would work out. I had a daily calendar on my laptop that divided the day into half-hour segments. I had the addresses and mobile numbers of all the guests. I had the accommodation booked, the restaurants booked as far ahead as possible and the tickets bought for the various sites where I was taking them. I could give up my ticket to Lionel if I wasn't able to purchase additional admission tickets. All should go well.

I pulled into the auto rental garage. My van takes only seven guests, so I'd rented a Mercedes Sprinter which takes nine. I would leave my own vehicle at the rental lot. I made the transfer, using my own supplies to clean the rented vehicle from stem to stern. I stocked a hand sanitizer at each seat along with a welcome package, containing the itinerary, chocolate, a thermal cup and tissues. I had enough extra supplies to add a package for Uncle Lionel.

I pulled away from the rental garage and into the line at the airport heading for my designated parking spot. I had a yearly permit to park outside the Arrivals' area where the vans from the hotels waited. I left the Mercedes there while I went into the terminal to meet my guests from Nova Scotia. After I collected them, we would have only a fifteen-minute wait for Judith Lloyd from Vancouver, Canada, then twenty minutes to pick up Dr. Clark from her American Airlines flight. She had flown from Sacramento, California, to Heathrow via Dallas, Texas—a long flight. Once I had that group, I'd fetch the couple from Montana who had arrived an hour ago. I'd sent them the code for the VIP lounge where I was a member. I hoped they were waiting there in comfort. Coordinating all the flights so everyone arrived in reasonably close proximity had taken hours of planning, but it would be worth it if all flights were on time.

I spared a thought for Mark on his way to the misery of those desperate immigrants. He'd sort it as best he could, but it would be heart-breaking.

My guests would be tired from long flights, particularly the Montana couple and Dr. Clarke, but they were the youngest. That didn't always mean they wouldn't be affected by the time change. I couldn't predict how people would react to overseas travel. Jet lag was an individual affliction, laying teenagers low and leaving an eighty-year-old alert and energetic, or visa-versa. My plan was to get everyone in the van, start the drive home, and take them to their B&Bs at Ashton-on-Tinch where we'd stay for two nights. While they were resting or exploring the town, I'd drive to the railway station in Basingstoke to pick up the Blighs from their Cornwall train. It looked totally possible to accomplish in my planner.

CHAPTER TWO

The first thing to disrupt my schedule was an hour's delay on the arrival of the plane from Nova Scotia. The one from Vancouver was on time. Mrs. Judith Lloyd was not happy.

"My plane was punctual," she said, as if her plane was virtuous, and the British Airways plane from Nova Scotia was delinquent.

I glanced at her. She was in her seventies, thin, still upright. She wore a soft green blazer over a cream-colored sweater, tailored trousers and Pikolinos trainers on her small feet––an elegant lady. My glance sharpened as I noted her diamond rings and perfect sapphire ear studs, probably a modest £2000 for the studs alone. She was an impeccably and expensively dressed older woman who was, at the moment, snapping at me.

"I am not accustomed to waiting."

I could deal with this. I *would* deal with this. I slid into tour guide mode. "I'm sure it must be annoying Mrs. Lloyd, particularly after a nine-hour non-stop flight from Vancouver. How was the trip?"

"Smooth. Over the pole is usually smooth. And the service was good." She admitted that a little reluctantly. I'd noticed she'd flown first class. It's a different world in first class. She probably had hot towels, a smoldering scotch, elegant meals, and cognac with her coffee. If the air was smooth, it couldn't have been arduous.

She flicked her hand toward the silver Cosmolite group of three suitcases on the baggage carousel. I got the message and hauled them off. I would have done it anyway—she was elderly, after all, but felt a prick of annoyance at being *ordered* to collect them. The suitcases were stylish with a curved design like a clam shell. Besides the three cases, she had a small leather knapsack hanging by one strap on her shoulder and a Voya Tote bag over her arm. What could she possibly be stowing in all those bags? Or, were they empty? Was she going to buy books? I hoped the other guests had not brought this much luggage. I could get sore muscles carrying it around. I'd have to be clever about asking hotel staff to help. For now, I'd deal with it. I loaded all her bags onto a cart, at least one bag felt empty, and shepherded Mrs. Lloyd to the VIP lounge. I stashed the luggage in the baggage room near the reception desk.

Heather Freeman and Matthew Dunn, mid-forties, tall, were ranchers from Chinook, Montana. They had arrived earlier, were sitting at a table near the window They had to fly from Helena to Salt Lake City before boarding a direct flight to Heathrow and that last flight was over nine hours. I hadn't had a chance to talk to them yet, so didn't know what they were like. Matthew rose when he saw us coming. I was impressed. I've found that men under the age of sixty seldom rise when a woman comes into the room, probably because women are part of their work environment these days and they'd be popping up like meerkats if they gave their work mates this courtesy. It seemed a little old-fashioned but courtly. Mrs. Lloyd smiled at them. Good. She was over her irritation.

"I will nip over to the Immigrations gate and meet Dr. Clarke the wait there for Mrs. Morrison and Mrs. MacFarlane. Please order anything you like."

Matthew indicated the coffee on the table. "We're good." The spicy scent smelled wonderful. I wished I had time for it.

"I'd like tea," Mrs. Lloyd said as if she expected me to get it for her. I was going to have to keep my temper with Mrs. Lloyd. It might not be hard if I could figure out why she need to be antagonistic, or if she even realized she was.

"I'll tell the wait staff," I assured her and left.

Dr. Clarke's flight was on time. I waited outside the Customs and Immigration gate until she emerged. She matched the picture she'd sent me which isn't always so, as some people send passport pictures which bear little resemblance to the real person and some send pictures that are years old. Dr. Clarke was about five-foot-eight, Chinese appearing, long, dark hair, light brown skin, and dark eyes with long lashes. She was the youngest on the tour, in her late thirties and a doctor of entomology at the University of California, Davis. She'd flown out of Sacramento. I wondered what she would talk about with my group. I expect she could teach me a great deal about insects if I only knew what questions to ask. She was wearing a loose, light grey tunic, black leggings and trainers. She'd had a fourteen-hour trip and had dressed for comfort. She, also, had flown first class.

"How's it goin," she called.

I grinned. It was lovely to hear her accent. She sounded like a typical Californian—breezy and cheerful with a sense of being in charge of her corner of the world. All that in 'How's it goin'. Dr. Clarke also had the dark, bright eyes of intelligence and the forward lean of a friendly soul.

"Hello, Dr. Clarke. I'm Claire Barclay."

"Figured that much," she said. "I'm starving. And it's Anna."

"All right, Anna. I can help with the hunger. We're going for lunch in about an hour, but I'll take you to the VIP lounge and you can have what you like there."

"Thank you," she said with real gratitude.

I collected her luggage, a small rolling suitcase. She had a knapsack and a smaller bag with her. We slid through the airport crowds to the lounge. I left her with the others and moved back to the Customs and Immigration gate.

The British Airways direct flight from Halifax, Nova Scotia, had finally arrived. I spotted the two older women outside the gate looking around at the crowds.

"Mrs. Morrison? Mrs. MacFarlane?" I reached for their wheeled suitcases.

"Oh, thank you. You must be Claire." That was from the shorter and wider of the two. "I'm Peggy MacFarlane. So nice of you to meet us. I feel I should apologize for the late arrival but really…"

"We had nothing to do with it." Nancy Morrison finished the sentence.

"Of course not. It happens." All international passengers poured through this gate, surrounding us with children clutching Paddington bears, adults in flowing robes of either white or black depending on gender, tall turbaned Sikhs, men in dark business suits and women in jeans and hoodies. I smelled overheated humanity, some musky perfume and chocolate. I shepherded my ladies away from the stream of passengers. "Everyone else is in the VIP lounge enjoying quiet and relaxation."

"Oh, good. No one standing around cursing us then."

"No," I laughed. If they could be this agreeable after a long flight in Economy Class, they were going to be good company.

"It's lovely to be in England again." That was from Peggy.

"Do you come often?" I asked as I led the way toward the lounge.

"I used to come every two years before the pandemic," she said. "I may have to curtail my travel a little until my savings recover from the wallop they got in the recession."

There was definitely a downturn in the economy—more a deep dive than a turn—which was still influencing tourists.

"I'm glad you could come this year. Have you been to the Cotswolds?"

"Well, I have," Nancy said. "But I just dashed through, you know the way you do when you're on a day tour. I saw the Cheddar Caves and Stonehenge. I can't remember what else. Were you with me on that trip, Peggy?"

"Not that one. I've been once before as well, but just to Bath and Lacock."

I led them through the VIP lounge door and put their luggage with the others. "We'll be going to Lacock. Are you all right with seeing it again?"

"Absolutely, it's lovely."

Lacock is a quintessentially Cotswold village, a period piece, like a miniature village in a diorama. It always seems a bit unbelievable to me, but the tourists love it. The ladies followed me to the lounge, chattering about the thrill of traveling after two years of restrictions.

I introduced everyone and waited while the Nova Scotia ladies collected a cup of coffee and a Chelsea bun. While everyone visited with one another, I piled all the luggage high on the cart. Matthew had his and his wife's luggage on a separate cart. Then, I announced our departure and led a procession through the terminal, out into the sunny May morning and to my parking spot.

Mrs. Morrison took a deep breath and exclaimed, "Ah, England!"

"Come on, Nancy. All you can smell is gas fumes." Mrs. MacFarlane tugged on her friend's arm, leading her to the van.

Mrs. Morrison laughed. "You're right. And it's petrol."

"Same thing."

"It smells different."

My guests loaded into the van and gave a collective sigh of relief. From now on all the travel arrangements were my problem.

Mrs. Judith Lloyd sat in the front seat. She pulled a map and a notebook from her tote bag. The notebook appeared to be divided into sections and contain hand-written notes.

"Where are we going now?" She had a pen ready.

I faced the guests and addressed them all. I'd answer her question in my opening bulletin. I took a breath. This was a new set of guests and a new adventure. Every tour was unique. "Welcome, everyone. You have at your places a bag of goodies which contains among other things, water, chocolate and the itinerary. I want this tour to be satisfying for all, so if you have requests or particular needs, please ask me. I will stop to take pictures if you give me enough time to find a layby. I will let you know as we drive, where we are going, what to look out for in terms of historic sites or points of interest, and I will let you know how we are doing on our schedule.

When we leave the airport, we will travel toward Ashton-on-Tinch where I live and where we will stay tonight and tomorrow night. On the way, I plan to stop for lunch. Does that suit everyone?"

Dr. Clarke leaned into the aisle from her seat near the back and waved a piece of chocolate at me. "Sounds good."

Everyone else nodded

I started to turn toward the driver's seat when Mrs. Lloyd stopped me with a touch on my arm.

"It says here," she checked the material I'd sent via email last week to all participants on the tour, "there are two more on the tour. Where are they?"

"Mr. and Mrs. Bligh are arriving by train a little later in the afternoon from Cornwall. There will be a third person joining us at Cirencester, Lionel Atkinson. He's not yet on the list." I hurried on with the plans. "We'll have lunch; I'll get you settled in your B&Bs, then I'll pick up the Blighs. We will all meet for supper." When tourists were this tired, it was best to be direct and firm.

Mrs. Lloyd was satisfied. I saw her check off the first item in the notebook and write what I suspected was Lionel's name, before she closed it. Oh, crikey. She was going to be my critic and taskmaster. I sighed. There was often one who caused trouble. Still, she didn't seem malicious, just fussy and super-organized.

In thirty minutes, I pulled into The Royal Oak, a typical English pub, just outside Farnham. The menu was varied and the food delicious.

There were two waitresses assigned to our table. One took orders from everyone *but* Mrs. Lloyd and one took orders *only* from Mrs. Lloyd. She had particular needs and was not shy about stating them.

"I can't eat dairy, at least, not most dairy. Which of these cheeses is goat cheese? I can eat that." She went through the menu asking the waitress questions until she finally made her selection. I was going to have to tip. Usually, in British pubs one didn't tip, but this waitress was going to need placating pay.

The meal was a little subdued as I assumed everyone was reacting to their flights. I'd leave the discussion of the itinerary until the evening when I expected the food and an afternoon's rest would give them some energy.

We were in Aston-on-Tinch fifteen minutes after leaving the pub. I pointed out my house as we drove by but didn't stop. I was proud of the brick and flint semi-detached and the tidy garden. I wasn't responsible for the garden as Peter Brown, the local handyman and jobber, "did for me", but I puttered around in it enough to feel proprietorial pride. The late daffodils bloomed under the trees near the street and the lilac, the official flower of Hampshire, was just beginning to flower showing a dusty purple close to the house.

I turned down the first road to the right. The sooner everyone settled into their rooms, the better. I left the Freeman-Dunn couple, Mrs. Lloyd and Anna Clarke at the Badgerhouse B & B. and drove down toward the river, and along Princess Street to Ivy Cottage. I'd booked two rooms for Nancy Morrison and Peggy MacFarlane at there.

"We've stayed friends over the years because we insist on having a room each," Peggy told me. "Privacy is very important in our selfish old age."

"Basically, she's a night owl and I'm a morning person," Nancy said, "so we'd grumble at each other at the beginning and end of the day if we shared a room." She looked at her friend. "It might even come to hair-pulling."

Mrs. MacFarland grinned.

"It's better to be separate." Nancy continued, giving me the reason for the added expense of separate rooms.

"Then there's the fact she snores like a freight train," Peggy offered.

"*I* snore." Nancy was indignant. "You could snore for Canada."

I smiled as I left them. They were going to be lively and easy to work with.

I dashed home, took Gulliver out for a short walk, made sure he had water and got in some petting time. I breathed the spring air suffused with wild garlic. They grew near the bluebells all around the village. Then I drove to Basingstoke. The train from Cornwall was on time and Mr. and Mrs. Bligh, carrying their two small bags and the English ubiquitous rucksacks, disembarked. They were both short, he about five-seven and she about five-foot. Both were wide, but his was the stocky width of a rugger scrum and hers a soft plumpness. They were both smiling.

"Hello," Mrs. Bligh said and shook hands.

"Aright, lover?" That casual designation flipped my mind straight back to Cornwall with its multicolored sea, steep cliffs and warm-hearted people. Mr. Bligh shook hands as well and brought me to the present. "I'm Branock and this is Eseld."

"I'm Claire Barclay. Welcome to The British Mystery Book Tour."

"I'm that excited," Mrs. Bligh, Eseld, chattered. "Branock is just coming with me because he doesn't know what else to do in his retirement."

"And they'll be birds, for sure," he said indicating the binoculars hanging down on his chest. Branock was like a bird himself, a solid crow; Eseld like a sparrow with its satisfied air of having much to do and doing it well.

"He doesn't like mysteries so much as I do," Eseld continued, "he got too many of real ones when he was working. He's so pleased Lionel is going to join us. The two of them can chase the honey buzzards, common kestrels and kites to their heart's content."

"As well as owls, eagles and ospreys," Branock said, amused by his wife. "We're not twitchers. We don't chase rare species. We just observe what's around us."

I took Eseld's suitcase and walked beside them. "What did you retire from, Branock?"

"Policing," he said shortly. That explained his friendship with Uncle Lionel who had also retired from policing.

"In Cornwall?"

"That's right."

"I know Edward and Chesten Tregere," I said, I didn't tell them I'd known them through my involvement in a murder investigation in Cornwall. "He's an inspector out of Penzance."

"I know him. Different constabulary. I was stationed out of Truro with Lionel."

There was a short silence. Possibly, Branock Bligh did not appreciate Inspector Tregere. The inspector could be blunt, opinionated and a little rough.

"He's right fond of his own way, that inspector," Eseld said with a bite to her tone.

"Aw well, he *is* an inspector," Branock said, as if belligerence came with the rank. Mark was an inspector. He didn't have an authoritative attitude, well, not usually.

"He couldn't have managed without his sergeants," Eseld insisted.

"We'll I wasn't *his* sergeant, Mother, so don't go on so. And Lionel was only his sergeant seconded for a few months."

"Lucky he survived the blighter." She sniffed.

I changed the subject. "I have you booked at The Gables, on Princess Street in Ashton-on-Tinch. It's a lovely B & B near the river and good walking trails. I guarantee birdlife." I smiled at Branock.

"Excellent. That'd be a proper good start."

I loaded their suitcases in through the rear door while they climbed into the front seat. At The Gables I introduced them to

Margery Calder, an unlikely landlady as she was in her late twenties and had full-time work as an infant school teacher. Rose told me Margery had inherited her house and took guests from the first of May to the end of July in order to pay her taxes, teaching school "not giving a body enough to keep flesh on her bones" as Rose put it.

Margery was welcoming, her house immaculate and the front bedroom attractive. It was a spacious pale green and white bedroom with an *en suite* bathroom for guests. I'd checked it out before I'd booked it, and the Blighs seemed as satisfied as I had been.

"I will collect you about six-thirty for supper," I said. "It will be casual, at the local pub."

Eseld looked a little disappointed but Branock brightened. "That'll suit me."

No doubt Eseld had a vision of elegant dining. I did say in the brochure there would be some sophisticated dining. Likely, Branock was not looking forward to that. Balance, the tour was all about balance. I wanted everyone to be satisfied at the end of it. As well as all the schedules and timetables I'd organized, I was now collecting the likes and dislikes of my clients. My brain was busy.

When I returned home, I walked Gulliver down to the park beside the river and let him loose. The ducks were agile and he missed every one despite his mad dashes and frantic barking. The peace of the afternoon descended on me. I could handle this tour. I'd done many and had some difficult people and situations. I'd be fine. I took Gulliver home, brushed and fed him. Then I changed into a fresh pair of long trousers, trainers, a flowery Holland Country shirt and light cardigan. I sent Mark a quick text to tell him I was home and my group collected. He sent back a thumbs up emoji. He was likely busy with the tragedy of human trafficking. I spared a moment to think of those migrants facing repatriation. All their efforts and probably all their money spent for nothing. I closed my mind to their plight. I trusted Mark to do the best he could for them.

At six-thirty, Nancy and Peggy were on the porch waiting for me, enjoying the sight of the bluebells near the river. From the porch it looked like an illustration from a book of fairy tales, the blue carpet spreading as far as we could see with graceful willows dropping fronds over the flowers. I spotted white garlic flowers among them.

"A sign of renewal," Peggy said. "We can use that after what the poor world has been through."

"So true." Nancy said.

"What was that?"

"I said, 'So true.' You have your new hearing aids in, don't you Peg?"

"I do. They are much better than the other ones."

Nancy grunted, obviously not convinced.

I'd have to pay attention to whether Peggy missed directions. I had a tourist once who was always late returning to the vehicle and for whom I often had to search all over the sites because, I discovered on the last day, she couldn't hear when I announced the time and place of the next meeting. At least, Peggy wasn't making a secret of her disability. Perhaps, her hearing aids gave her normal hearing, or almost normal hearing.

The Blighs joined us and we headed for Badgerhouse. The Montana couple and Anna Clarke were waiting, but Judith was not.

I left all the guests in the Badgerhouse lounge and walked to the kitchen with Carol Badger.

"Judith? Mrs. Lloyd?" I asked with some apprehension.

"She's coming. She had a little trouble with the kind of soap we supplied. She wanted lavender soap. Not just our lavender soap but one that was naturally handcrafted, cold processed and expensive. I gave her Yardley's. She also wanted," Carol dropped her voice, "thicker towels, the bed stripped so she could be sure there were no bed bugs, then remade. She wanted 500 thread sheets."

I stared at her. "I'm so sorry."

"There's got to be one like that a season." Carol was philosophical, but there was definite irritation seeping through that philosophy.

"What did you do about the sheets?" I didn't imagine Carol had sheets that fine.

"I lied," she said. Her voice dropped even more as we spotted Judith at the top of the stairs.

"Oh, good," I said with as much cheer as I could infuse into my voice. "We're all ready, then."

"I didn't keep you, did I?" Judith glanced at her watch. "It is exactly 6:50 which is the time you stipulated."

It wasn't the time I'd stipulated, but I didn't argue with her. I hustled everyone out the door and down the streets to the pub. We settled around the table.

Jack did us the favor of bringing menus. Usually, in this pub, people ordered from the bar.

"Everything's fried," Judith said with disapproval. "I don't care for fried food. It's usually fried in old oil which is carcinogenic."

There was a short silence, then Matthew looked up. I don't think he'd been listening to Judith. "This is fabulous," he said. "Fish and Chips. My mother told me about these."

"They are a speciality here," I said willing to go with Matthew's conversation rather than Judith's.

"Here," Eseld said, quite kindly to Judith, and pointed out items on the menu. "There are several salads and there is a slow cooked beef stew and oven baked chicken, even a veggie Thai stir fry. Lots for you to eat here."

Judith raised her eyebrows but stopped complaining.

In true tour guide style, I jumped in with a panacea. "I'd like to offer you a drink on me tonight. Beer or wine is available."

Everyone ordered. Judith stopped the conversation with her clear, incisive question, "The wine? It says red or white. That's it?"

"It will be quite acceptable wine," I said.

She rolled her eyes.

It was a lovely French Bordeaux. She couldn't complain about it. All the men had opted for beer as Jack had his own product. I had a half-pint of it. It was a dark, nut-flavoured and unique.

Between praise for the food from everyone but Judith—whom I noticed ate all her portion and drank all her wine—and the get-acquainted small talk of international travelers, the meal went well. No one wanted pudding.

"I want a bed now," Anna Clarke said. She'd had a long day. From her brief biography supplied on my form, she was a research professor of entomology and had a husband and a child, so she had probably worked hard to get away.

I passed out another copy of the itinerary to everyone.

"We will just go over tomorrow, then we'll leave," I promised her. "Tomorrow is a late-starting day, and we will end early so everyone who has traveled from afar can recuperate. Although," I nodded at the Blighs, "there will be interesting things to do around here. I you'd like, a short drive, I can accommodate that."

They studied their itineraries.

"Breakfast is supplied by your B & B, so you can make your own arrangements about what time you want it. The Mystery Book Sale sponsored by the local Mystery Book Club will be held starting at ten in the morning. It is a huge event, and since they couldn't have it the last two years, they have a mountain of books for sale this year."

"I'll need to buy another suitcase," Eseld said.

Her husband shook his head, but smiled. If she wanted another suitcase, I expect she'd buy one.

"There will be other books available as well," I told him. "Perhaps even bird books."

"That looks entirely satisfactory," Anna said. "My apologies. I'm off to bed."

I paid the bill. Jack thanked me. We were old friends.

"Hey, dude," Matthew said to him. "Fabulous fish and chips."

"Yes, very good," said everyone but Judith.

Jack smiled at me. He was always pleased when I brought customers. He and his wife worked hard.

"I'll take you out for dinner tomorrow evening at a restaurant near here," I told my guests as I drove them the few blocks to their temporary homes. "And the next day we are off to the Cotswolds."

"I know I'll be thrilled tomorrow," Anna said. "But right now, my bed is calling."

I deposited everyone at their designated B & B and parked the Sprinter in front of my house. Mark's car wasn't in the driveway, so I assumed he'd stayed in Southampton. Gulliver was ecstatic. You'd think I'd been gone for days. I sank into a comfortable easy chair in the living room. Gulliver bounced onto my lap, and I stroked his silky coat. His delighted welcome made me feel loved. I knew he loved me, and I felt guilty for leaving him. But I needed a life away from home, so I had to leave him occasionally. I suppose mothers felt this way about going to work and coming home to their children. There would never be a perfect balance that suited our dependents and us. I talked some sense to myself. *Guilt is unreasonable here, Claire. Ignore it.*

"Come on, Gulliver. Up to bed. I will herd my group through the book sale tomorrow. I need my sleep."

He trotted up the stairs in front of me with no thought of tomorrow.

It should be fine. We were just going to the book sale and for a drive around the countryside. All would be well.

CHAPTER THREE

The Mystery Book Fair was held at the parish hall, where all events in the village take place: parish meetings, flower shows, dog shows, Morris dancing, formal balls and contentious debates of public interest. It's located next to the church at the top of the hill, an easy walk for my guests. The hall was decorated with a few colorful posters and, on the stage, a swath of big, bountiful peonies of the deepest burgundy color I'd yet seen.

"Like them?" Mary Greenwood moved up to stand beside me. She had been a friend since I'd moved here and was a proficient gardener. I guessed those peonies were her contribution.

"They look like wine," I said. "Good wine."

"They're my lovelies. Herbaceous peonies *Rubra Plena*. Early flowering. Very Edwardian and lovely." Mary's brown eyes beamed with affection as she beheld her prodigy.

"Wonderful." I gave my adulation to her peonies.

"Thomas brought some early roses."

Her husband Thomas, had a spectacular rose garden. I spotted some cheerful yellow roses on the window sills. They looked like the wild roses I'd seen in America, but I didn't think they grow wild here.

"They're floribunda," Mary said. "Very hardy. They light up a corner of the garden reliably every year." Although both Mary and Thomas worked as teachers, they spent their spare time in their back garden and were the acknowledged experts in the village—not that some people didn't constantly vie with them for the position.

"Isobel Paulson used to organize this book sale," Mary said. We shared a moment of understanding. Mrs. Paulson died from poisoning, a drastic method of removing her from her position of influence. She'd been noted for her community involvement and had been a long-time family acquaintance of Mary's. Although I hadn't known Mrs. Paulson before she died, after her death I'd become well-acquainted with her activities. I wasn't surprised she'd been active in the Mystery Book Fair because, at the time of her death, she'd been president of the society.

I slid my eyes over the scene. It looked festive and busy. Whoever was in charge of it this year was producing a lively event.

"The flowers make a difference," I said.

"We aren't supposed to wear perfume in here now-a-days," Mary said," but nobody seems to mind the scent of real flowers."

I glanced at Judith to be sure she wasn't button-holing someone to demand the flowers be removed. She was engrossed by a row of books.

The "stay home" directive during the pandemic had encouraged book buying, as readers could order from independent shops which would deliver and from online stores which would send books through the post. It was one of the few entertainments we'd had and attracted new readers. Now, those readers were shopping in person for novels and non-fiction to fill their bookshelves.

Someone, likely Mrs. Helen Taylor who had taken over the president position, had created a useful shopping plan. Helen, the mother of Rose my cleaner, was the post mistress and a determined woman. She was always happy to organize as many lives as she could, but the village was used to her and often resisted. She'd had several skirmishes over the annual garden party and the method of collecting donations. I hoped she'd have fewer contretemps as she learned how to be an effective leader. Her organizational skills did make it easier to find the type of mystery each person wanted at this event. The signs designating genres were clear and obvious from across the room. The cozy mysteries attracted my group, particularly the women. There was a section for "Other Books". Bran and Matthew headed there.

Surprising me, Judith headed for the thrillers. They were side-by-side with the True Crime books where Anna stood. I'd have to add some different authors to my plans if those two were interested in mysteries that weren't cozies. I needed to learn who wrote thrillers and True Crime in the Cotswolds. I knew some of them—Colin Dexter's were classics. In the meantime, some of that research was in front of me. I glanced over the titles that interested Anna. Then, the ones that interested Judith. Anna reached across the books in front of Judith and picked up one, *Madness and Murder* by Jenny Hilborne.

"I haven't got this one," she said. It was a thriller with an earthy red cover, a faded picture of a woman's head and the title set out in pale gold, a more attractive cover than the usual black and silver of thrillers.

"I don't have it either," Judith said. "That's the first of a trilogy. I need it to complete the set." She held out her hand, expecting to receive the book.

Anna glanced at the title, smiled and said. "I can understand that," and turned away, heading for another section, taking the book with her.

"Well!" Judith was fuming. "She certainly is used to getting what she wants."

That could have described Judith exactly. I hoped there wasn't going to be open warfare between those two.

Nancy and Peggy hustled past me, each with an armload of books which were mostly paperback and light to carry. Peggy grinned at me. She was slipping through the crowds, picking up what she wanted, like an energetic robin after the perfect worm. Nancy was following behind, a little bent, perhaps with osteoporosis, but she still walked quickly and had the steely eye of a determined shopper. I watched them for a moment as I ambled through the aisles. I was counting my tourists to be sure they were all present, a habit ingrained in all tour guides, and was not paying attention to my near surroundings when Helen Taylor grabbed my arm and stopped me. She wore a long turquoise tunic over loose black trousers. Because she was short, the outfit looked like a billowy tent. She had a new perm for this event and her hair curled tight to her head like a crocheted cap. She edged me into a corner.

"Your tourists have descended like a plague of locusts. Don't let them buy all the books," she commanded. "We're not here to support your company."

"Why, Helen." I was startled. "Whatever do you mean?"

"If they buy all the books you'll get up the nose of the local people and they'll stop coming."

"Pardon?" My guests were going to irritate the villagers? I couldn't understand her concern. "For heaven's sake, Helen. It's not as if they're backing a lorry to the door and loading pallets full of books. My guest are just buying for their own use. They can't carry enough to put a big dent in the sales here. Even if they did, why wouldn't you encourage it? That's why we have a book fair." I was a member of Ashton-on-Tinch's Mystery Book Club, and I objected to her dictates both as a tour guide and as a member of the club. She was not going to interfere with the group's pleasure here.

Mary Greenwood, slipped in beside me and faced Helen. Mary is an old resident; I'm a new resident. Her words carried more weight. "The point is to sell books, Helen. We don't care who buys them. We need the money and Claire is doing us a favor by bringing her guests. You're cutting off your nose to spite your face here. Now, just stop complaining. You're working too hard. Take time for a cup of tea. I'll watch the floor."

Helen looked startled. "I was narky?"

"A bit," Mary said.

Helen exhaled a deep breath. "I'm that sorry, Claire. I got carried away."

"Apology accepted. Go for that cuppa, Helen. You have a long day ahead."

"True. I'll do that." She addressed Mary. "Keep your eye on those kiddies by the door. We don't want books walking away."

"I don't think they are going to steal books, Helen."

"They might," she said glumly and left us.

"She isn't used to being in charge of such a big event," Mary excused her.

I understood. "She's doing a good job, but I can see it's upsetting her. I expect she always wanted to run this then found it a be overwhelming when she had to." I was willing to give Helen some slack, as I had no desire to run this sale myself.

I scanned the room, finding all my tourists engaged in studying the books. I saw Peggy search out Anna and bring her over to one of the book bins. She held out a book to her.

Anna smiled, nodded and put it in the bag she was carrying. It looked full. When she pulled out her books at the cashier's table, I saw one of the books was titled *The Nature of Life and Death: Every Body Leaves a Trace*. It wasn't a mystery I was familiar with. I'd ask her about it later.

The Mystery Book Club provided lunch with the admission price and, since it included an abundance of homemade sandwiches, biscuits and cakes, I encouraged my group to sit at the long tables near the back of the hall and scoff the lot.

Matthew called me over. "Just like home," he said. "We call dinners like these 'county socials'. Usually, some group is raising money for something." He gestured with his fork. "Same atmosphere. I feel right at home."

He was about six-foot-four, stocky, wearing jeans and a studded shirt and, most noticeably, what I'd call a cowboy hat.

Not huge, but definitely different from any hat worn here. He didn't *look* at home, but as long as he *felt* at home I was happy for him.

"People like to gather in any country," I said.

"Yeah. That was what was so bad about the last couple of years. It felt like you were on an iceberg, just sailing past people and never talking to them."

The pandemic had been hard on people who counted a day without friends or family in it as a day lost.

"I bet you got lots of work done," I said. Heather had told me they lived on a huge ranch in eastern Montana.

"We did. The work didn't change much for us because the cattle had to be fed, but, man, we got tired of each other's company." He smiled at his wife.

Heather shook her head as if she'd just as soon forget those days.

When they had had enough lunch and enough shopping, I drove everyone to their B & B with all their newly acquired books where I gave them an hour to rest before picking them up and driving them on a short tour around the countryside. I stopped at vista points so they could see the green and rolling countryside of Hampshire with it's hedgerows dividing the fields and its villages nestled along rivers.

"It's so *English*," Peggy said.

"Beautiful," Nancy agreed.

I deposited them back at their lodgings and left them to find supper on their own. It was a mild night and the pub and café were within walking distance. I hurried home to Gulliver and took him for a long ramble across the river and up the footpath to the bench at the top of the hill. I sat there for a few minutes while Gulliver nosed in the bushes, always hopeful he would flush a pheasant. It wasn't quite dusk, so I was surprised to hear the shivery "whooo" of a tawny owl. It's long quavering call rang out over the woods below me. Every mouse and mole in the area would be diving for cover. A robin sang a musical chatter from a nearby hedgerow. They will sing day and night. I sat for some minutes hoping to hear more night birds: a Little Owl who sounded as it were saying "*What's going on*" over and over, or a nightingale with its liquid notes that covered a range an opera star would envy or even a night jar that sounded like a rattling motor, but there was silence.

We ambled home. I fed Gulliver and brushed his coat. I made myself an omelette, had the last three ounces of Sauvignon Blanc in the refrigerator and packed my suitcase. I like being married to Mark, but I also like the occasional time alone.

Mark rang as I was getting ready for bed and told me about his case.

"Wicked situation," he said. "I'll be a few days straightening out all the paperwork on the charges."

"You caught the trafficker?"

"The local police did. They were right narked about the deaths, so they worked overtime. They caught the local trafficker. There are others who transport and distribute immigrants all over Britain who are still free to reorganize. It's a *diras* business. I need to get some social services people in here and the refugee organizations."

Diras must mean evil or wicked. Even after all his years of policing Mark still hated the horrors that some people had to endure.

"What are your guests like?" He changed the subject abruptly. Sometimes, Mark doesn't want to talk about his work, particularly when there is something disturbing he can't fix. He'll tell me eventually but not immediately.

I told him about my tourists and my impressions. We murmured to each other for a while, getting our dose of love and support, then bade a good night.

In the morning, I packed up Gulliver's accoutrements: comfy bed for napping, bag of treats, dog food, comb and brush, rain coat and toys. I delivered it to Rose's house and watched as her kids hugged and petted him.

"He'll be fine," Rose reassured me. Of course. I knew that.

I collected my tourists. They expressed pleasure at their stay. I paid the bills and thanked the hosts. When all were settled in the van, Nancy Morrison waxed enthusiastic about the book fair. "What a treasure trove," she said. "I could have spent days there."

"You're going to have to carry those books," Peggy admonished.

"I can mail them home for you," I said.

"Wonderful. Then I can keep buying."

"I found a book of Cotswold's birds," Bran Bligh announced with some incredulity. "Imagine that?"

"A lucky fine," Eseld agreed. "You'll be a happy man for weeks." Eseld was the one who looked happy. She had some wrinkles around her eyes that made her seem as if she was going to smile at any moment. She had retired from her nursing work about eight years ago, she'd told me, at aged fifty-five and had been happily sitting her grandchildren and gardening since. It must suit her.

"I found a rare green and white Penguin, an Agatha Christie I don't have," Judith said. "Of course, it wasn't the one I wanted, but it will do."

That was a dig at Anna for snatching a book from under her nose. I doubted there was anything of "rare" value at the book sale. Thomas and Mary Greenwood would have combed the donations for anything that could add to our Mystery Club's library. Still, they might have let a duplicate slide though to the sale. Perhaps there really were finds in that lot.

We left Hampshire behind us and headed for Gloucestershire and the Cotswolds.

"Tell us about Cirencester," Nancy said. "I read M. C. Beaton's Agatha Raisin, so I have a picture in my mind of a pretty little town with an impressive church."

"I read the Miss Read stories when I was much younger," Peggy said. "I've always thought it sounded ideal. Of course, those stories were set in the 1950s. She certainly described the area and the people. I suppose it's all changed." She sounded wistful.

"Not so much you won't recognize it," I promised.

"What was that?" she asked.

I repeated myself.

"I'm sorry. I'm trying out new hearing aids and what with the noise of the van, although it is fairly quiet, I'm distracted. Nancy, be my translator."

Obligingly, Nancy translated.

"Oh, that's wonderful," Peggy almost gushed. "Years ago, when I was a young woman, I used to hide near the filing cabinets in the library trying not to be caught while I was supposed to be working. I'd keep one eye on the front desk in case anyone arrived who needed help, and I'd read for as long as I could. That's when I read Miss Read. It's exciting that I'm finally going to see the places I read about. I'm sure I'm going to love the Cotswolds."

I'd have to remember she didn't hear well. I knew from experience with my brother-in-law, Michael, settings that were noisy, such as a pub, made it difficult to hear. As long as Nancy would repeat things for her in the van, she'd probably catch most of what I said and everything when I was miked. She'd let me know if she wanted something repeated. She was a lively speaker with a bit of a Scottish or Irish lilt in her cadence. I'd noticed people from the Maritimes in the eastern part of Canada, pronounced "sure" as "shore". It was charming.

"I've never been to Cirencester," Eseld said. "Is that how it is pronounced? *Sigh wren cester*?"

"You can pronounce it that way and some do. The local people call it "Sister" or" Siren".

"Sister?" Nancy Morrison said. "That isn't even close."

"Well," I said "Gloucester is pronounced Gloster, so there isn't a lot of logic in how names are pronounced here."

"Oh, my," Anna, contributed from the back seat. "I don't think I'll manage to work that out. No rational to it."

"Spelling is often loosely related to pronunciation, I agree. Often, there *isn't* any logic to it. I found some of the names in America interesting but confusing when I lived there. I was always making mistakes. Heather, how do you pronounce Puyallup, Washington?"

"*Pul-all-up*. I get your point."

"Or Arkansas? It isn't Ar Kansas. It's Ar kansaw. Right?"

"Right. We'll just have to get used to each other's idiosyncrasies," Anna said.

"It's a bit mucked up in Cornwall," Bran said. "You have to throw in the Cornish language to make any sense of it. Fowey, for instance is pronounced Foy. Tourists are always stumbling over that one."

"And Wales is totally confusing," Eseld added. "They have an entirely different way of spelling. Two "Ls" equal an "F". At least, I think they do."

"It's part of the joy of traveling," Nancy added her bit. "Often confounding."

"What about you, Matthew?" I asked. "Are you familiar with the place names here?"

"Nope and never will be. I'll let you lead me around. You and Heather. She's quick at that sort of thing."

I smiled to myself. Matthew's attitude to place names was like my attitude to rugby: others might find it fascinating.

I drove into Cirencester on the A429 which turned into London Street. I had to mind the one-way streets and didn't head directly to the hotel. I took them on a short tour of the town center.

I chose the market town of Cirencester because of a delightful hotel smack in the center of town. My guests could wander without having to make arrangements for a lift. They could go to their rooms and rest whenever they liked or nip out to the shops or museums as they wished. That was no doubt why Uncle Lionel had chosen it as well. Cirencester was a centuries old Roman settlement, so there is much of historical interest. There are also bookstores, shops, hiking trails, pubs, a theater, even an old Roman amphitheater and gorgeous Cotswold scenery.

The hotel, a grade two listed gem, was just off Cricklade. The owners had found a parking spot for me a few blocks away. For now, I parked in the street and helped the guests unload their baggage. The owner came down the steps. He was about forty, dark, trim, and muscular.

"Robert," I said as I approached him. I had not yet met him.

"Bob," he responded offering his hand. "You must be Claire. Thanks for choosing our hotel. We'll make you comfortable, never you fear."

The previous owners had been about twenty years older and experienced hoteliers. I hoped Bob would be as accommodating.

"I'll introduce everyone when we register. Right now, we need to get unloaded so I can park the van. Perhaps the guests can wait in the lounge while I do that."

"For certain. Shirley has tea ready in the lounge so the guests can be comfortable. She made a couple of cracking good cakes as well."

He turned then and headed for the back of the van to help with the luggage. Dr. Clarke was standing on the sidewalk staring up at the Tudor half beams and stucco walls.

"Wow. What a place," Dr. Clarke said and turned to smile at Bob.

He checked his gait, just a half-hitch in his step but it was noticeable.

He said nothing to her but brushed past and reached for the luggage.

She looked at me and raised her eyebrows. Those were expressive eyebrows.

It took me a moment to realize Bob had reacted to her color. I felt a burn start low in my belly and move up. This was not going to happen on *my* tour.

"Bran," I said, "Could you stay with the van for a moment in case any officers come along. I will be right back to move it."

"For certain, I can do that," he said.

I marched up the stairs after Bob. He set down luggage near the reception desk and turned to go back for more.

I motioned to him to step aside. He did.

"What is it?" His voice was mild.

Mine was firm, my anger only barely controlled. "If there is any hint, any trace of racism against my guest, in particular against Dr. Clark, I will remove my clients from your hotel and register a hate complaint with the local constabulary. Am I understood?"

He flushed. "I haven't done anything."

"And you shan't, or I'll have your head."

I could tell he was furious. But so was I.

At that moment, a woman came through the swinging door from the back of the hotel.

"Hello," she said, "and welcome. Bob is looking after the luggage is he? I'm Shirley James. Welcome to Queen Bess Inn."

I glanced back at Bob, but he had turned away from me and was descending the stairs, heading for the back out to the van.

"I'm Claire Barclay. Lovely to meet you." I was pleasant. She wasn't Bob.

"We are so excited to have you," Shirley said. "We haven't had this hotel long and we want to make a success of it. A satisfied tour guide gives us repeat business. If there is anything I or Bob can do for you, just ask. Any special diets?"

"Mrs. Lloyd doesn't tolerate dairy from cows. She's okay with goat milk. I think that's all. If you give my guests tea, I'll go park the van then come back and help you get them settled. We can discuss anything you like then."

"Right you are. I'll go out and welcome them and help with the luggage."

"Ta."

I followed her down the steps, nodded my thanks to Bran and got in the van. I'd find Uncle Lionel as soon as I returned. What a way to start a fortnight in one hotel! I suppose the Anderson's who had been the last owners had enough during the pandemic and sold. The new owners were not what I'd expected. I breathed deeply and slowly, trying to control my anger. I could look for an alternative place to stay but that would be difficult, considering how hard it would be to find one that would take all the guests and had, at least, an eighteenth-century charm. Now there was the complication of Uncle Lionel. He wouldn't want to move. I'd like to stay here, but I'd have to remain alert. Dr. Clarke was not going to be treated as if she were invisible, not important, or worse. Not if I could help it.

When I arrived back at the Queen Bess Inn, everyone was congregated in the lounge. Uncle Lionel met me at the door. He looked just as he had when I had seen him last: a little stooped, but still with alert eyes and a hint of a smile. He wore a hand-knitted vest over an open necked sports shirt and jeans. I would report to Mark that he was looking after himself.

"Hello, Uncle Lionel," I said and hugged him

He patted my shoulder. "*Hwegan*."

I was sure that was Cornish for "my dear".

"Lovely to see you." It was. He looked contented. I hoped he finally was accepting Auntie Addie's death.

"Kind of you to take me on at such short notice."

"Delighted I could." I smiled at him. I don't know how he survived a career as a sergeant and still maintained his gentle attitude.

I turned toward the room with the intent of introducing him. He took the introductions right out of my hands.

"Well, now," he said loudly. "As I live and breathe, if t'aint Bligh himself. Wasson, me cock?"

Bran stood and rushed over to shake the newcomer's hand. "Lionel! Aright, my 'ansum? Wasson shag?" While the words seemed to be Cornish and not intelligible, the meaning was clear. These two were old friends.

Bran brought the older man to our group. Eseld stood and greeted him with a firm handshake. "Lionel Atkinson. You'll keep Bran occupied now, won't you?"

Bran took Lionel around the group introducing him. Lionel shook hands politely, and I am sure totally forgot their names. I'd have to get him an itinerary with everyone's name on it.

Bran brought him back near me. I had, by this time, helped myself to tea and some delicious Victorian sponge cake.

"I've been here a over a week," he said, waiting for Eseld to sit herself before he sat beside her. "The nosh is good here," he said. "I like that about it."

That implied there were things he didn't like about it.

"The new owners aren't the same as the old?" I prodded carefully.

"Not a tetch on them. Mind you, the place is convenient and central for birdwatching."

"What have you seen?" Bran asked.

Eseld stood. "I will give you my seat, Bran. I don't plan to be the pillar around which you and Lionel here talk Zebra finches, dunnocks and yellowhammers."

Bran agreed. "Good idea."

Eseld sat beside me and joined the conversation around our table. We left Lionel and Bran to their lapwings and wagtails.

A young man, an employee of the hotel, arrived with a full tea pot and refilled cups.

"What's your name," Heather asked him.

"Dylan, mad'am," he responded.

"Dylan's new here," Lionel said, breaking off his conversation with Bran. "The other young man---Richie?" He raised his eyebrow at Dylan.

"Richie Stonehouse," Dylan said. "He just didn't show up for work about a fortnight ago, and I got the job. It was totally like him. I had my eye on this job because Richie, like he only ever works one job for a few months. His mom's right narked about it."

"Didn't he tell her where he was going?"

"Nah. That was like him too. He'll be all right. Always turns up when he's broke."

"You don't think anything bad happened to him?"

He considered that. "Could be jud or wuss, but I don't think so."

Dead or worse, I translated the Gloucestershire dialect.

"Where do you think he's gone?" I asked, only idly interested.

"Maybe to another job, or a lark. Who knows? Sailing around the world, no doubt."

He caught Bob's eye and quickly cleared the table.

We moved our chairs a little closer, so we could talk more easily. Lionel and Bran moved to a separate table.

"Lionel's a lovely man," Eseld informed us. "He worked with Bran in Truro and left the constabulary just before his wife died. It's too bad she couldn't have had more time in their retirement. She was a great one for the birds, as well. She liked them in her garden. She didn't hike out looking for them. She had a crow that used to visit her. She called him Charlie. She'd leave peanuts and sunflower seeds out for him. He brought her a present once, a piece of shiny paper, a candy wrapper. Crows are canny birds."

I agreed. They were highly intelligent and could work out problems, such as how to open garbage bins.

"Bran and Uncle Lionel will have lots to talk about," I said, observing the two men poring over a small book, possibly the bird guide to the Cotswolds that Bran had purchased. As I watched, Lionel pulled a blue book from his jacket pocket and opened it.

"That looks like his official blue book," Eseld said following my gaze.

"The constabulary official record?" I asked. Mark had used one, he told me, when he was a constable. Constables had to hand them in at the end of every day. Inspectors could use a tablet.

"Well, it wouldn't be the official one. They have identity numbers on them. It must be one that looks much the same. Bran is just as bad. It seems that having had to write everything down, every day, for so many years, they can't think without one. It's like a second brain."

The two men were bent over the blue book. Lionel had no doubt documented the birds he'd seen.

"They are going to be right tedious, those two. Bird talk from morning to night, but that will keep Bran happy and I can read, search for and talk about mysteries to my heart's content."

Shirley and Bob were circulating through the lounge, adding tea and offering more cake. Shirley approached us just as Eseld was saying, "At least they aren't talking cases. It was bad when they were both working at the station in Truro. Addie and I felt like widows sometimes with all the police talk at the table."

Shirley started and almost dropped the cake. She recovered. "I'm sorry. I must have stumbled on a loose board. I'll have to look for it later." She smiled and Anna took another slice of cake.

"Delicate flavor," Anna said. "You're an excellent cook."

"Thank you," Shirley murmured and left us.

I glanced at Shirley. Was Shirley reacting to Eseld's mention of the police? I shouldn't put too much meaning on it. Everyone has something to hide: late payment of car insurance, a few bottles of wine bought from an unlicensed source or unpaid utility bills from twenty years past…or nothing like that. Perhaps, she just thought of something.

Bob came to our table and offered everyone more tea, even Anna. He was polite. I met Anna's eyes. Those expressive eyebrows rose, and she smiled.

Bob seemed more at ease with the men, offering them tea and encouraging them to come to the bar for an evening drink.

"You should join Lionel here. He's our steady customer."

"I'll have to check with the missus. Thank you." Bran was comfortable with his old friend and with the host.

After Bob and Shirley left, I outlined the plans for the afternoon. Everyone had an itinerary. I handed out another list of points of interest to look for in Cirencester.

"We'll meet at seven at Jesse's Bistro on Black Jack Street. Lionel, you can now join us on all our activities. I've added another place to our reservations."

"I'd take that kindly," he said.

Bran sent me a warm smile.

I was looking forward to getting to know Lionel better. We had a short chat in the snug before dinner.

"It's nice you and the Blighs are old friends," I said.

"I'll try to enjoy them without intruding on their holiday too much," he said. "Bran and I miss working. All this idle time isn't what we're used to. I have no idea what's going on at the station, just what I read about cases in the newspapers. No one tells me about cases over coffee. No one asks for advice. I play Bocce at the local seniors' center. Darts at the pub. But no one needs me. It's a hard thing, after being needed every day of my life, to not be needed."

I nodded. A pension can't compensate for a purpose in life.

"Hobbies. That's what Bran and I are doing, looking at birds."

"Aren't you interested in them?"

"I am. I'm interested in their family life and how they communicate. Maybe I can learn something from them. And they're beautiful, amazing creatures."

Birds instead of people occupied his time now. "It's a new life, I suppose," I said.

"That it is, maid." He changed the subject. "When's that nephew of mine arriving then?"

"I'll let you know as soon as I can." Mark had said he might join us if his Southampton case wrapped up in time.

"He's a good man."

I agreed that Mark was, indeed, a good man. The light from the lamp glinted off my new wedding ring. It fit closely to my engagement ring and caught my eye unexpectedly, reminding me that I was married. It still seemed surprising.

I saw a man walk through the lobby and head for the stairs.

"Who's that?" I asked Lionel.

Lionel turned slightly to watch the man's back as he moved up the stairs.

"That's Mr. Buchanan, Alistair Buchanan. He is a businessman. He's here to oversee his transport company."

I looked at Lionel.

"He bought me a drink one evening in the bar. Nice man. If a little boring."

"You wouldn't think this part of the country would need a transport company: no motorways, little industry."

"Lots of farming. Lots of produce that needs transport."

"Oh, I see."

"He's friendly enough when he isn't busy. You'll meet him. He seems to be regular here, coming every month or so for a day or two."

I had a few hours left in the afternoon to shepherd my guests. I proposed a walk around the town to orientate them to the shops and attractions. The cathedral in particular was my favorite of all cathedrals. I'm not sure why. Undoubtedly, it was beautiful, but so were many others. The music was wonderful and I'd been to many concerts here and heard their choir. I was a member of the choir in Ashton-on-Tinch and appreciated the altos in particular. They had made me cry with the emotions and clear beauty of their song. I wouldn't take my tourists inside the cathedral on this outing; we would stay out in the fine weather. They could explore the cathedral in the coming days. Now, those who wished to do so could join me in a longer walk into the nearby Abbey Park.

"What's with the rabbits?" Matthew pointed at the statue of two hares over six feet tall in fighting stance at the junction of roads in the marketplace.

"Hares are a symbol of Cirencester. They appear on a mosaic Roman floor preserved in the museum and have been recognized here for centuries. You'll see hares on cups, plates, buildings and even in fabric on chairs."

"Charming," Judith said. "Luckily, they don't grow that big in real life."

She had a point. Six-foot tall hares would be a menace. I wondered why the statue depicted the hares fighting. Did it symbolize the fighting spirit of the Cotswolds, not something I saw here. Laid-back, tranquil almost placid was my assessment of Cirencester.

CHAPTER FOUR

I made sure everyone had a map of the town, although it was hard to get lost where a church spire marked one end. Still, some people had a directional gene missing and needed a map, a guide and a possibly a GPS tracker embedded in their skull.

We walked up Cricklade to the Market Street Corner. I pointed out the Church of St. John Baptist, not St. John *the* Baptist. The name makes one think it's a Baptist church called St. John but its Anglican, once Catholic, built in 1125 on top of an old Saxon church which had been built about 600 A.D. The twelfth century church was added onto with carefully planned improvements until the fifteenth century, resulting in this lovely church which had stood here since. I often felt as if my feet were reaching down though centuries to touch my ancestors in ancient times. The mellow Cotswold stones glowed in the afternoon sun.

"Notice the flying buttress that supports the tower," I said. Dutifully, all my guests studied the architecture of the church. When I thought enough veneration had been given the magnificence of the planners and builders of the past, I pulled them back to the present.

"Now, about our plans for the rest of the afternoon. There are shops along here," I gestured to my right, "if you'd like to explore the town. I propose a walk into the park just beyond the Abbey Grounds, so I'd be happy to have company. We have about two hours before we need to gather for supper. What is your pleasure?"

The shops did look enticing, jostling cheek by jowl along Market Place. Peggy, Nancy, Heather, Judith and Eseld opted for the shops. Anna, Bran, Lionel and Matthew joined me in our hike north of the church and along the path at the edge of the Abbey Grounds Park.

I notice a bulge in Anna's vest. For a moment I worried: she was from California—murders, guns. "You need a licence to carry a gun here," I said.

"I know." She looked surprised.

I gestured to her vest.

"Oh, that. I carry specimen bottles and a small microscope always. Never without them. Some things stimulate my curiosity and I want a better look. I know there's a Roman wall around here somewhere. I'd like a specimen of that."

"There is," I said with some relief. I had only once had to deal with a gun-toting tourist, and I didn't want a repeat experience. Guns are illegal here unless you have a licence which is hard to get. I pointed her along the path to the west and told her where to meet us.

"Ten minutes," she said.

The rest of us walked slowly along the broad path as it angled in a typically Roman geometrical pattern to Abbey Lake where we stopped. Bran and Lionel scanned the lake with their binoculars. Anna caught up with us there.

"Did you get a specimen?" I asked.

"I did." She beamed. There was a woman happy in her work. Perhaps she examined the specimens she'd collected in the evening in her room and made notes on her computer.

"What are you looking for?" she asked Bran.

"Anything, really," he said. "Someone saw a white swallow here, near the reeds," he gestured to the wild bushes before them. "It would be lucky to see one."

"Without pigment?" Anna asked.

"Yes. Entirely white."

"That happens sometimes in seals around San Diego and L.A." She gazed over the field but the white swallow never appeared.

Bran and Lionel didn't delay us long and we went across Grove Lane which is a fairly busy road and onto the treed path. The forested strip angled east between the cricket field and the rugby club as the path entered Harebushes Wood. Here, the bluebells lay an abundant carpet on either side. The air was filled with bird song, which kept Bran and Lionel fascinated. I heard a chaffinch and a blackbird. It might have been a Mistle thrush; they sound similar. Matthew took pictures of the trees and the bluebells.

"We have forget-me-nots at home," he said. "Never seen so many bluebells before."

The path angled east then in a gradual 180 degree turn to the west. We lost the woods and came out along the farmer's field, lush now with grass, beside Burford Road. There were a few cows grazing some distance away.

"They look like Red Angus," Matthew said. "I wonder how much protein they get in that grass."

"Want to find out?" Anna asked him.

"Sure."

Anna picked a few blades of grass and secured them in a specimen bottle.

"Thanks," Matthew said with a grin. "I've always been interested in Red Angus and the new breed, Speckle Park. I want to check them out. We have some in the country that are grass-finished for the quality market, but they barley-finish them here. I'd like to see if they're a possibility for us. But, you know, I'm not sure there is going to be a market for beef in the future."

"No?" Anna said.

"Well, maybe in my life time and Heather's; we have good sales. We've got Herefords with some black Angus. But our kids better get into something else. We thought we'd take some time on this trip to talk about it. We've got a farm tour booked after this one. We may have to plan for a future without beef."

"No oil consumption. No beef consumption. It's going to be a big shakeup for our country." Anna said.

"It is. A rancher has to plan years ahead, even decades."

"There's a businessman, Mr. Buchanan, who is staying at the hotel who meets with a farmer sometimes. Perhaps you could talk to them about how the farmers here are coping with change," Lionel offered.

Matthew looked interested. "That's be great. Could you introduce me?"

"First chance I get," Lionel promised.

I heard them continue their talk as I waited for Bran and Lionel to finish their visual sweep for grasslands birds.

"There's a lapwing," Lionel said.

"Yes and over there by the chestnut tree, that's got to be a coal tit. See, you can barely make it out." He pointed and Lionel moved his binoculars to find the tiny bird.

Satisfied, they joined the rest of us as we trekked along the field towards the A417 then under it and over the River Churn. I knew there was a path that took us to the Corinium Gate Road thence to Market Place, but we didn't get far.

Lionel stopped and pointed. "Look at those crows. Right at the river's edge. What are they up to?"

We'd stopped on a small bridge where we could see the river beneath us and the leafy path in front, leading to the town.

Bran snapped his binoculars to his eyes and focused them on the column of rising and falling crows. They looked to be quarreling about something and darting to the ground, then up and attacking each other, then back to the ground.

"Hmmph." Bran started to the other side of the bridge and into the bushes beside it. Lionel stayed on the bridge guiding him with, "A little to your left. Now straight ahead."

We could see Bran's gamekeeper's cap at about the same height as the reeds beside the river. We saw when it stopped. We all waited.

"Better get here, Lionel. We've got a body."

I stood perfectly still. A body? I did not want to encounter a dead body on this trip. I could handle Judith's demands, changes in plans, weather problems and arguments between guests, but I did not want to deal with bodies. *Take a deep breath, Claire. You don't have to deal with it. You have two retired coppers here.*

But I knew that such a discovery meant police involvement, statements to give, hours tied up with officialdom. *Spare a thought for the poor victim, Claire. You're not the center of the universe. You will help if you can.*

Lionel moved toward the break in the bushes where Bran had entered. Anna was directly behind him. I stayed with Matthew on the bridge.

"Do you want me to ring the police?" I shouted at Bran.

"Yes, luv. Give them a ring. Young man, early twenties, fair-haired. Been here a few days by the look of him."

"Any evidence of foul play?" I asked. I was sure the police would ask me that.

"Some," Bran said, after a pause. "I don't want to get any closer and muck up the scene."

"Are you all right?" Matthew asked. "Want me to come?"

"No, lad. We're fine."

I was happy not to observe the body. If the crows had been picking at it, it would not be something I'd forget. I could feel my breath quicken and my hands shake a little. I did not want to imagine that body. I dialed 999 and slowly and deliberately waded my way through the questions. Yes, police. Yes someone was with the body. Yes, they were sure he was dead. A young man, fair hair. My name. My address.

"Can you advise the way in which the emergency vehicles should come?" the dispatcher asked.

"The best way would be off Corinium Gate Road, then along past the houses there. The path comes off it just before the river." My breath was more even now. I concentrated on answering the questions.

"I see it on the map," the dispatcher said.

"I expect it's Richie Stonehouse," I said impulsively.

"What makes you think that?" her voice was cool.

"Just how many fair-headed, twenty-year-olds are missing in this town?" I snapped.

There was a pause which gave me time to be mortified. Honestly, that was rude.

Before I could apologize she answered, "Three, at present count."

"Sorry," I mumbled.

"Hold it together, madam. The officers will be there as soon as possible. Please make sure no one leaves the scene."

I tried to be more helpful. "The two with the body are retired coppers," I said. "And the other is a forensic entomologist on holiday. They'll know how to behave at the scene. I will stay on the bridge along with another of my guests. We'll be obvious."

"Thank you." She maintained her polite demeanour which made me feel even more ashamed of my comment.

This was going to disrupt the tour. Bran, Lionel and Anna would have to have their fingerprints taken and submit their shoes so the forensic officers could eliminate them. That would take time.

"We have to stay?" Matthew asked as I disconnected.

"Yes." I looked up at him. "Are you okay?"

"Yep. Fine. I'm not looking at anything gross. Just appreciating nature right here. I'd better let Heather know I'll be a little late."

"Please do that. Could you just say we are delayed because we are witnesses to an accident and that everyone in the group is fine?"

"Then tell her everything when I see her?"

"If you would."

"I can do that. She'd get it out of me anyway."

I left him to his mobile call and texted Judith, Nancy, Eseld and Peggy.

We heard the siren as it approached the wood then silence as the police vehicle could not proceed onto the walking path. In minutes, a constable and a short, stocky, uniformed woman strode into view.

"The body?" the woman asked. Sergeant from her badge. D.S. Thompson," she said and proffered her warrant card. "SIO."

Senior Investigation Officer.

"Already?" I asked. Usually the responding officers call in a SIO.

"I was in the office when the call came in. The dispatcher said the witnesses were coppers."

"Retired," I said.

"I've called in the Scenes of Crimes Officers."

The SOCO were civilians employed by the police to collect evidence. Not to analyze or give any opinion, just collect it.

Sergeant Thompson was my height but broad-shouldered. Her uniform strained across her bust. Her short, fair hair was scraped back from her face which was shiny and unlined. Although she had offered more information than I'd expected, she wasn't friendly. There wasn't any expression on her face or in her eyes. I definitely was going to cooperate with her.

"Here." I showed her where my three tourists had entered the bushes. The branches were broken, and we could see their footprints in the mud.

"Just follow that path. They aren't far. Perhaps fifty yards."

The sergeant indicated the constable should remain with us. "Get their particulars, tell the SOCO people to secure the area then get to the site," she told him. Then commanded us, "You both stay here," before she headed off toward Bran and the others.

The crows were perched on the branches of a nearby chestnut tree. I waited for one of them to intone, 'Nevermore'. Then shook myself. Death was a natural order of life for them, not anything macabre. Although, from what Lionel had said, this wasn't a natural death.

The constable spoke into his mobile, then walked over to us.

"Name?" he asked as he pulled out his official notebook. He was tall and thin with big brown eyes, older than his sergeant and with lines around his eyes.

We gave our names, addresses and mobile contact numbers. I glanced at his name badge.

"Thanks, Constable Green. We'll remain here." I wondered if the dispatcher had warned him about me: *sarcastic woman, could be trouble.*

He nodded and disappeared into the brush. We could see the bushes further along the river moving as the constable approached the crime scene, like a wave in the tall grasses and reeds, but we couldn't see the scene itself. In about twenty minutes, the sergeant returned with everyone but the constable following her. The SOCO team still hadn't arrived. Sergeant Thompson took Lionel to one side and spent about fifteen minutes talking to him and making notes. Constable Green did the same to Anna. Then the Sergeant took Bran aside and took information from him. They would compare their stories later. *Keep all witnesses apart and take individual statements.* I'm sure it was standard procedure, but Matthew and I had to wait.

Finally, the sergeant walked over to us. "Constable Green has your name and addresses. I may need to get more information from you, but I will be tied up with the forensic team here for a few hours."

She addressed me. "You're the tour guide?"

I nodded.

"Can you keep everyone at the hotel," she checked her notes, "the Queen Bess Hotel, until I get there?"

I thought about it. "I have reservations for everyone at Jessie's Bistro for seven. We'll be there until about ten. Then back to the hotel. Can you accommodate that? My guests have to eat, and the Queen Bess doesn't serve an evening meal."

She considered it. "All right. "

"We're free to go?"

"Yes. But not far."

"I'll keep you informed." I said. The first on the scene are always suspects. I did not want to be a suspect. It would take time to extricate myself. I hoped she wasn't going to keep us away from the itinerary I had so carefully arranged. I imagined the destinations, dates and times rising from the page, whirling in the air and dropping back in a disordered mess. I'd work hard to avoid that. I definitely didn't like the uncertainty her command caused. We left her turning back into the bushes while we started down Corinium Gate Road to Market Place then down Cricklade to the hotel. I had expected to appreciate the warm May afternoon, the honey-colored stone of the houses and the bustle of the market town, but what I felt was worry about the threat to disrupt my tour and kind of detached sadness for a young life lost. I dropped back to check on Lionel.

"Are you okay, Uncle Lionel?"

"Dandy," he said. "I'm sorry for the fellow, but it's nice to be part of a team again."

"Are they going to use you?" I asked in some surprise. Sergeants and inspectors were usually reluctant to share their territory.

He looked at me. "Not likely, but Bran and I can have a good chin wag about it. Might even talk to Mark. He's coming tomorrow, isn't he?"

"He said he was, but you know his superintendent. She can call him out on another case at any time."

"You tell him to look me up when he arrives."

"Of course," I said. Lionel's eyes were brighter, and he walked with more energy than he had previously.

"Oh, Lionel."

"Yes, my lover."

"What did the boy die from?"

"Looked like a stab wound to the heart."

"Oh, my word!" I stared at him.

"Right nasty," Lionel said.

CHAPTER FIVE

We met in the lounge at the Queen Bess for a quick drink before dinner. I thought it best to let the group know about the death of the boy and the police investigation. We'd managed to put two tables together so we could chat. I didn't want to talk about Richie Stonehouse, if the body *was* Richie Stonehouse, but I needed to keep my group informed. Matthew would certainly have said something. They would be curious.

"We had a rather difficult afternoon," I started. Anna, Eseld, Bran and Lionel were quiet. The rest looked at me with interest in their expression.

"We found the body of a young man near the river." I kept my voice low.

"No!" Peggy stared at me. "Dead, I take it."

"Very."

"How distressing," Judith said and leaned over and patted my hand. "I take it you informed the police."

"I did. You should know it might be a former employee of this hotel."

"Ah," Matthew said, "the boy who's missing."

"That's right."

"Sad. Overdose?"

"I've no idea," I lied. A stab wound to the heart was definitely not an overdose, but I didn't want to cause any more distress than necessary. "There may be police around, but I doubt they will want to talk to any of you as the boy's death occurred before we arrived."

That wouldn't stop Sergeant Thompson from interviewing those of us who had discovered the body, but I wanted to be clear this murder need not concern them. My guests had paid for an interesting and relaxing trip.

"As a parent and a grandparent, it's scary," Nancy said. "The young seem to live dangerous lives."

Some did. The young are notoriously risk-takers, in any era. I remember not having the best of judgement when I was a teen, but I didn't die because I was stupid. I thought of my niece, Kala, and my nephew, Josh. I hoped they'd survive their teen years. Nancy was right. Life for teens was scary. This young man might have done something stupid, or at least, risky.

The group around me were sorry for Richie, or whomever the dead man was, but they hadn't known him. Neither had I, but I'd been too close to the body to just dismiss him from my mind. It reminded me of other deaths and was part of accumulated sadness around a deliberate murder. *Get a grip, Claire. You don't have to ladle your sorrow over the group like an unwanted sauce.* They were on holiday. They didn't need to feel any responsibility. I tried to be informative without being morose. They accepted there was nothing any of us could do and let the subject drift away into talk of the Romans in Cirencester.

Shirley came from the kitchen and stopped me as I was headed up the stairs. "What happened? I heard the guests talking about a body?"

I looked around me and nodded toward the kitchen but Shirley took me to her office, a small room under the stairs.

"What's going on?" she asked.

I told her about our discovery.

"Was it Richie?" she asked. "He hasn't shown up for work."

"I don't know Richie, and I never saw the body."

We didn't get a chance to discuss it further because a woman pushed open the office door, talking as she arrived.

"God Almighty, Shirley! That gormless little shit is causing trouble."

She stopped when she saw me.

She was a short woman, a little plump with dark hair and snapping black eyes. She was dressed in tailored black trousers, a silk shirt and a conventional but expensive camel blazer. Her shoes were Fluvogs, black and white and must have cost close to three hundred pounds. They were beautiful shoes.

"My mother, Lydia Harris," Shirley said.

Her mother stood straighter, took a quick breath and apologized. "I *am* sorry to jump in like that. I had an irritating encounter with one of my salespeople, and I am used to complaining to Shirley."

She offered her hand and I shook it.

"Claire Barclay. I'm a tour guide, and I have my people here."

"How nice to meet you. Are you staying long?" Lydia Harris's diction gained a couple of classes from her initial outburst. I had a hard time reconciling this posh-speaking, well-dressed woman with the woman who'd burst into the room with her council house accent. What a character! She might be fun to know.

"I was just leaving." I smiled at both women and let myself out.

I met everyone in the foyer on time and we walked to Jessie's Bistro. The route took us up Cricklade which turned into Dollar Street, then left onto Black Jack and there it was, in the courtyard behind Jessie Smiths Butchers. No apostrophe on Smiths. We're losing the battle of apostrophe. The bistro was in an eighteenth-century building made of warm, yellow Cotswold stone. Inside, the exposed stone continued, creating the cozy atmosphere. I had a reservation, so we were shown to a long, bare, dark wood table in the private back room. The shiny silver and blinding white napkins added refinement without formality. The chairs were upholstered in a deep cognac-colored leather. The sorrow around the young man's death, the worry about my tour being disrupted and the niggling irritation of tour details slipped from my shoulders. Ah, there would be elegance and most likely excellent service. I could relax. I ordered two bottles of wine, Châteauneuf-du-Pape and Chateau Fargueirol 2015, for the table—that ought to satisfy Judith—and passed around the menus. This meal was included in the tour fee. They could order an expensive meal here, but, usually, people didn't do that. They simply ordered what they liked, and I found the bill close to what I expected.

I chose a seat strategically at the middle point of the table where I could partake in conversations on either side. Eseld, Bran, Heather, and Matthew sat at my left and Peggy, Nancy, Anna, Judith, and Lionel on my right. There was little conversation until we'd ordered. The menu took concentration because the offerings looked fit for the King—and Queen Camilla who was reported to be a fussy eater. Judith should be fine here.

The farms from which the chef purchased his or her supplies were listed next to the item. We weren't offered simply pork tenderloin; we were offered Bythburg pork tenderloin. The same applied to the lamb and the chicken. The cheeses looked delicious. I would have to try the Welsh Peri Las "strong and creamy and a gold medal winner at the World Cheese Awards 2015". It would be exceptional.

After everyone had given their order and the wine had been poured, conversation started to bubble. I heard Lionel explain to Anna how he came to know me through my relationship with his nephew.

"Both you and your nephew are in the policing field?" Anna asked.

"That's right. I made sergeant but me *noy* is a detective inspector."

"I do a little work for the police back home in California."

"You do? Now, I'm right interested in that."

I lost track of their conversation because Nancy who was sitting next to me started talking about mysteries.

"I've found a new writer for this area," she said. "I think he self-publishes and only e-books. I might be wrong, I often am about that sort of thing, but I buy his books on line and read them on my tablet."

"Who is it?" I might not have found this author.

"T. E. Kinsey. His protagonist is Lady Emily Hardcastle, but the story is narrated by her maid, Miss Florence Armstrong."

"I've read him," Judith said from across the table. "Competent and lively writing. Set in about 1905 or so."

I'd enjoyed his books as well. I thought they were published by a Seattle company but I didn't correct Nancy.

"That's right," Nancy said.

"I like the ones set in the 1920s and 30s," Heather offered from my left-hand side. "I've read a lot of them, but I found *Cold Comfort Farm* by Stella Gibbons with an introduction by Lynn Truss truly funny."

"It is hilarious," I agreed, "but set in Sussex."

"Oh, yes. That's right. It makes fun of the genre."

"It does that." I had laughed aloud while reading that book.

"I've read all the Agatha Raisin books," Nancy said. "I enjoy her and the writing is excellent, but Agatha never seems to have any emotional development. You almost want to take her out for a drink and explain life to her."

I agreed with Nancy. "I think the author knew how flawed readers are and thought she'd keep her protagonist limping through life emotionally the way most people do." I'd the same problem with reading her Hamish Macbeth series. He never learned anything about his emotional life.

"It's discouraging," Nancy said.

"In what way?" I asked.

"You keep hoping that the next book will give Agatha, who is by this time almost a friend of mine, some idea about how to grow up."

The main dishes were served just then and everyone was distracted by the impressive presentation of the food and the subsequent tasting experience. The staff were attentive, but didn't rush us, so it was about nine-thirty when we rose from the table and wandered out to Black Jack Street.

The night air was crisp but not cold. The street was paved with flagstones with a brick walk on one side. The flagstones were easier to negotiate than the brick which had heaved a little in spots and pushed up toe-stubbing edges. I was wearing my Roger Vivier low-heeled pumps so was relatively safe on the flagstones.

We proceeded in crocodile fashion two-by-two with Lionel and me at the tail. The couples paired off as did the ladies from Nova Scotia, leaving Judith with Anna. I'd have to see Anna didn't have to partner Judith all the time. She might get quite tired of that.

Everyone said a mellow good night, the Chateau de Neuf, no doubt, working its magic. We agreed on the time to meet at breakfast in the morning. Mark had still not arrived.

Mark and I had met over a body shortly after I returned to England. I'd moved to tranquil Hampshire only to discover a murder victim. Mark had been the investigating officer on the case. At first, I found him aloof, but he proved me wrong about that. As I got to know him, I discovered he'd been married and divorced ten years earlier, had a couple of relationships immediately after the divorce that had died natural deaths and hadn't been with anyone for years before he met me. I'd had a disastrous relationship with Adam, an abusive, narcissistic mistake, and steered clear of men for ten years. Neither of us was looking for romance or commitment but found ourselves involved without deliberately planning it. I was not prepared for love and was gobsmacked. Who would have thought I'd meet such a man—and in my late forties?

Mark moved in and enriched my life for a year. Living together without legal ties suited me, but Mark wanted marriage. I dithered. Living together was fine.

"He's not Adam," Deirdre, my sister, had said with some irritation.

"I know that."

"Stop acting as if he is!"

I married him on September 16th in the garden of my house. We made our commitment official with Mark's parents, Deirdre and her family and, possibly, the entire village of Ashton-on-Tinch at our wedding. Even Superintendent Addison came. She wore an elegant grey suit; I hardly recognized her. I'd tried to make the wedding causal but traditions dictated some formality. I wore a smart, creamy yellow suit and no veil, just a barely-there fascinator. Mark resurrected his uniform and looked handsome and somehow stiff. His sergeant Andy Forsyth, also in uniform, stood up with him. Deirdre supported me, as she always does but she couldn't resist the drama of the ceremony and wore a stunning royal blue shirt-waist with the obligatory fascinator. We could have slipped off to a garden party at Buckingham Palace. Someone put a white satin bow on Gulliver's collar and he joined us. The decorum didn't last. We adjourned to Jack's pub after the brief ceremony for beer and fish and chips which was my idea of a satisfactory wedding breakfast. So far, I had no regrets. I still looked forward to our time together and I hoped he could make it to Cirencester soon.

The breakfast room smelled of bacon, ham, and spices. We must be having muffins which is not the usual fare at a guest house. I joined Lionel at a table for two. The Blighs arrived and found a two-person table. They nodded to me. We were served by Bob while Dylan hovered nearby. It was Dylan's job to bus the tables. He said nothing to us, just concentrated on his work.

"I don't want Eseld to have to put up with me first thing in the morning," Lionel explained why he wasn't sitting with the Blighs.

"But I can?" I teased.

"Aye, but you're family." He smiled.

I noticed Mr. Buchanan, the man who had a transport supply business, sitting by himself, reading the paper and sipping coffee. He looked liked something from an old movie in his impeccably made grey suit and white shirt, a caricature of a precise, English, fussy, bank employee, although from his name he was likely Scottish. He didn't look like an aggressive, entrepreneur who managed companies.

Lionel and I ate in companionable silence until we were down to coffee.

"Have you enjoyed this hotel, Lionel" I asked him. "You've been here about ten days now, right?"

"Well, I like it fine. The food's good, more than good—bleddy 'ansome, it is. And not having to make it is a treat. I go tramping around the countryside looking for birds, so that's healthy, and I'm finding some and that keeps me looking."

Bob was waiting on the tables. I presumed that meant Shirley was cooking. Even though I'd eaten a week's worth of food last night at Jessie's, I ate every crumb of her marvelous spice muffin. Lionel was right. The food was 'bleddy 'ansome'. I watched Bob punctiliously pour coffee and take orders. He hesitated at Anna's table. I narrowed my eyes and watched him. If he said anything to her that was the least bit aggressive, I'd do something about it--but he didn't. He pulled out his pen and politely asked for orders. I let out a sigh.

Lionel raised his bushy eyebrows. "What is it?"

I waited until Bob had disappeared through the swinging door.

"That Bob, Lionel, what do you know about him?"

"He's teasy as n'adder at times," Lionel said.

Angry he meant.

"Dangerous?"

"Hmm." Lionel reached for his blue book and thumbed back a few pages. His voice changed as he read what he had written with, what I surmised, was his sergeant's voice.

"Robert Simpson 42. Burly, fit, does weights, runs, handles the bar, able to subdue boisterous revellers, boxes in a local league, has a cupboard full of protein and health food supplements. Plays football for the local league. Has some shifty mates. No prior convictions that I know of." He looked over at me and said in his usual voice, "But then, I might not know, eh, maid?"

He returned to his book. "Suspect he hits his wife. No real evidence, just something in her attitude toward him." He shut the book. "If he was squatting on my patch, I'd keep an eye on him."

I really didn't care about Bob's life or his philosophy as long as he treated my guests respectfully and gave them good hotelier service. I would care if he was hitting his wife, but there wasn't any real evidence of that. I respected Lionel's suspicions, and I'd pay attention. But I was most concerned about Anna. She was my immediate responsibility. She gave me the impression of capability. She undoubtedly knew how handle racist situations when she met them. I got that, but I didn't want her to *have* to deal with them.

I watched Bob as he brought the food to the tables. He was polite to Anna and Judith, who were sitting together. Anna was also polite. He was more friendly to the Blighs, but as long as he wasn't rude to Anna, I could cope with him. Bloody hell! That's all I need. An idiot racist! *Don't forget a murdered man,*" I told myself. "*Well, yes. But he doesn't have anything to do with me.*" That was true. He wasn't my responsibility, but involvement with the police could interrupt my tour.

"Here's the agenda for the day," I said to Uncle Lionel. "You might want to continue bird watching because you may have already seen some of the sights I have listed here. Just let me know what you decide."

I stood and made the rounds of the other tables, handing out the agenda. I had included a map of Cirencester.

"Since we have independent time, I am going to wander down Black Jack Street," Peggy said. "I saw some fascinating shops there when we were walking home last night."

"I'll do that, as well," Nancy said. "Get my present-buying over with at the beginning of the trip."

Judith held up my itinerary and her own notebook. "I have a few different places than what are listed here. I'd like to check those out with you to be sure they are still open."

She had a point. Many shops and businesses had closed down during the pandemic and never re-opened.

Mr. Buchanan folded his paper, and stood.

"Good morning," he said to me and smiled. He had twinkling blue eyes behind those glasses.

"Good morning," I responded.

"Welcome to Cirencester,"

"Thank you. It's lovely."

He smiled and walked toward the stairs and the rooms above.

Anna stood. "I'll see everyone at supper tonight," she said. She murmured to me as she passed, "I'm off to the Roman Museum."

I assumed she'd said that quietly because she wanted to prevent Judith from following her.

I sat down with Judith as Dylan cleared the tables around us and reviewed her choices. Judith had done her research and had an intelligent interest in the town. I dutifully checked on my mobile to see if her choices were still open and mapped out a day's sightseeing for her. She could have done that herself. I could see she was capable of it, but she wanted special attention from me and she got it. It was easy to do, and it was my job. In a way, it was soothing as well.

"Ring me on my mobile, if you want a lift anywhere and I'll come and get you," I said.

"Well, thank you," she said quite graciously then took herself off to prepare for her day.

Matthew and Heather had left to find presents for their children who were staying with grandparents.

"Maybe a cricket bat and ball," Heather said. "And a set of instructions."

"We'd better buy something spectacular for Mom and Dad," I heard Matthew say as they left the breakfast room. "Those two boys will be turning their hair even greyer."

I returned to my room to find a message from the constabulary requesting I attend along with Dr. Clark at the station sometime today to give our statements. I'd look for Anna in town and we'd go together--or, if I missed her, we could go before dinner tonight. There was no hurry. We weren't crucial witnesses.

I fired up my computer and checked out my emails. There was one from Mark. He usually texted me, but when he wanted to say more, he emailed.

I studied his report of the wild time he'd had in Southampton. He didn't give me specifics, places, names or results of their raids, but he told me enough so I got the sense of what his life had been like the last few days. As well as finding all the caches of humans trafficked into Southampton, he had been trying to get government agencies and a private refugee charity to talk to the illegal immigrants to see if any of them could remain. It wasn't really his job but he was a compassionate man.

"Coming up your way today," he said. "On route to a hastily arranged meeting in Birmingham where we will try to do something about these illegal immigrants. I don't think the MCIT will have much influence."

The Major Crimes Investigation Team was an innovative idea, but establishing lines of authority and funding it had been a nightmare. Still there were many good brains working on that team so a meeting to try to create a better policy could make a difference.

"Lovely," I emailed back.

"See you at dinner time. Send me a text where you will be."

I smiled to myself. We grabbed time together whenever we could. I'd let Shirley know Mark might be joining me overnight. There would, no doubt, be an extra charge.

I checked online to reassure myself that everywhere I'd planned to take my group tomorrow would be open and expecting us. Miracle of miracles, all were as advertised. That done, I shut down my computer and headed out the door. I wondered if my careful planning meant I was trying to control the future. Possibly; I did know that without planning the future would be chaos.

I caught Shirley at the door to her office and told her about Mark's arrival.

"I think there is an extra charge," she said and turned into her office. I followed her.

"That's fine. Just add it to the invoice."

"I'll do that." She looked around at the office a little helplessly.

My sympathies stirred. "You haven't owned the guest hotel long?" I said.

She turned sharply. "We don't own it. My mother does. She thought it would be a good investment, and I could run it. 'It will keep you busy and you can do some cooking but you'll be the manager not just a cook.'" Her voice dropped after she had mimicked her mother.

I was still for a moment. Bitterness had filled that comment.

"You'd rather cook."

"Much rather. But you don't cross the great Lydia Harris." She took a deep breath. "To be fair, she's been good to me, but this hotel is her interest, not mine." She clicked up a file on her computer. "I'll run it for a while then I'll persuade her to buy me a *boulangerie*." She smiled. She was shorter than me, broader too with a practical aura about her that would be an asset in a bakery. She looked like nursery story typical baker with an open face, clear blue eyes and rosy cheeks. Her blond hair hung in a simple plait. I could see her in her French-style bakery.

She clicked the information about Mark into her computer and turned back to the door. I walked out in front of her.

"I'll still do my best for you," she said from behind me. "I can learn a lot here before I get Mummy to change her mind."

"I hope you get your bakery," I said.

Bran and Lionel were leaving with binoculars and notebooks.

"We thought we'd drop into the nick," Bran said. "Read our statements, sign them and maybe pick up some gossip."

"I'm going to the station later," I said, "although I won't get any gossip."

"They might come around here to interview you," Lionel said.

I didn't think they would, as neither Anna nor I could to add much to their investigations. Perhaps Anna could. I wondered if she'd picked up specimens while she was at the river where they found the body. She was quick with her tweezers and vials. But I hoped I would be seen as a bystander. I liked the puzzle of solving a murder, but I didn't want to be involved. That, I knew, could be dangerous.

They waved, and I was off to the shops. My quest today, in the few hours I had away from my tourists, was purchasing a pair of shoes, preferably Italian, mid-heel, suitable for dancing. Mark had decided we should learn to dance. I agreed with him. I was tired of seeing everyone float by me in respectable romantic foreplay. I hoped we'd find enough holes in our schedules to give us time to learn the steps. For dancing I needed shoes. To be honest, I always needed shoes. There seems to be a direct link from the pleasure center of my brain to my feet, a phenomenon well-understood by Italian shoemakers—psychologists, every one.

I cruised through Dunne's, Sassy's, Moda in Pelle and finally shopped for an hour at Jones Bootmaker. I dithered for ages between a black and white-speckled, satin sling-back pair with a bright pink elastic strap and a white satin pair with pearls in the heels. They were both stunning, but satin stains easily and it would be hard to make either of them work for more than one outfit. I decided on a leather shoe, still a sling-back, but more substantial. The heel looked as though it would take some tough treatment. I imagined I would be turning awkwardly on it before I learned grace, and this shoe might survive it. It was black with a white band on the toe and a silver button on top. But what entranced me was the red sole at the open-toe and the red trim around the heel. I couldn't leave it in the shop. Luckily, it wasn't expensive compared to what I usually bought. I still thought about price, even though I had enough money from my stepfather's legacy to buy a closet-full of Italian shoes. I loved shoes, but I wasn't buying them today because they were a good price or because the red trim called to me. I was buying shoes because I didn't want to think about murder.

I walked up Dyer Street, satisfied with my purchase, casually looking at beautiful dresses on the mannequins, lounging in impossible poses in the windows of the shops. If real people posed like that, they'd have aching joints and torn muscles. I considered a late morning coffee and turned to the New Brewery Café. I could browse in their shop as well. It was a combination of art show and merchandize, and always interesting. I wasn't far from the Corinium Museum so wasn't surprised to see Anna drinking coffee at one of the outside tables.

"Hello, Anna. Can I join you?"

"Absolutely," she said and moved packages off the chair beside her.

I set my precious shoes on the ground beside the chair and went inside to get a latte. When I returned, I eyed her parcels. "What did you buy?"

"A fabulous scarf." She showed me a bright red, silk scarf, with startling yellow lilies on it.

"Dramatic," I said.

"Occasionally," she agreed, "I am dramatic. And I bought a vase. Art really. They're shipping it."

"Did you take a picture? "

"Of course." She activated the gallery on her mobile and showed me the vase.

"Stunning. It looks like someone scooped up a bit of the ocean, froth and all, and immortalized it in a vase. It's even poised as if it's going to curl over at any moment."

"Amazing, isn't it to get such movement in a bit of glass?"

"Truly."

I showed her my elegant shoes and she smiled. "Sexy."

"That's the idea," I said.

She leaned back in her chair and let out a satisfied breath. "This is the life. It's really cool to get away from my work and my family for a while."

"You have children?"

"I have a husband and one son who are rafting down the Colorado River right now. Mom's not needed."

I raised my eyebrows. Was she sorry she wasn't with them?

She understood. "I'm happy to leave them to their bonding time. I could have stayed home and got relief from their company. But they aren't my only family."

"No?"

"No. I have a mother and father, four sisters, three aunts and their families, two uncles and their families and numerous cousins, nieces and nephews. All of them seem to be in my life a lot."

"I have a sister, and," I added as an after-thought, "two step-brothers. I have a niece and nephew. That's it."

"Well, you're not Chinese-American. We hyphenated citizens often have a lot of family who want to GET AHEAD." She said that in capitals.

"A bit of pressure, is it?"

She shrugged. "From here it looks supportive. When I'm home and trying to conduct two big research projects, supervise grad students, teach, then go home and deal with a teenager, family seems oppressive. It takes a holiday away to appreciate them. But you're working now."

"Not right at this minute." We smiled at each other and sat back in our chairs, enjoying the warmth of the spring sun and sipping our coffee.

"Tell me about your work," I said. "You study insects?"

"And pollen, and spores."

"For what purpose?"

She was silent for a moment.

"If you'd rather not talk about work because you're on holiday, I understand. I'm interested, but I don't need to know."

"No, I like my work and I'd like to explain it. I have what many PhDs don't have and that is a research lab at a university. So, I feel supported. I still have some teaching load but it's mostly with grad students now. I don't have to correct 300 first-year papers, and I can encourage the grad students' research. It's pretty fascinating most of the time. The purpose of my research is to establish ways in which the police can access the knowledge we have at the university to answer the questions they have about a case. They often ask us the same questions: How long has the person been dead? Was the body moved? Does the material gathered from the suspect's clothes match the material gathered from the body?

"We should be able to take those usual questions and put them into a systematic process that will give answers quickly. Now, it takes an interview and usually one of us has to go and collect the data."

No wonder she was interested in Richie Stonehouse's body.

I imagined her with tweezers hovering over a corpse. She'd be important to the prosecutors. "Because the case will go to court, you have to be sure the data collection is secure? That is, no one could have monkeyed with the samples?"

"That's right." She seemed pleased I was following her. Mark had complained bitterly about lost evidence and evidence that had been contaminated in some of his cases. All his painstaking work had gone for naught when some careless officer had lost evidence or contaminated it.

"Do you get called out often to a police case?"

"Often enough that my department thinks I have a second job. It's California, you know. Lots of murders."

"Did you find out anything yesterday?"

She toyed with her coffee cup. "I took samples from the clothes and skin and found fungi that grows in dark places and some yeast spores, no tree pollen. That's enough for the investigating officer to call in a forensic entomologist of their own. Richie Stonehouse, if that's who he was, was lying among the trees and bushes when we found him, not on a dirt floor, or a cave."

I felt a shiver run up my spine. Richie hadn't died in a fight in that meadow; He hadn't brawled with someone from a pub, walking along, arguing and ended up dumped beside where he was killed. He had been killed somewhere else, somewhere hidden like a cave, and transported with what Mark would call 'evil intent'. His death might have been planned. Was it an execution by a drug gang? A revenge killing by a rival of some kind? Did he see something that endangered him? I couldn't know any of that.

"So, the specimens you took from his clothes don't match the area in which he was found. You can tell he must have been moved." I assumed she'd taken the specimens from his clothes.

"I can't know if he was moved after he died, or if he was transported and killed at the site we found him. Their own entomologist will take samples from his shoes and his clothes. I hope they tell me what he or she found. I guess I'll mosey down to the cop shop and let them know what *I* found. Purely as an interested observer."

Anna impressed me. She had so much knowledge and must have worked hard to get it. She was tall, willowy and utterly feminine. She must also be tough, determined and opinionated. I wouldn't have to protect her. I expect she could deal with police, obstructive clerks and Bob the idiot without my help.

"Are you okay with staying at the hotel? Bob seems a right bigot."

"Yes, he is. A fifth-grade asshole. But he knows you have the power to withdraw a lot of money from his business if he offends me. And I'll slap him with a harassment charge if he's a nuisance or dangerous. I won't put up with it. I won't have to. Any overt remarks or actions and I'll report him. Shirley seems okay, so I'll deal with her and avoid dear Bob. I think he's making an effort to be neutral."

"He has to." I was firm about that.

"It takes some people longer to evolve than others. Not much prejudice in the medical world where I work any more. Most of the time, other docs are interested in what they can find out from me, not what I look like. There was a little increase in prejudice during the pandemic. Some thought I might have inside information about the virus because it came from China. I was born and brought up in L.A., for God's sake —a California girl. What did I know about Wuhan, China? That's prejudice of another kind, but it has a grain of reason behind it and isn't hard to deal with. It's just thoughtless. I tell them I've never been to China, have they? Most people realize when they're being idiots."

"Something like Americans saying, 'Oh, you're British. Do you know the King?'"

She grinned. "Something like that. Bob's different. His prejudice is grounded in emotion. Nothing I can do about that. He wants to hate someone of color, and I'll do."

What did it feel like to be hated because of the color of your skin? How did I feel about being white? I had a sense that white was normal. Did that mean I thought brown was not normal? I hoped not. I could think white was normal and also think brown was normal, just as blue, green and brown eyes were all normal. In Britain, even in Hampshire where I lived, people were mixed colors, races and cultures. But people can hold contradictory thoughts in their minds. It was possible I intellectually thought all colors were normal but acted as though only white skin was. My business was founded on British history and an out-dated view of Britain where everyone was white. Did I present Britain as white? I was shaken by the thought I had been unwittingly compliant in prejudice. I shoved that concept into a "to be examined later" box in my brain.

"How was your visit to the museum?"

"That was awesome. I managed to take scraping from a Roman artifact. Can't wait to see what's in it."

"After 1800 years?"

"You never know. It was the tombstone of Bodicacia. What do you think of that?" Her eyes brightened with excitement.

"I think that's bloody marvelous," I said.

"The epitaph read in Latin *To the Shades of the Dead. Bodicacia, spouse, lived 27 years.*"

"She died in battle, didn't she?"

"No, that was Boadicea. Queen of East Anglia. A similar name. This woman, while probably wealthy, wasn't the warrior queen."

"Just a young, rich Roman."

We smiled at each other, in sync with our insatiable curiosity. Nosey parkers, both of us.

I blinked, returning to the tasks of the day. "We'd better get over to the station and give our statements. They may want all the information you have and be glad of your advice."

"Not likely," she said cheerfully. "Most cops don't appreciate outsiders, but I'll give them my notes."

We stopped at the Queen Bess Hotel to leave our parcels and for Anna to pick up her notes on what she'd found at the site.

The police were polite. The constable at the front desk took our statements and said she would see they were typed. We would have to return to sign them.

"I also have some notes." Anna fetched the papers from her rucksack. The constable looked skeptical.

"Notes?" she said, accepting the paper Anna slid across to her.

"Yes, just preliminary on the yeast, spores and pollen found on the deceased clothes. But you will want to call in your forensic entomologist to take their own specimens. I'm unofficial in this country. You'll need to trace the line of evidence gathering and my notes won't do that."

The constable stared at the papers Anna had passed to her.

Anna continued. "It appears that the body we found was moved from someplace like a cave or a basement—someplace dark and probably cool. Good luck with it." She then turned, and we left the station. It felt as if there was a stunned silence behind us.

My mobile binged with a text. Judith. I guided Anna until she could see the hotel then walked to the car park to get the van and fetch Judith.

I was intrigued by Anna. She had casually gathered evidence then almost as casually dropped it off at the station. I wondered if they would examine it and call in that specialist she requested. It wasn't her job, and she was clear she didn't expect to be involved. She was curious, though.

I never knew what was going to interest my tourists besides mystery novels. Anna was not only interested in current homicides and willing to lend her expertise if needed; she was interested in Roman artefacts and the lives of people who lived long ago. I wondered if she read Aaron Elkins' novels with his skeleton detective and forensic anthropologist Gideon Oliver.

CHAPTER SIX

I took a few minutes to text Rose and ask about Gulliver. She responded immediately with pictures of Gulliver draped in children. They all looked happy. He was definitely getting hugs and love. I thanked Rose and disconnected. I wished I could give Gulliver a hug. I missed him. *He's fine. You're fine. Stop being maudlin.*

Judith's call for a pick-up from the Abbey Grounds Park was equivalent to a royal command. I moved quickly to retrieve the van and collect Judith. She was waiting in front of St John Baptist Church, bundled against the breeze with a trim cranberry-colored, quilted jacket, a Liberty silk scarf with a hint of purple in it, light grey trousers and her sensible but elegant Pikolinos trainers. She had her leather rucksack and was carrying a notebook. I'd like to look like her when I was older, but the chances were slim. I didn't have her notion of style or attention to detail—except for shoes. My shoes would always look fab.

"Did you enjoy that?" I asked her as she climbed into the van and settled in the front left-hand seat.

"Indeed, I did."

She settled her notebook on her lap. "The present Abbey House is very recent, about 1964, but the past history of the house and grounds is intriguing. The original abbey was St. Mary's, an Augustine abbey, built and consecrated in 1176. That was the reign of Henry II. Henry VIII grabbed it and deposed the monks around 1530."

She told me all this without referring to her notes.

"Richard Master was the physician to Queen Elizabeth I and was rewarded for his service with the property which included farms and substantial acreage. He didn't live long after he received it and it was his descendants who built the original Abbey House, most likely from the stones from the deteriorated monastery."

I had been to Cirencester many times, but I hadn't heard this story before. "Was there a museum there or a kiosk where you got this information?" I asked her.

"No, I researched this before I left home."

I had a new respect for Judith-the-scholar. "Please continue."

Judith was enjoying educating me. I was happy to be educated and I didn't have to be back at the hotel for an hour. I had time. She had been on her feet for a few hours. She'd welcome a comfortable ride.

"Would you like a short drive to the cricket field and the Bathurst Estate?" I asked her. "It's a lovely park."

"That would be very agreeable," she said.

I drove in a wide loop north then alongside the cricket fields while she told me about the beautiful Abby manor house which survived until the 1770s.

"The Master family replaced it with a new house which survived with modifications and variations until after the Second World War when it was torn down and flats built for the elderly and a park established in the Abbey House Grounds. The farms remained with the family."

We talked about the influence of such a prosperous family on the community.

Judith referred to her notes only a few times as we discussed English death duties and their contributing role to the demise of stately homes.

When we arrived back at the hotel, I opened the door, and allowed her to alight.

"Did you see the Roman wall?"

"Yes. Very interesting. Third Century. Cirencester was the second most populated town in England in Roman times. Only London was bigger."

She could have told me much more about the Roman world of Cirencester if I hadn't been holding up traffic.

After I parked the van, I took a shower, entered expenses into my spread sheet, dealt with emails, set up our trip to Lacock for tomorrow and checked in with Rose again. Gulliver was fine. I was ready for a drink and joined everyone at the lounge bar at six-thirty.

Bob was busy with locals who found this bar to their liking. Our group was waited on by Dylan who was concentrating so hard in getting the orders correct he said nothing at all. He was efficient with the delivery of the drinks and got them to the correct customers

"Thanks, Dylan," Heather said, ever-friendly. "Are you still in school?"

"Yes, madam," Dylan said.

"Got plans?"

He looked at her blankly.

"I mean are you going to go on to college or training of some kind?"

"I'll work here until September," he said reluctantly. "Going into second year at the uni."

Dylan needed to learn to deal with inquisitive questions waiters were asked. The secret was to be friendly without telling anything you'd rather keep private.

"For what?" Matthew said with interest.

Dylan shrugged. "Medicine."

Medicine. That would be an expensive education.

I could see the questions hovering on Matthew's lips. What kind of medicine? Trauma? Family? But he realized Dylan didn't want to talk about himself and stopped. Dylan's bedside manner was going to need some work.

We were gathering our various rucksacks and handbags, preparatory to leaving the hotel for our dinner reservations, when we heard tromping in the hall. Six young men swaggered toward the back of the hotel. They weren't speaking to each other and appeared intense. Perhaps they'd had an argument outside. They looked between eighteen and thirty and fit as a rugby team. Maybe they *were* a rugby team?

Shirley came to the table to make sure all was well, and get my signature on the bill.

"Are they a rugby team?" I asked "Don't they have a club house?" It seemed to me rugby teams had a club house with a bar, catering kitchen and a party room.

"No. No," Shirley said. "It's Bob's philosophy group."

I stared at her. Philosophy group?

Uncle Lionel raises his eyebrows. "I've seen them before. They meet here twice a week. Tough looking boys."

Shirley gave Lionel a sharp look.

He smiled at her blandly as if he hadn't said a thing out of the way.

I thought of a robbery gang...or drug dealers. They looked a bit tidy for roughnecks, and not sophisticated enough for gangsters. But how could I tell? They did *not* look like a benevolent society. I didn't have children. I didn't know how respectable young men dressed these days. I'd pay attention now that my nephew Josh was approaching fifteen. So far, I'd only seen him in sports togs, his school uniform or jeans and a hoodie. These men were dressed in jeans, but with sports shirts and jumpers or sports shirts and jackets--respectable, but somehow they were too quiet.

"No, truly." Shirley said, "They argue ideology for hours. It keeps Bob happy. He wanted to be a barrister but couldn't manage it. Doesn't do exams well, but he's ambitious, my Bob. Always trying to improve himself. I'm happy he's occupied."

I exchanged a glance with Alistair Buchanan who had come in and sat at a nearby table. I raised my eyebrow and he smiled. A philosophy club? Who knew?

A stocky man in his mid-fifties entered the lounge and strode over to Mr. Buchanan's table.

"A pint of bitter, Dylan" he said and sat down.

"Ah," Lionel said and stood. He walked over to the table and spoke to Mr. Buchanan. "Excuse me, mate."

Mr. Buchanan smiled, "Yes, Lionel?"

"I have a fellow here from America who runs beef in Montana. He's interested in talking to a local farmer. Perhaps, when you finished your business, you could talk to him." He nodded at the newcomer.

"Lester Wright," Mr. Buchanan said. "Lester is indeed a local farmer. Lionel Atkinson, retired police sergeant and a birder."

"Pleased to meet you," Mr. Wright said and the men shook hands. "A rancher from America?"

"That's right.".

"Be happy to talk to him. Maybe tomorrow?"

Lionel nodded. Obviously Mr. Wright was not going to take the time right now. Mr. Buchanan was working a transport business. Mr. Wright, no doubt, had produce to transport. There were no good rail links to the Cotswolds so the farmers must depend on lorries.

"I need those workers now!" I heard Mr. Wright say.

"A short delay," Mr. Buchanan responded.

They were both quiet as I passed their table. I hoped the farmer would talk to Matthew tomorrow. It sounded as though he had to juggle getting workers and moving product. I expect Matthew had some of the same problems.

We assembled outside the hotel. I gave the directions to Igloos Restaurant on Black Jack Street. It wasn't far, and by now most of the group were familiar with this area of Cirencester.

We paired up again and walked crocodile style to leave room for others on the pavement. The restaurant was about a ten-minute walk up Cricklade, through the maze of shops to the back side of the restaurant on Castle Street.

Lionel and I led the way as cutting through the lanes could be confusing. We talked about Bob's group as we walked.

"People can get intense," he said, "about almost anything. It's a stress-reliever, no doubt. When the stay-at-home pandemic orders were on us, a load of people, like Bran and me, got interested in birding. I tellywot, it was a time to take up hobbies, almost anything would do for some. Maybe those young men started reading when they had to stay home. Like-minded people gather around a passion and can be as single-minded as a cat at a mousehole. These men *might* be talking about changing the rugby rules, or organizing for better wages. But philosophy? Giss on!"

I didn't believe it either. "Rugby or union problems sounds more likely than philosophy."

We found the Igloos Restaurant and were welcomed by the head waiter who gestured toward the stairs. We followed the brick wall up the stairs and into the private room I'd booked, the red of the brick giving a warmth and cozy atmosphere to an otherwise plain, rectangular room.

Everyone found a place at the plank table. I sat beside Anna. Lionel sat further down the table. Judith sat on my right. She immediately busied herself with scrutinizing the menu. It was a lovely menu. I hoped she wouldn't find fault with it.

Anna turned to me. "How are you doing? Did this morning upset you?"

It was kind of her to inquire.

"I'm all right," I said. "Not as used to finding bodies as you are." I gave a fleeting thought to the five I *had* found. That didn't come close to the many she must have examined. I hadn't seen this corpse, so I only had my imagination to contend with. I wasn't going to think about it now. "Did you get a chance to look at your pollen from the museum?"

"I did."

"What were you looking for?"

"I'm looking for sea silk made from byssus. It's the right period, third century AD." She smiled at me, prepared to let the subject drop if I wasn't interested.

"What is byssus?" I'd never heard of it.

"It would be a rare find, but it did exist. It's the filaments of Pinna nobilis a giant mollusk, a clam, that attaches itself to the sea bed by long, strong, silky threads. They made a cloth from it way back then. A luxury cloth so not readily found." As Lionel said. People get passionate about their interests. Anna's eyes sparkled.

"The woman was rich. Did you find it?" I persisted.

"No. Disappointing but not unexpected."

I supposed the life of a scientist was full of disappointing incidents. Only occasionally would they have eureka moment. She'd look at thousands of ordinary microscope slides before she discovered one that interested her.

"What *did* you find?" She had taken specimens, so she must have seen something. I suppose she might just find dirt. Of course for her, dirt might hold many surprises.

"Barley pollen. Some grasses as opposed to tree pollen which makes sense because they must have had farms."

"True. They had to feed the people in the settlement."

"Yes." We were quiet for a moment, no doubt both imagining Cirencester in the third century, fields of barley, workers scything the tall grasses, horses grazing in the distance, mill wheels turning. I wrenched my mind back to the present.

"I'm sorry you didn't find your sea silk."

She smiled at me. "It's out there somewhere. I'll keep looking."

I could see her going around the world from Roman ruin to Roman ruin, extracting tiny bits of dust to study.

"What happens if you find it?"

"If I do, I'll ask for official permission to study the site and 'discover' it."

I supposed she saved herself a great deal of time by doing preliminary pilfering. I glanced at the rest of the group. They were studying the menu. It was extensive and took some concentration. We gave our drink orders and, when they had been served, our menu orders. Mark hadn't arrived. I hoped he would come some time tonight. He might have been held up by another murder...or not. I've wasted a lot of time worrying about that in the past only to find he was delayed by paperwork. I needed to pay attention to my guests.

"You were a nurse before you retired, weren't you?" I asked Eseld who was sitting across the table from me.

She took an appreciative drink from what looked like sherry. "I was a nurse, yes. Lovely job, it was. Lionel's Addie and I worked together at the doctors' clinic. Agreeable hours. Proper good'uns to work with. I've been retired six years. I miss it. And I miss Addie." She glanced down the table at Lionel.

He smiled but didn't respond.

"Well, now," Peggy said. "You've had an interesting life. Was it exciting being married to a policeman? That's was what you were, weren't you, Bran?"

He nodded.

"Sometimes," Eseld agreed. "We tried to keep our professions separate—as you do I expect?" She glanced at me.

"I try to stay out of Mark's investigations." I didn't add I wasn't always successful.

"I imagine your nursing profession made you a supportive helpmate to your husband when his job got stressful," Nancy suggested.

"You imagine wrong, my lover." Eseld snorted. "If I'd stayed home and supported my husband every time life got stressful, I'd never have left the house. No, I looked after my stress, and he looked after his. No point in compounding it."

"Did you read fictional mysteries so you didn't have to deal with the ones on your doorstep?"

Eseld looked pensive for a moment." Perhaps. But there now, I think I read them for the humor."

I laughed. "Really? Such as T. E. Kinsey's books about Lady Hardcastle?"

"Love those," Nancy said.

"I like Ann Granger's characters," Peggy said. "The Mitchell and Markby ones are set in the Cotswolds, aren't they?"

"They are. The Campbell and Carter ones are set there as well."

"So you didn't involve yourself in Bran's cases," Nancy persisted.

"No." Eseld was definite.

Nancy laughed. "That's refreshing. Didn't you want to know all about them? I'd have pestered the man with questions."

"I had enough 'cases' of my own. Still," Eseld took a small sip of her sherry. "I'd like him to write about his life. I'd find it interesting—in retrospect, as it were."

"I'm not a writer," Bran protested. He'd been listening but not participating until now. "I tell her that, but she won't accept it."

"You've been writing every day of your constabulary life," Eseld said. "Every constable in the country writes every day. Sergeants and inspectors as well."

"They have to record everything," I agreed, thinking of the ubiquitous constabulary notebooks and Mark's tablet.

"You did that Lionel, didn't you?" Eseld called down the table

"Very likely," he said. "Did what?"

She smiled. "Had to write down everything you did in the day in your official notebook."

He nods. "Still do."

"I know. So does Bran. Every bird he sees goes into his notebook. So both of you should have excellent recall of what happened during your police career."

"I don't know about that," Lionel said. "We wrote it down so we didn't have to remember it."

"Hmmph." She turned back to us. "Addie used to complain that Lionel didn't get on with computers when he was a sergeant, no he didn't, so wrote everything down in a police journal."

I nodded.

She went on. "Bran used to carry one. When *he* got promoted he used a tablet; he's a dedicated computer geek now. What about your Mark?" Eseld asked me.

"Mark uses both a tablet and a blue book."

"That's not the official notebook," Bran said. "The blue book isn't so regulated. You just keeps notes in it. It isn't required for evidence."

"Really?" Nancy said. "I wonder if our Mounties have to do that? You wrote in them every day?"

"When he was a constable, he had to hand them in at the end of the day," Eseld answered for him as she often did. "Those pesky official note books have serial numbers. They're registered and have to be accounted for. And they have to be written so they can be used as evidence. Very time consuming and tedious."

"Just like your nurses' charts," Bran said.

"Oh, I expect that's so." Eseld gave up.

"One of the joys of being retired," Bran said. "I don't have to file those notebooks."

"You still use them, though, the unofficial ones," Eseld said. "Like a second brain."

"I was like that in the library," Peggy said. "Everything was tabulated, categorized and filed, and I came to depend on the system."

"I volunteer at the local vet clinic," Nancy said. "They file all the information on the animals so nothing gets lost. They do it on old-fashioned paper files and also on computer."

"Before computers we had systems of keeping and retrieving information. Computers are just faster. I think most professions use that 'second brain' Eseld talks about," Peggy offered.

"You volunteer at an animal surgery?" I asked Nancy.

"I lived on a farm, well an orchard in the Annapolis Valley, most of my life. We had lots of animals, and I missed them when I retired to the city after my husband died. The vet clinic helps with that."

The conversation moved on to the itinerary then to almost silence as all enjoyed the elaborate meal. It was a shame Mark missed it. I imagined he got supper somewhere.

Over the tea and coffee, I heard Lionel explaining to Heather and Matthew further down the table about his relationship to Mark and Mark's to me. "She's my niece-in-law."

I was good with that.

"My nephew, an inspector with the Major Investigations Team. Very talented bobby, my nephew."

Mathew was interested. "You were a bobby yourself."

"I was. A good life. You are a rancher I hear. Tell me about Montana."

Matthew was happy to do so and the conversations became more general.

I left early to get the van because Judith refused to walk back to the hotel. I thought Bran, Eseld and Lionel might appreciate the ride as well. I didn't know if Lionel had any underlying health conditions. I should ask Mark. Somehow asking Lionel seemed presumptuous. I'd like to know, though. The others had filled out a form that asked that question, and so far no one, except Bran who had high blood pressure and Judith who had the same listed anything that might cause alarm. I had aspirin in my first aid kit for those who might suffer a stroke, and naloxone if anyone overdoses on opioids, something that was highly unlikely with this group, but I was not equipped for any other kind of emergency.

They headed up the stairs. I peaked into the lounge, hoping to see Mark, but only Dylan was there, sitting at a table drinking tea. He looked tired.

"Still here, Dylan?" I said, stating the obvious.

He half-rose then sunk back in his chair,

"Lots to do now that Richie isn't here. To be fair, he did the lifting and hauling."

"He's not coming back?"

"Naw. The cops were here. He's dead."

"I'm sorry. Were you close?" I pulled up a chair and sat across from him.

"Not so much. I mean I've got good parents. I live in Chippingham. He lived in The Dells. Not much chance for someone from The Dells."

"A rough neighborhood?" I'd heard The Dells was a district in Cirencester and I had a vague idea it was a place to avoid.

"More or less. Not much going for him there."

"What was he like?"

"Lazy to start." Dylan drank from his mug of tea. "Chippy. Fun in a way. Always had a grin and always looking for a way to make money. Not that I blame him for that. I'm always looking for a way to make money, but Richie didn't much care how jubby his deals were. He'd been dealing for years. Probably started in infant school."

"Drugs?"

"Maybe. But I mean he was always making a deal. Little things: watches, bikes, chargers for mobiles, mobiles, anything."

"He sounds a bit dodgy."

"Yeah. That he was. And he was young. Twenty. That's too young. He was murdered, the cop said. That's weird. He wasn't important enough to be murdered. That sounds naff," His voice drifted to quiet. "He was kind of a cheerful guy and I didn't think he'd make enemies. He didn't deserve to die like that."

We sat in silence in a short wake for Richie.

I broke the silence. "You find it hard to work here?" I was curious about this hotel. Dylan might have some insight into why I felt as if there was an underlying story here.

"I have to work somewhere. Shirley's all right." He shrugged his shoulders, then gave me a smile. "Thanks for listening. I'd better get on home."

I left him then and went to my room.

No Mark. If he got in before midnight we'd had time for some conversation and I could get his ideas on the murder of Richie Stonehouse. At least I knew the identity of the dead man. I wondered if Richie had any connection to Bob's group. Those menacing young men trooping through the hotel to the back room worried me. I hoped there was nothing nefarious going on. As my mother would have said: I'm not so green as cabbage-looking. Philosophy indeed!

CHAPTER SEVEN

Mark did get in about midnight, but we didn't take much time for conversation. We were still newlyweds, after all. In the morning, we had coffee in our room and talked. I'd been feeling relaxed, my toes even felt soft, when the caffeine began to percolate my brain. I sipped the coffee, trying to get more cognitive cells firing. I noticed the leaded windows were not authentic, but a replica with shiny vinyl sashes. It made sense. They were longer-lasting and didn't leak the way the old wooden ones did. I'd thought about replacing the ones in my house when I bought it but couldn't bear to get rid of hundreds of years of solid workmanship. Perhaps this hadn't been solid. I wondered what kind of flooring was under the bright red, patterned carpet. I distracted myself for a few seconds with the design on the cornice that ran around the top of the walls. Grapes? Ivy? Then I faced what had been whining for attention at the back of my mind.

"I'm worried about those men who tramp through the hotel on their way to a 'meeting,'" I said. "Is that just prejudice against strong, young men who look intense?"

"You might be prejudiced but possibly with good reason. I'll ask Uncle Lionel what he's noticed."

"He keeps notes, you know."

Mark laughed. "That's an old copper, for you. It's habit."

I brought up another subject that had been simmering in the back of my mind. "What do you know about The Dells?"

"Here in Cirencester?"

"Yes. Here."

"It's an old council housing site. It's been the subject of renewable efforts several times but nothing seems to improve things there."

"What's it like?"

"A bit of a rabbit warren. Streets go off into closes, tiny alleyways snake off into who knows what."

"Crime?"

"Lots of it. The police don't go in there if they can help it. Petty crime abounds. Kids are recruited at a young age to run drugs."

I sipped my coffee and thought about it. "Because they won't get charged if they're caught."

"That's right. There's not much choice for them. Their parents or their neighbors lean on them and we can't do a thing about it. There are hell holes like that in many cities."

"Cirencester looks so peaceful."

"It is, in most places. Just not The Dells."

Richie Stonehouse had come from here. I wondered if he had a family. I sipped the last of my coffee. It was good but not as good as I make myself. "I'll go knock up Lionel now," I said. "He asked me to let him know when you arrived."

Lionel followed me back to Mark carrying his own cup of tea. Mark gave him his chair and sat on the bed. I poured myself a second cup of coffee and settled back in my chair.

"Got anything on those yobs that are meeting here, Uncle?"

"Might have," Lionel said and pulled out his blue book. "Don't know if they are just local idiots who do a lot of talking, or serious goons. They meet once a week at a regular time, like cows for milking. They swagger in; Shirley herds them to the back and leaves them alone. They don't get loud or angry. I've loitered with intent a few times but didn't hear anything of interest." He studied his notes for a moment. "No insignia on their clothes. No common tattoos. Maybe gormless."

"Don't put yourself in harm's way," Mark said.

"Na likely." Lionel sounded amused.

"Some of those 'philosophy' groups are hate groups," Mark reminded him. "They don't have a lot of common sense or respect for others, including old coppers."

Lionel raised his eyebrows. He'd been dealing with malefactors for fifty years. I don't suppose there was much Mark could teach him. Still, the world had changed in fifty years and the young men of today were much different from the young men of years ago. Lionel knew this. I expect he would be open to any ideas from Mark.

"This hotel isn't just a hotel," Lionel continued. He read his notes again. I looked up to see the door moving slightly inwards just as Lionel said. "Shirley is running another business."

"Just a minute." I stood then opened the door and saw Shirley standing outside with a full tray.

"Did you order tea for this time?" Shirley asked.

"Not us," I said.

"Drat that Dylan. He has the wrong room. Which one of your guests do you think would have tea at this time? I'd hate to go all the way back to the kitchen."

"Not Heather and Matthew. They'd be coffee drinkers. The Nova Scotian ladies would drink coffee as well. Try the Blighs." I turned back to the room. "Are the Blighs morning tea drinkers, Uncle?"

"Of course," he said.

"Thanks." Shirley hefted her tray and started down the hall.

"She heard you, Uncle Lionel."

"Her business is na a secret. She makes hand sanitizers in plastic bottles with the spray on it. You know the kind that all of us were using during the pandemic. Most people still spray their hands. It's a little business she runs from the wine cellar. She's a smart woman. She wanted to be a great chef, but isn't above making a shilling or two from a trend."

I'd noticed the hand sanitizers with the toiletries. "Good for her."

"I'm off to Birmingham soon, love," Mark said. "I'll grab a quick breakfast with you and be gone."

We ate breakfast with Uncle Lionel at a table for three. Mr. Buchanan arrived and stopped to say good morning. Lionel introduced Mark. "My nephew, another copper."

"And my husband," I interjected.

Mr. Buchanan commented. "A family of coppers. What's the collective noun?"

I laughed. "A cadre of coppers?"

"A platoon of police?' he suggested.

"Mark outranks me." Lionel said with obvious pride. "He's a detective inspector on the Major Crimes Investigations Team."

"Very impressive," Mr. Buchanan said and moved to his table.

A red tinge appeared at the edge of Mark's cheeks. He should be used to Lionel's praise.

"I think they're going to disband The Major Investigations Team," Mark told us.

Uncle Lionel shook his head. I know he enjoyed the constabulary talk with Mark.

"Glad I was only a sergeant," he said. "I didn't have to attend as many meetings as the brass did. Bran was an inspector for the last two years of his work. They couldn't get anyone else so he was a stopgap, and it did good things to his pension. We both 'ad rather be sergeants. Na so much paper work, nor meetings."

"You've got a point," Mark said. "But I like being in charge and solving puzzles when I can. Claire's good at that as well."

I took the praise, undeserved as it was. I clearly remember being convinced the wrong person was a murderer and only disabused of the notion when the real murderer tried to kill me.

All my tourists came down for breakfast.

Bob took the hot meal orders. I noticed. While he stood beside Anna, he didn't look at her, just studiously ignored her.

I took a deep breath and started to rise. He was not going to be discourteous to my guest. Before I could do anything, Anna suddenly stood up close to Bob, her coffee cup in hand, ostensibly heading for a refill at the carafe on the counter. She was about two inches taller and looked down on him. She gave him her breakfast order with crisp authority and great detail. "Two poached eggs on avocado toast, shrimp, with melted butter in a small cup on the side, whole wheat toasted lightly buttered, and a latte. No cinnamon on top."

Bob had to concentrate on his writing as she delivered the complicated order quickly.

Anna smiled. "Thank you, I'll looked forward to it." She turned her back on him and left him to take the orders from the others. Anna poured herself more coffee and looked up. I met her eyes and smiled. Of such small things is satisfaction rendered. No one else noticed anything.

Mark stopped me as we were leaving the hotel.

"That Mr. Buchanan," he said. "What does he do?"

"He has transport lorries and is looking to set up an office here."

"What does he transport?"

I thought about the little I knew. "Calves. Furniture."

"People?"

I remembered Mr. Wright's question to Mr. Buchanan. "Workers."

We looked at each other. A transport company could bring illegal immigrants to an area as well as take livestock like calves away.

Mark nodded decisively. "I'll get Andy to investigate him. We might find something." He bid me a hasty goodbye and disappeared up the Birmingham Road. I stood for a moment considering the idea of Buchanon and Wright as traffickers. They could be bringing in legal farm workers. They didn't have to be transporting illegal ones. I shrugged off the problem—Mark would deal with it—and concentrated on being a tour guide. I passed out the daily itinerary. We were going to Lacock.

Lacock is twenty-seven miles south of Cirencester down the A439 to the A350, then south-east onto the Cantax Hill Road. We would park nearby and spend the morning at Lacock Abbey and the Fox Talbot Museum. I had everyone's National Trust passes, so they would not have to wait in line. We'd lunch at the Lacock Abbey Courtyard Tearoom on the grounds. After lunch, those who wanted to wander around the quaint village could do so. The others might want a ride to the edge of the Lover's Walk and make their way back to town through the pretty path there. We could meet at King John's Hunting Lodge for high tea.

"Cucumber sandwiches when we get there?" Peggy asked.

"Guaranteed," I assured her.

"After tea, we'll travel back here arriving about five-thirty then go out for dinner about eight-thirty. Does that suit?"

"Will they have dairy free at these tea rooms." Judith needed to know she would get exactly what she wanted.

"They will," I said. If she ordered plain tea, that would be dairy free.

We'd just finished our breakfast and were gathering our bits and pieces when Sergeant Thompson arrived followed by Constable Green who was carrying a file full of papers.

Sergeant Thompson appropriated an unoccupied breakfast table. "If you could come here one at a time, you can sign your statements and be on your way."

I calculated the time that might take and how that would impact my schedule. As one person read their statement, signed it and left, the next filed in to do the same.

Anna positioned herself at the end of the line after me and, when I had signed, settled down to read her statement. As I was leaving, I heard her speak to the Sergeant.

"Did you call in a forensic entomologist?"

"We did," Sergeant Thompson said. "She was miffed we'd moved the body but the day was warm, and he'd been there a few days, so he had started to .." she hesitated.

"Started to..?"

"Pong a bit. He was a public safety hazard. Dr. White will be out to take samples from the area then go to the morgue to take them from the body. She may be out later today; she's that keen. Would you care to observe?"

Sergeant Thompson was much more accommodating that I'd expected.

"You don't have any status in the UK," she told Anna, "but we'd be foolish to turn down your expertise if you're interested."

I looked back to see Anna's eyes brighten as she answered with some enthusiasm. "Love that. Do give me a call." She handed the Sergeant her business card. "Here, I'll circle my cell phone."

"Is that long distance?"

"Oh," Anna's face fell. "It is. California. Could you let Claire know if you have anything for me? I'm sure hers is local?"

I nodded and the Sergeant sent me a corresponding nod in acknowledgement. "I have her number."

Anna looked a little startled. In America, 'I have her number' meant Sergeant Thompson had assessed me and didn't trust me. Here, it simply meant she had my mobile number.

Shirley arrived to assist Dylan in clearing off the crockery. I'd noticed Bob took orders and served food. I'd yet to see him clean up.

Lionel and Bran stopped just outside the lounge to chat. I heard Lionel say, "I might go down to the nick with my observations."

Bran gave him a warning look. Lionel turned, saw me then saw Shirley who had come up behind me. I stepped aside.

"Sorry to be in your way," I said to her.

"You work hard," Lionel said and smiled.

Shirley stopped for a moment, adjusting the heavy tray so her hip took some of the weight. "You're off to Lacock?"

"We are," I said, "Most tourists go there."

"True enough, and it's well worth it. I'm off to Bath today to load up on supplies."

"Lionel tells me you make those hand sanitizers that are in the guestrooms."

"I do. It's a bit of trouble, but they sell well, both here as guests buy them to take with them, and at the local chemist's and gift shops."

"I imagine this place takes quite a few provisions as well. You must spend a day in Bath buying what you need."

"I'm used to managing a restaurant," Shirley said. "I was on my way to being a master chef when the pandemic hit. I'll get back to that when the trade recovers. Making hand sanitizers is just a stopgap."

"You're a marvellous cook," Lionel said.

She smiled faintly. "Thank you, but I really want to create great pastry, not just breakfast. Maybe next year."

The pandemic had shoved many a career from its path. Shirley must be in her forties. She might feel there wouldn't be many more years of opportunity left for her. The younger chefs with new ideas would be snapping at her heels. The pandemic had been like a giant earthquake, shaking people out of their positions and scattering them into new ground. Shirley didn't seem happy with where she'd fallen.

The day trip to Lacock was a success. The abbey was impressive, the grounds, lovely, the lunch satisfying, even to Judith, and the walk through town enjoyable. Bran and Lionel elected to trek through Lover's Lane and meet us for high tea at the hunting lodge.

We were back at the Queen Bess hotel in Cirencester around five-thirty.

"You won't believe all the amazing pictures I got," Peggy said. "I will bore my neighbor witless, the way she's been boring me with her photos over the last few years. I'll enjoy doing that." Her eyes danced.

Nancy smiled at her and shook her head. "It was almost like a fairy-tale village. Everything was so perfect."

"I agree," Peggy said. "You almost wanted to see vulgar graffiti just to remember which century you're living in, you did." Occasionally, Peggy sounded Scottish. Nova Scotia meant New Scotland. I suppose some of the accent came down through the families.

"We are eating later," I reminded them, 'around eight-thirty. So, you have time to have a nap or take a walk."

"Let's sort out our treasures," Peggy suggested and they went off with their full shopping bags to their rooms.

My mobile buzzed and I saw a message for Dr. Clarke.

"The police would like you to attend at the station, if you could," I told her.

"I'll be there."

I texted that information back to the constable.

"Where's the station?" Anna asked. "Will I need a cab?"

"No, it's close. I'll walk you over." Because the lanes and streets curved and wound through the town, directions were difficult to follow.

"Thanks. Let me get my recorder and my notebooks."

"I take it you have your specimen jars."

"I do."

"Did you get some samples from the abbey in Lacock this afternoon?" The abbey was begun in 1229 by Ela, Countess of Salisbury.

"I did. They weren't Roman, but interesting in any case." She smiled at me and was gone only a few minutes.

The rest of my guests made their plans. Eseld decided to take a nap in her room and Bran and Lionel said they'd go back along Bufford road to the river to look for Mandarin ducks.

"They will be breeding now, so we might catch the male patrolling around the nest," Lionel said. I noticed he had a small camera in his hand. He stuffed it into his old, tattered and probably much appreciated vest.

"Good time of the day to catch them." Bran agreed. They disappeared through the front door with their binoculars and notebooks.

Heather and Matthew retired to their room. Couples needed to grab their privacy when they could.

I led Anna through the streets to the Gloucestershire Constabulary, a distance of less than a city block, but not in a straight line from our hotel. The route required weaving around buildings and choosing the correct lanes. Sitting on the North Way, the station was a distinctive building, a rectangular made of Cotswold brick, not stone, so while it reflected the warm glow of the eighteenth-century buildings nearby, it had none of the charm. It was neat and looked serviceable. It had bright blue, freshly painted doors and sparkling white window sashes—all with paned windows. I wondered about that. There were no security bars, and the window and door panes looked decorative rather than substantial. There were buildings behind this entryway that were part of the compound, so perhaps the secure rooms were there.

We were obviously expected by a constable, who greeted us, and ushered us into an interview room. It looked like all the interview rooms I've seen on films: square, small, a table with two chairs on one side and one chair on the other, with one more against the wall, and a high window battling feebly to bring light into this dark space.

Sergeant Thompson stood as we entered the room, but the other woman remained seated. The constable left us and the seated woman introduced herself.

"Good afternoon, Dr. Clark," she said. "I'm Amy White. I'm the environmental entomologist assigned to this case."

"Glad to meet you," Anna said, looking eagerly at the papers in front of Dr. White. Then checked herself as good manners prevailed. "This is Claire Barclay. She's my guide. She brought me through the lanes."

Sergeant Thompson raised her eyebrows but brought the fourth chair forward so we could all sit. I was staying.

"Tell me, Dr. Clarke," Dr. White said. "You were at the scene before me. If that had been me, I wouldn't have been able to resist picking up a specimen or two. Do you have anything for me?"

"Anna. Call me Anna."

"Amy here."

They were interrupted by Sergeant Thompson.

"I am afraid we cannot give you any consultant fee, Dr. Clark. You're not licensed in Britain, and we don't have a budget for two entomologists. Anything you contribute will be gratefully received but not compensated."

"Understood," Anna said, directing her attention back to Dr. White. She pulled some papers from her rucksack. "See here, Amy. I picked these up right here." She had a printed Google map. She must have brought a small printer in her luggage. She had marked spots on it with a pen.

"Aha! And you found …?"

"Spores. Mostly Ascomycota, oligotrophic—psychrotolerant fungi. No Histoplasma capsulatum, no bat guano, so likely a dry cave."

"Yes!" Dr. White said. "Not typical at all of where he was found, so I understand. Let's go see."

She stood quickly, a small woman with short blond hair that stuck out in spikes. Her blue eyes snapped; she radiated energy.

"Okay!" Anna said. Shoving back her chair and standing. "Lead the way."

"No. No. We'll have to get Maisie here to lead the way." She gestured to the sergeant.

Sergeant Thompson was Maisie? I wouldn't have guessed that. The sergeant smiled with genuine affection at Amy.

"Need anything?" the sergeant asked her.

"No. We can go in my car. I have Wellies, bottles and protective gear in the car."

We trooped out behind her, through a connecting passageway to another building then to a private car park.

Dr. White drove a Land Rover which was covered in mud. She shot out from the car park into the street, paying scant attention to the traffic.

"Amy, slow down. I should have driven." Sergeant Thompson slunk down in the front seat and braced her hand on the dashboard.

"Close your eyes," Dr. White said.

We left the car on a lane just off Corinium Gate Street and took the time to let Dr. White don her coveralls and wellies and stuff gloves into her pockets. She handed Anna identical gear while the sergeant and I waited until they were ready. The sergeant led the way to the bridge. It was as beautiful and as peaceful as it had been yesterday. The late sunshine filtered through the lime trees and the day became brighter as the trees thinned out near the river. Lionel was in the center of the bridge binoculars in hand.

"Hello," he called.

The sergeant waved but didn't stop and stepped off the road just before the bridge, following the now obvious path to the site where the body was found.

I waved to Lionel but hurried after the investigators, picking my way around the oozing mud, trying to go from grass clump to a stone, to any piece of dry ground I could see. When I reached the site, Anna and Dr. White were crouched over a patch of ground where the grass had been flattened. It had been taped off with blue and white police tape and was obviously where the body had lain.

"When those dry cave spores fell off the body where did they land?"

Anna studied the patch, no doubt envisioning the body as she had last seen it. She indicated several spots and Dr. White took samples.

"We'll need to take samples and plot their location so we can show the difference between what flora occurs naturally here and what was introduced by the body." Dr. White tossed that over her shoulder to Sergeant Thompson.

"I need to take samples from—what was the boy's name?" She asked Sergeant Thompson.

"Richard Stonehouse." Dylan had been right. The body *was* the Stonehouse boy, not one of the other two the dispatcher had mentioned.

"Ah. We'll have to take samples from Richard's clothes. Where did you take yours from?"

She nodded as Anna gave her the information. "I'll take them from those spots and replicate them so we can use them in evidence."

Anna and Amy were thoroughly enjoying each other's company and what they were doing. I hoped Anna would continue with the tour, as I appreciated her as well, but she may want to leave it to stay with the investigation.

"What we have here then, Maisie," Dr. White said to the sergeant. "is a body that has been killed somewhere else, somewhere dry and dark—a cave or something cave-like—then dumped here. Very little blood here. So dead already."

"Thanks, Amy." Sergeant Thompson wrote down the information.

"I'll get the report written as soon as I can. I'd invite you for a drink, Anna, but I have to get back to Bristol. Another meeting. I hate meetings."

"No problem," Anna said. "Thanks for including me."

"Ta for taking those first specimens. It puts me on the right track. Do you have a card? We'll keep in touch."

After they had stripped off their protective clothing and bundled them into the back of Dr. White's vehicle, they exchanged business cards.

"Want a lift home?" Dr. White asked us.

Anna looked at me.

"No, thanks. We're close to the hotel here, so we can walk."

"Thanks for coming," Sergeant Thompson repeated their gratitude.

We shook hands all around. I appreciated shaking hands. For almost a year after the pandemic, no one shook hands, and I'd missed the friendliness of it.

I checked my watch. "Fancy a walk around the field?" I asked Anna.

"I'd like that. I'm wired up after that foray into my professional life. I'm supposed to be holidaying. A walk will wear off some of that adrenalin."

We strode off quickly along the Roman Wall then across the end of the grounds to the river, back along the river and approached the bridge from the other side. I looked for Lionel as we had left him still searching for his Mandarin Duck on the bridge. There was no one there. Then I saw a man crouched down at the side of the path. It didn't look like Lionel, too broad.

He straightened when he heard us approach. "Claire, good to see you, maid."

"Bran! What's the matter?"

"It's Lionel." He pulled out his mobile. "I just found him."

I froze for a second. It couldn't be Lionel. I'd seen him earlier looking for birds. He'd been fine. Heart attacks happened suddenly. I knew that. He could have had a stroke. Just about anything.

I left Bran phoning 999 and rushed to Lionel huddled on the ground and unconscious. I could see a gash on his forehead, but I didn't know what was wrong. Did he get that when he fell, or did someone hit him? I couldn't tell. I felt incompetent. I didn't know enough.

"Anna. You're a doctor." I stood up and stepped back. She would be able to find out more than I could.

Anna knelt beside Lionel and felt his pulse. She put her ear to his chest and listened. Bran moved away so his low-toned instructions to the ambulance wouldn't interfere with Anna's diagnosis. I leaned forward.

"Surprisingly strong heart beat for an old man. Looks like head trauma, but I can't tell you more. He needs treatment for shock, and a CT scan." She relinquished her position to me. I was relieved to hear that he was alive, that his heart was strong, but I was almost thrumming with worry that his age would push him into death. Someone hit him? He was a gentle man. Not at all argumentative. Why would someone hit him? He'd been studying the bushes with his binoculars. Had he seen something? Had he heard something that made him a threat? Was this what the police called 'targeted" or just random violence? What there something about this site that evoked danger? It looked so peaceful.

I took off my light jacket and draped it over Lionel as we waited. He looked old, ashen face, still and unconscious. I stopped thinking about why he had been attacked and just wallowed in worry. He was such a dear man. I sat on the ground beside him, holding his hand and willing him to breathe, to keep a steady heart beat and stay with us.

CHAPTER EIGHT

The ambulance arrived at the end of the road. The siren cut into silence. We waited as the paramedics hiked in and watched as they carefully loaded Lionel onto the gurney then into the ambulance. He still hadn't regained consciousness. Bran climbed in and sat beside him.

"I'll ring Mark," I told Bran before the doors closed. I should be with Lionel, but I couldn't leave my group. I had reservations for them for supper, and they didn't know where to go. "I will be at the hospital as soon as I can."

"Na to worry, lass. I can give the doctors his particulars likely better than you. Tell Eseld. I'll put Mark down as next of kin, shall I?"

I gulped. That sounded ominous. "Yes, Yes. He is that."

Bran left with Lionel. He would be more competent than me if competence was needed. I hurried back to the hotel with Anna at my side.

"His color was fine," she said offering some reassurance.

"He's an old man," I said.

"True, but, I think, a healthy old man. What can I do for you?"

I turned at the steps of the Queen Bess Hotel and looked at her. "If you could tell the others, I'll tell Eseld and ring Mark." I glanced at my mobile for the time. "We can still make it to our dinner reservations and, since everyone needs to eat, we will meet here at eight fifteen and make our way there. "

She patted my shoulder. I felt her warm concern. It helped.

I went to my room first and texted Mark. "Please call. Lionel's been hurt."

Then I went to Eseld's room and told her.

"What did the doctor say?" I stared at her. Doctor? Oh, Anna. "She said his heart was fine, his color was all right, although he looked pale to me, and he was breathing. He was just un..un.. conscious." I could hardly say it. My eyes blurred, and I felt my lip quiver. "Uncle Lionel is a healthy man but an old man. This might be too much for him."

Eseld said briskly. "He's is only old to you because you're young. He isn't old in terms of frailty." She was a recently retired nurse; I could believe her. "This is what I'll do. I'll take a thermos of coffee and some biscuits for Bran as he will stay there until Mark arrives. I may not make it to the restaurant. Where is it?"

I told her.

"We will have a meal somewhere but perhaps not there. It depends on what I find out at the hospital and how long Bran will need to stay. We will look after Lionel. Bran knows what questions to ask, and I'll nosy in and read the chart. You do your job and try not to worry, lover."

I hugged her. It was like having a mother beside me. She was giving me practical support which was emotionally comforting. I *did* have to look after my tourists, even though I was totally distracted by worry about Lionel.

Mark called.

"Lionel was attacked," I told him and gave him Anna's assessment.

There was silence. I waited.

"I'll go straight to the hospital." I heard him let out a long breath.

"The hospital is just off the A429 and Bristol Road."

"Yes, I know where it is, *cariad*."

I let out a long breath. I was his dear, and it helped me to know that just now. "Bran will stay until you get there. Text me and let me know how he is. I'm so worried."

"Me too." He disconnected. I could imagine him shoving aside his feelings for Lionel and getting on with making arrangements. Neither of us could fall apart right now. It would take him about a half-hour to extract himself from his meetings on compassionate grounds then an hour and twenty minutes on the M5 to get here. He had responsibilities in Birmingham. He wanted to help those illegal refugees. He wouldn't be able to do it if he was with Lionel—but Lionel had no one else. Mark would give detailed instructions to his sergeant, Andy, and stay connected by mobile to the investigation.

I splashed water on my face, applied a little make up, sent my sister, Deirdre, a text but told her I couldn't talk until later that night. She would be upset if she didn't hear this from me. I joined my group in the lounge.

"What happened?" Matthew asked.

I ordered a half-pint of lager and looked around at my group. They were subdued, likely concerned about Lionel. This was not turning out to be the tour of their dreams.

"Lionel was attacked while he was birdwatching. Bran had gone to look for a particular bird, and Lionel remained on the bridge. Between the time Anna and I went for our walk and returned to the bridge someone hit him with," I shivered, "a blunt instrument."

"Is he alright?" That was Peggy.

"Concussion?" Nancy asked. I expected a high school teacher knew about concussions as sports teams had their share.

"He was unconscious but Anna said his breathing and heart were fine." I looked up as Anna arrived. She sat beside Nancy and indicated to Bob she'd have what I was having.

"Anna, you're a doctor. He was stable, wasn't he?" I tried not to sound as if I was pleading for a positive prognosis.

"Hard to know with head injuries, but I'd say his chances were good," she said.

There was a collective sigh of relief.

"Bran is staying with him until Mark returns from Birmingham. Eseld took some coffee to the hospital. She'll order a dinner for them both and not come with us."

"Lionel is such a charming man," Peggy said. "I wonder how he managed to be a police sergeant. Don't they have to be grumpy?"

"They are certainly grumpy in mysteries," Nancy said. "Just think of how many of them are annoying, like Sergeant Caldwell in Jacqueline Winspear's novels."

"He got promoted," Peggy said. "He's a Detective *Inspector* in the later books."

"Or that Sergeant in Kinsey's novels," Nancy continued, "who is always trying to exert power."

It warmed my heart how this group who didn't know me well were trying hard to distract me and comfort me.

"Well, Lionel isn't a sergeant any more," I said. "He directs his energies to recording birds, not catching criminals." He shouldn't have been in any danger.

Matthew leaned forward, "I never paid much attention to the birds around the ranch, except if they were taking too much grain from the hoppers, but Lionel made me think about them. He was really dedicated to conserving the bird life here."

I didn't like the past tense Matthew used. "I expect he'll get back to it."

"Oh, for sure," Matthew said. "I hope so."

I turned to Anna. "I didn't see his blue bird book, did you?"

She thought for a moment. "No. He always had it with him, and he was writing in it when we left him to go for our walk. I think he put it into his front vest pocket."

I remembered. "Yes, he did. But it wasn't there when we found him injured."

"Who would want his bird book?" Matthew asked.

Who indeed? I puzzled over that.

Everyone went to their room to collect their few items for the evening, so I was alone in the foyer sitting against the wall in one of the ladder chairs when Shirley's mother appeared. I saw, through the narrow entry windows, that she'd arrived in a black, chauffer-driven car. I'd had the impression that Mrs. Harris was wealthy; her clothes reflected wealth. I glanced at her as she walked quickly into the foyer and stopped when she met Shirley coming from the kitchen.

"Hello, mummy."

"You got to get a business head, Shirley. What is this nonsense about an ex-rozzer pitting out? That surely wasn't…"

Shirley interrupted her. "You've met Claire before, mummy. You might want to say hello."

Mrs. Harris turned abruptly. Her accent climbed a class or two. "My apologies, Ms. Barclay. I didn't see you there."

I nodded and smiled.

She turned back to Shirley. "Could you spare me a few minutes, luv?"

"In my office, mum. Excuse us, Claire."

I nodded again. Obviously, Mrs. Harris had an issue of some urgency to discuss with Shirley. She'd said 'That surely wasn't…' What would come next? Necessary? That surely wasn't necessary? That implied Shirley might have had something to do with Lionel's attack. What else could she have been going to say? Usual? That surely wasn't usual? That surely wasn't good for business? The last one might be the most accurate. Lionel was staying at the hotel. He was attacked. *That* wasn't good for business. Lydia Harris was a concerned mother, but Shirley might resent her interference. She implied that Shirley was incompetent, and I didn't think she was. Maybe Mrs. Harris wanted to control her daughter. She owned the hotel and perhaps controlled many aspects of it. I thought fondly of my mother who was loving and supportive of my plans to the day she died. I'd been lucky.

I headed to the car park, collected the van and was parked outside the Queen Bess when my guests appeared. I drove them to the restaurant. It wasn't far, but they were tired after their long day and with the worry that had capped it.

The Fleece on Market Place was Tudor style, looking as if it was built in the seventeenth-century, but modern inside. It had been renovated to a spare and almost austere standard, but the beams overhead and touches of wood throughout retained the cozy feel. We had a long table and sat in the order we arrived. Anna was at the other end of the table from me. I ordered two bottles of a robust Burgundy and hoped that would help our anxieties.

The menu was excellent. I didn't think the beef industry was going to suffer from a downturn in consumption if Matthew was anything to go by. He ordered steak again. It would be good here and also expensive.

"Oh, look at this," Heather said. "'Roasted venison haunch with Jerusalem artichoke puree, honey glazed Chantenay carrots, game chips, red wine jus'. I could never cook that!"

Matthew looked at her and said with an intense look. "I wouldn't want you to spend that much time in the kitchen. You have so many other things to do. Just enjoy someone else's cooking."

She beamed at him. "That was the perfect thing to say. Thanks, I will. Claire, what are Chantenay carrots?"

"Short carrots, stubby even, but with great flavor."

"That's what I'll have."

Judith was beside me and studying the menu as if she was going to take an exam on the contents.

"This fishmonger's plate. Squid, salmon, prawns Marie Rose?" She waited for an explanation.

"Marie Rose are prawns with a Marie Rose sauce which is a spicy tomato sauce."

"I see." She continued. "Whitebait, marinated anchovies, capers, tartar sauce and granary bloomer."

She paused, looking directly at me, waiting again as if I were her private thesaurus.

"Granary bloomer is a small loaf of whole grain bread."

"Ah. That sounds very good."

"It's a large platter," I warned her. "That's why it's under 'sharing plates'. Would you like me to share it with you?"

She considered that. "No. I will eat it all."

I'd be surprised if she did. I ordered the chicken, gammon and thyme pot pie. I didn't want anything fussy, and I knew I wouldn't be able to eat much. The wine went well with it.

I offered to get Judith, who was the only one eating fish, a glass of white wine. She agreed, and I ordered it for her. If I made sure she got some kind of special attention at least once a day, it soothed her and kept her from being too critical.

Everyone enjoyed their food. Judith was working through hers at a constant rate, a little like a rabbit, nibbling steadily. Perhaps she *would* eat it all. Nancy and Peggy were arguing about the merits of real books versus e-books.

"You can't carry all the books you're buying," Nancy complained. "You can get some of those on the internet and load them into your tablet. You don't need to buy them all here."

"I need real books," Peggy said. "I hate the way the libraries are going theses days. We have so few real books now with so much online. I agree it's more convenient, but I need the solid book in my hand to be connected to the author. I feel as if a hardcover book has been slaved over, and produced just for my hands. Books sitting on my real bookshelf make me feel more secure, safer in my world, as if no one can take that away from me. Storms can come, the power can go out, the wifi can be down, and I can still read. On my tablet? If I lose the tablet what then?"

"Oh for heaven's sake, Peggy. They're in the Cloud. You get another tablet, and there you are. All your books are available."

Heather laughed. She enjoyed the two older women and their frank friendship.

"What did you do this afternoon after we returned from Lacock?" I asked her

"Matthew and I got into a real parley with a local. Matthew was so indignant. It was funny."

Matthew looked embarrassed. "I feel a bit of a tenderfoot, but how was I supposed to know?"

"It was like this," Heather said. "I finally found the cricket set I wanted for the boys and asked the clerk to mail it. He said he'd put it in the post, and he'd knock me up when that was done and could he have my mobile number? Matthew reacted. He leaned forward and had his fists up before I could translate for him. I managed to whisper, 'Knock me up,' Matthew, means 'phone me' or 'call me'. It's not an indecent proposition."

"Well, Matthew," I said amid the general laughter, "you aren't the first person to misinterpret that word."

"It does remind you English isn't the same everywhere," he said. I drove them home and everyone dispersed to their rooms.

Shirley was there to greet everyone and convey her concern about Lionel to me.

"I am so sorry to hear he was hurt," she said. "Will he be all right?"

I didn't know if he'd be all right, and I was suddenly almost overwhelmed with worry for him.

"I don't know," I said. "He was unconscious, and he's old."

She patted my hand. "I'm sorry."

Anna stopped by me for a moment. "I expect the police will be around again tomorrow for our statements."

"Did they say so?"

"Amy said it was possible."

"We didn't see anything, but we did know he was standing on the bridge when we went into the field and on the ground when we found him. So we can narrow down the time of the attack. Do you have to attest to anything else? Bugs? Spores? Pollen?"

She laughed. "No, Amy will do that. No point in having me hang around for a trial. They'd have to pay me."

When I arrived in my room to find a note had been slipped under my door.

"Come to our room when you get in," It was signed by Eseld.

I found Bran there, just finishing a Thai take-out and sipping tea.

"How is he?" I asked.

"Still unconscious but doing fine. Mark's there."

I checked my mobile. There was a text from Mark. *I'm staying with Lionel.* He had made the trip quickly.

Bran gave me more information. "They did a CAT scan, and it doesn't look as though there has been internal trauma. There must be some or he would be conscious, but no big bleed or damage that needs surgery."

I sat down with a thump. "Good. But why isn't he conscious?"

Eseld answered. "Sometime the body just cuts out for a while when you've had a shock. Just gives you relief from dealing with anything by keeping you unconscious. Mark is with him so he may feel secure enough to come back to us soon."

I stared at her somewhat bland, ordinary face, mousey hair, and those sharp, intelligent, almost black eyes. She was immeasurably comforting.

I stayed with them for about an hour, accepting a cup of strong tea, listening to them talk about their days with Lionel and his Addie, and the plans Lionel and Bran had to compile a list of the birds they have seen.

It occurred to me that, if Lionel had died, there would many people who would care: Bran and Eseld, his work mates in Truro, his neighbors. Lionel had a capacity for friendship, and he must have hundreds of friends. I wondered who would care about me if I died: Mark, Deirdre, and her family, perhaps Rose and her mother, Robert Andrews, Mary and Thomas Greenwood but not many others.

Reminded of Deirdre, I rang her from my room. If she didn't hear about this soon after it happened, she would give me grief. I sent her a text first; in case she'd gone to bed. She was up.

"What now?"

"How's everyone?"

"Fine. What's up?" I seldom rang her this late, so she knew something was wrong.

"Uncle Lionel was attacked."

She was silent for a few seconds. "How is he?"

"Surviving, we believe."

Again another short silence. "Do they have a guard on him?"

"No. Not an official guard."

"Why?"

"Why was he attacked? That we don't know."

"Where's Mark?" Sometimes my sister's barrister attitude is annoying.

"He's here with Lionel at the hospital."

"That all right, then."

Her voice warmed and she said, "How are you doing? You're rather fond of Uncle Lionel?"

I started to cry. "Yes, and I haven't even seen him since he was stricken, and I'm worried about him."

"He's a tough old boy. Is there any advocate at the hospital who can give you the true picture?"

"A retired nurse, Eseld. She thinks he will recover. And Dr. Clarke on my tour can interpret medical jargon for me. She has an in with the local sergeant, so I might find out more information tomorrow."

Deirdre always wanted more information. It was her way of keeping the world on an even keel.

"Will you carry on with your guests?"

"I have to."

"Yes, of course. But it's tough when you want to stay at Lionel's bedside."

"That is it exactly."

We didn't solve my dilemma, but I felt better for having told Deirdre about it.

Rose had sent more pictures of Gulliver. He looked happy. I did have people and a dog who loved me.

I was in bed, reading because I wasn't calm enough to sleep when Mark arrived. He kissed me. I clung to him for a moment then sat back on the bed and watched him fish his keys, mobile and change from his pockets and dump everything on the dresser..

"How's Lionel?"

"Awake," Mark said. The relief was amazing. I just melted for a second. Even with Eseld's reassurances, I hadn't thought Lionel would recover until he was conscious. I cried, again. Mark sank down beside me and gathered me in his arms.

"I was so scarred we'd lose him," I whispered.

"Me too," he said. He sniffed. Tears ran down my cheeks. Mark handed me a tissue and picked up one for himself. We wiped our eyes.

"I'm glad he's conscious. That is so much better. Is he in pain?" I relaxed a little more.

"A little headache, but nothing major."

Mark hugged me once more, then rose, stripped off his clothes and headed for the shower.

I composed myself, blew my nose a few times and waited for him.

"Did the police talk to you," I asked him when he slipped into bed with me.

"Yes, there was a Sergeant Thompson."

"Maisie," I said.

"Really? That's her name?"

"It is."

"Doesn't suit her. Anyway, your Maisie came up to interview me at Lionel's beside. She did a good job."

"Why interview you? You weren't there?"

"I inherit."

I rolled on my side and stared at him. "You inherit? As in you might kill him so you could inherit? What is she thinking?"

"She's thinking like a good officer. Of course, she would interview me. I don't mind that. It's her job. What I mind is, I can't work on finding out who did this to Uncle Lionel. It's frustrating."

"Why not? I'd think she'd want you to work on it. The more intelligence on this problem the better."

"*Because* I inherit," he said patiently.

"Much?"

"Yes, quite a lot. They had no children and two properties."

I was indignant. "You wouldn't hurt a hair on his head."

"But they don't know that. You're a suspect as well."

"Why me?" But I saw the reason. "Because I'm your wife and, if you benefit, so do I."

"That's right."

Of course I would be a suspect. But not a likely one. "And I found him. I'm glad Anna was with me. She's a credible witness." I couldn't have attacked Lionel.

"I think they got that clear." He shook his head. "I was with a group of officers in Birmingham. They'll check and find that's true. Even so, they aren't going to let me near this case. I hate being out of the loop."

It would be frustrating to have your skills and expertise ignored while others investigated the attack on someone you loved.

"There are some things we can do." I scuttled back until I was sitting against the headboard with the covers pulled up to my neck. Mark mimicked me until we were side by side.

"Who would attack Lionel and for what reason?" I started.

"To steal something from him." Mark gave the most likely reason.

"His blue, bird book is gone."

Mark turned his head and stared at me." That's ridiculous."

"It is. But the book is gone. That was theft. Give me other reasons why someone would attack him."

Mark looked away and was quiet for a moment, then said, "Hate. Prejudice. Someone he knew in the past. Someone he found evidence on and who bore a grudge. He has information someone wants to stop him from revealing."

"If someone is targeting him," I asked, "could they get at him in the hospital? Deirdre suggested the police put a guard on him."

"I checked out the security," Mark said. "After the Covid pandemic, hospitals have more stringent guards against unauthorized people entering. You have to stop and have your temperature checked, so no one can wander in. There are cameras everywhere. He should be all right."

I worried about that for a moment.

Mark continued. "Lionel won't be able to continue on the tour; he'll have to rest and recuperate. But we can't let him go back alone to his house at St Mawes."

He was right about that. Lionel was ours to love and look after. We'd have to plan who would do that. "Did you get some time off?" Getting time off always depended on what jobs they had for Mark to do.

"Yes, compassionate leave. He's my closet relative, and I'm his. So I've got a fortnight."

That was a relief. I couldn't leave my tour yet.

"You'll have to leave your investigations of the refugees."

"Andy's working on it. I know it's the slimmest of leads, but I put him onto investigating your Mr. Alistair Buchanan. He's turning out to be interesting."

"He is? He's left the hotel, by the way."

Mark nodded. "So Andy said. We've had someone shadowing him. It seems Mr. Buchanan's transport company has been in the vicinity when refugees turn up to work on farms. We sent someone to follow one of his lorries. It started in Southampton and headed into the country. A few workers were dropped off on seven different farms, some of them in the Cotswolds. I've got an inspector from Southampton leading the investigation now. If those workers are in the country illegally, we have a case. Andy's reporting to the local inspector. They're hoping to get enough evidence to shut down Mr. Buchanan."

"So it will help?"

"It will help a little to stop the trafficking. If there's no one to receive the refugees, they will bottleneck at the docks. It won't stop the trafficking, but it might slow it down. In any case, I'm off the job for a fortnight."

Mark could spend time with Lionel and look after him.

"You could take him to our house. I'll finish my tour then come home and stay with him. That will give us both a week with him."

Mark reached over and hugged me. "Thanks."

"My pleasure." I loved Lionel. It wouldn't be a hardship. I sat up straight and stared at Mark. "Tomorrow, we will search his room. Maybe there is something there someone was looking for."

Before I slept, I thought about Mr. Alistair Buchanan. How odd that a chance conversation about calves and workers encouraged by Matthew's interest in farming should be enough of a clue to send Mark investigating. Serendipitous? Or just the methodical way the police put together scraps of information, trying to complete a puzzle.

CHAPTER NINE

In the morning, the first thing Mark did was to ring the hospital to ask about Lionel. The reports were cautiously optimistic. He was still conscious, was coherent, but drowsy. We both knew he might have serious consequences such as bleeding on the brain, a stroke or loss of memory. The list was as long as my imagination could make it. I took a deep breath and swallowed.

"He's tough. He'll be fine," I said.

Mark's face was set, as if he also was repressing his fears.

I made coffee in the French press in the room and left it to filter as we started down the hall to Lionel's room. We needed to see if there was any indication of a motive for the attack on him There might be something in his room that would tell us.

"Do you have his keys?"

"I do. We'd better get in there and out before Sergeant Thompson sends someone to search—if she does." He was frustrated with his fetters. If he had been part of this investigation, he would know what was being done and when it was going to be accomplished.

"*Cachu!*"

When he's swearing in Welsh, he's angry. "Ask Bran to infiltrate for you."

His mood changed and he smiled at me.

"Good idea."

Bran had contacts in Cornwall. Gloucestershire was not this jurisdiction, but he was an old copper and deserved respect. The local constables would most likely answer any questions Bran put to them.

Mark opened Lionel's room with the key. No fancy pass cards for this hotel, just a large, old-fashioned key. The room was as Lionel had left it. Everything was either neatly hung in the closet or aligned carefully on the dresser. Nothing seemed out of place. We both donned rubber gloves. Everyone had them now. During the pandemic, we used them routinely when grocery shopping and dealing with strangers. I still used them when filling up at the petrol tanks, because those pin pads were filthy. The gloves were handy right now; we didn't want to leave any fingerprints for Sergeant Thompson.

"We should look for his blue book," I said. "He had one where he noted observations. He read me a description of Bob from it."

"He had a separate blue book for birds?" Mark asked.

"Yes. He had that with him. It was in his vest pocket, but it's gone. Whoever hit him, took it. At least, that's what I think."

"Who would want it?"

"I doubt they'd want the bird book, but they might want his book of observations, his copper's diary."

Mark looked around the room. "Where would he put it?"

"To hide it, you mean?"

"He might want to hide it. After all, if he was writing down his observations of Bob, he wouldn't want the cleaning staff—who might be Shirley—to read it."

"True."

We searched under the mattress. "Not a likely spot. Too obvious. Lionel has conducted many searches in his time. He'd know all the best spots."

"So have you."

"Also true."

Mark concentrated a moment, then turned and stared at the old-fashioned fireplace. It was no longer operative, just decorative, adding a bit of seventeenth-century ambiance. Mark knelt in front of it and reached inside the chimney.

"Addicts sometimes stashed their product up these things." He wiggled a little trying to get the angle of his arm straight so he could reach high into the flue. He finally lay on his back and reached up.

"Hah!"

He brought out the blue book. We grinned at each other.

"Tricky, Uncle Lionel," I said with some admiration.

"Cautious," Mark said. He sat back on his haunches and stared at the book. I know he was anxious to read what was written. He pulled out his mobile and glanced at the time.

"Here." He stood and handed me the book. "I'd better not take it to the hospital. If Sergeant Thompson asks for it, I don't want to be forced to hand it over before we read it. And I don't want to be accused of withholding evidence."

"I can keep it and claim Lionel lent it to me, and I didn't see any significance in it."

"Don't lie. Just don't offer information." Mark locked the door behind us. "I feel as if I'm hiding behind your skirts."

What? Were we equal partners or weren't we? I stared at him. "We're doing the reasonable thing here. It's no different from me being the designated driver on a night out together."

"It feels different."

That was interesting. Maybe we were only equal in his personal life, not in his professional one. He wanted to be in charge of the investigation, and he couldn't be. I wondered how he'd deal with that. Without discussing it any more, we knocked on Bran's door.

Bran and Eseld had a charming room at the front of the house. It was larger than ours and decorated in pale green with cream accents and floral Chintz curtains. Bran was buttoning his shirt as he opened the door.

"I'm off to the hospital," Mark said. "I'll stay with Lionel today."

"I can come over in the afternoon," Bran said.

"Can you arrange a roster of old coppers to come and sit with him? A kind of unofficial guard? I don't think Thompson and her crew are going to spare any officers to do that." Mark was definitely worried Lionel had some information someone wanted to supress.

"You think whoever whacked him will try again?"

"They wanted something. Or Lionel might have seen something. There are lots of reasons to be careful here."

Bran nodded. "I'll see to it."

"Thanks. I'm off."

"The coffee will be ready in our room," I said. "Fill up a thermal cup and take it with you."

He gave me a quick kiss on my forehead and headed back to our room.

"I'll arrange snacks for the men," Eseld said. "including your man."

I smiled at her. "That would be wonderful."

"I'll get that all sorted. Bran here will see it's all delivered, and I'll join you on the expedition today."

"Wonderful." I was grateful, but glad she could manage to come with us. This was supposed to be her holiday.

I stashed Lionel's blue book in my rucksack and thought about him. I mulled over who might want to kill him as I headed to the breakfast room. He was lucky not to have died in the attack. Perhaps someone didn't want him to share information. What information? Lionel wasn't a devious man. He shared information with Mark. I doubted he was concealing anything. So who thought he was? Did Lionel write more about those men who met in the back room of the hotel?

I had a quick word with Anna as we loaded into the van for our trip to Stowe-on-the-Wold.

"Anything new from the constabulary?" I asked her.

"No. They know Richie was killed somewhere like a cave and transported to the river. They're not going to put any more officers on it or much more time. No budget for it. How's Lionel?"

122 EMMA DAKIN

"He's conscious."

"Good. That's a relief."

It was kind of her to be concerned. "I've no idea why he was attacked. It must have something to do with Richie's death."

"According to the Law of Interconnected Monkey Business?" She raised her eyebrow.

I laughed. Aaron Elkins wrote mysteries featuring a forensic anthropologist who quoted the Law of Interconnected Monkey Business that affirmed coincidences are rare. Odd happenings are likely connected. "I love those Gideon Oliver books."

"Yeah. Me too." Anna was basically a happy woman. It seemed incongruous that her professional life involved death.

Anna joined the others in the van and we were off to Stowe-on-the-Wold. This was the day of the biannual Gypsy Horse Fair.

I activated the mic and gave my group the potted version of the history of Stowe-on-the-Wold. True to her word, Eseld had managed to get everything done and joined us.

I drove out of town, then started my spiel. "Stowe-on-the-Wold is situated at the conflux of seven roads. From a thousand feet up, it looks like a spiderweb, although many of the roads are straight, so perhaps a many-pointed star. It used to be the center of trading with the second largest population in England. The fair has been held since 1476 with the exception of 2020 and 2021 when everything was closed because of the pandemic.

"In the Medieval Days, traders came from Italy, France and Belgium and many other countries to trade for wool, meat and horses. There were six monasteries not far from here, so the monks came to buy and sell. Thousands of head of sheep, at one point twenty thousand sheep, were funneled along the roads in the center of town and sold here. As well, it was an employment center where people were hired and contracts for employment based on the date of the Gypsy Horse Fair."

"Why is it a *Gypsy* Horse Fair?" Nancy asked.

"Because the Romani came in their colorful caravans with their horses. Their horses were well trained, tough and eagerly bought by buyers who came from long distances. There used to be hundreds of caravans, the old-fashioned kind pulled by horses. Over the years, the market for horses drifted down and the Romani now often arrive in Airstream caravans and sell clothing and household goods. They used to parade the horses through town, but they don't do that anymore. But we will see some decorated wagons with their horses grazing nearby."

"I'm looking forward to the horses. Is the fair in the town center? Where do they graze?" Matthew asked.

"The fair is in the south part of the town on the Maugersbury Road. There's plenty of grass there."

It wasn't far from Cirencester to Stowe-on-the-Wold, about twenty miles. I pulled the van into the parking space I'd booked. It was in the driveway of a big house. The teenaged daughters of the well-to-do owner were running an entrepreneurial parking business. No doubt without a permit.

I handed over the hefty price in cash to the teen. Over her shorts she wore a small apron equipped with pockets. She had long earrings that brushed her shoulders and sandals on tiny feet with black lacquered toenails. She smiled.

"Have a good day."

It may have been an illegal car park, but it was handy to the fair, and I doubted any officials would concern themselves with it.

"Oh, look!" Peggy almost squealed.

"Oh my, Matthew. Look at that." Heather also had caught sight of the elaborated decorated Romani Vardo caravan.

"The wagon is such a bright red with all those intricate designs on it. I'm going to take a picture."

The red of the bow-top caravan was embellished with elaborate patterns in gold paint. The curved roof was bright turquoise. It was a beautiful and cheerful sight.

Heather rushed over the path to stand in front of the caravan, holding her viewfinder up to her eye. Her elaborate camera took snap pictures and more carefully constructed photos using the viewfinder.

I walked up beside Matthew. "The young woman standing near the caravan will want about five pounds for the privilege of taking those pictures."

Matthew raised his eyebrows but put his hand in his pocket and ambled over to the girl who was about fourteen. She smiled and held out her hand. Matthew put the five-pound note in it. She looked at it and nodded. Heather hadn't noticed.

My group spread out. I heard Nancy trying to persuade Anna to have her palm read.

"See," she said. "'Romany Rose. Palmist and Crystal Gazer. I can read your future.'"

"You are the single one, Nancy," Anna said. "You go in there and see if there is man coming into your life."

Nancy look surprised then intrigued.

"Go for it," Peggy said.

"Come in with me?"

"Sure."

Anna left them to it and wandered off to visit the stalls that lined the edge of the field.

We had established a mustering point. One p.m. at The Old Stock Inn on Digbeth. If lost, they could text me and I'd find them. Until noon, I was free. I looked for a coffee trailer where I hoped to find a chair and a few minutes on my own. There was one parked angled between tents with its side open and a coffee urn bubbling.

"Ta," I said to the attendant and took my coffee to one of the three chairs at the side. I gazed around me, noticing all the horses, little bigger than ponies, with shaggy coats and what looked like feathered feet and hair growing in long tresses to the ground. They were being led, ridden, loaded and unloaded all around me. Most of them seemed to be tough-looking black and white ponies. They had an enviable reputation for hard work, endurance and even temperament. The Romani must have an effective breeding and training program. One day, I'd like to ride a horse. That passed me by in childhood. I've never had a chance to learn.

There were children everywhere, Romani children and tourist children, playing in and around the modern Romani caravans, riding the horses and climbing the temporary fences. Several clusters of caravans including a few of the old colorful ones, surrounded an outdoor fire. Seats around the fire were taken by the owners of the caravans. Without signs of any kind, it was obvious tourists didn't sit there.

It was colorful, noisy and reassuringly normal. I'd been afraid the fair would not continue after two year's cancelation. Lovely to have it back.

I turned to my mobile and texted Mark. "How's Lionel?"

He answered immediately. "Much better. Good prognosis. Will be leaving tomorrow. Bran has a guard roster until then. Lionel is enjoying the visits from all his old friends. We may have to have an open house when he comes to us."

"I'm so relieved. Be sure to get instructions, medications, appointments like physio, GP and specialists."

"Will do. I had to get Lionel a new blue book so he could write down all that information."

I sent an emoji. That was so like Lionel. My eyes teared for a moment. I was grateful he was conscious and recording details in his new book. I wanted to read the one I had, but felt exposed here with so many people around me. I finished my coffee and wandered up Park Street, bore right 47 up Digbeth past the Frock Shop and Bridal Boutique to Market Square. I knew it would be busy today, so I'd booked a table at The Old Stock Inn, a building of ancient Cotswold brick. It had a mellow, warm, golden ambience on the outside. Inside, like many restaurants in the Cotswolds, it had been renovated. The dining room was bright and clean, with high ceilings. A long table in the center had our "Reserved" sign on it. Floor-to-ceiling windows let in the sun from the garden beyond. Floor to ceiling Cotswold stone on the far wall reminded us where we were. My tourists dribbled in around one, the time agreed upon, and all had arrived by one-fifteen. The menu was varied and the food excellent. There were vegan choices so Judith could avoid dairy. I'm sure the wait staff would spend time with her. I left them to it. She was at the other end of the table. I wasn't captured by her menu.

The conversation was full of talk about the horses, their size or lack of it, the way they were ridden, bareback for the most part, the trading which fascinated Matthew and the history of it all. There was little talk of mystery writers. I was relaxing in the news that Lionel was recovering. Eseld had chosen a seat beside me. After ordering, I spoke to her.

"I just heard from Mark. Lionel is much better."

"So Bran texted.," she said. "Good. He doesn't remember the attack which is normal, my lover. You mustn't worry about that. It's common in cases of concussion for the victim to remember nothing."

"Oh, I see. I've heard that."

Eseld smiled at me. "I'd worry about that man living alone, but he says he's going to you."

"To Mark until I get back."

"Good."

I reached out and patted her arm. "Thanks, Eseld."

"For what?"

"For being there. For being strong. For propping me up".

She smiled. "Easily done, my maid. Easily done."

Now that the worry of Lionel had abated. I itched to read the blue book. I hadn't wanted to pull it from my rucksack when I was at the Fair. Somehow I didn't want anyone to know I had it. I might not have time until we returned to the Queen Bess tonight to even skim through it. After lunch, I walked up to the van and drove back to the restaurant. Everyone loaded for our afternoon excursion to the Broadway Tower, about a fifteen-minute drive from Stowe-on-the-Wold.

"Tell me about this oddity," Eseld said from the front seat. "I remember reading about it in school, but I've never been here before."

I activated the mic. "This was conceived by Capability Brown, designed by James Wyatt, in 1794 and built for Lady Coventry in 1798. Finished in 1799. She wanted a beacon she could see from her house in Worcester, about twenty miles from here."

"Can it be seen from Worcester?"

"It could in 1799. I'm not sure about now."

"Have any mysteries been set in it," Peggy asked. "It looks like the perfect place for a Victorian. Maybe a group of invited guests who get knocked off one by one."

"Like Christie's *Then There Were None*?" Heather suggested.

"Good plot," I agreed, "but I don't know of any. There is a novel *The Owls of Gloucester* by Edward Marten that takes place in a tower, but in Gloucester, not in Broadway tower which is in Worcestershire."

"I know that one," Peggy said. I doubt there was a book I could think of that Peggy didn't know. She had extensive knowledge, but most librarians I knew remembered reams of books. A friend in Seattle who was a librarian told me they have to recount the plot and synopsis of many books to their library patrons and so cemented the book in their memory.

"It's set in the eleventh century. A couple of Doomsday taxmen find a body."

I agreed. "Somebody *should* set a mystery here."

I parked the van and we wandered around the tower for about a half-hour. It was a beautiful building. A little odd because it didn't seem to serve a practical purpose. I felt a frisson of disapproval of Lady Coventry because it was a symbol of frivolous spending.

Couldn't she have spent her money on something more worthwhile? I pulled myself up mentally. Shouldn't something beautiful be honored simply because it was beautiful? Am I so handicapped by generations of struggling middle class ancestors that I thought something impractical was therefore immoral? Could I be so narrow-minded? Crikey. That might be the case. Surely I could appreciate and value art and architecture for its beauty alone? I'd better pay attention to my attitude.

The next stop was Blenheim Palace. The men were entranced by its connection to Winston Churchill and the history of the palace in both the First and Second World Wars. The mystery buffs tried to think of books with war themes. There were many.

"Jacqueline Winspear's," Anna said.

"Christie for sure," Nancy contributed.

"Oh yes. Tommy and Tuppence," Peggy agreed.

The palace was impressive. It wasn't possible to see all of it, but I'd arranged a quick tour and a stop at the café and gift shop. There were several tours to choose from. Matthew and Heather chose the Churchill Exhibition tour, Nancy and Peggy the "Downstairs Tour".

"We watched Downtown Abbey," Peggy said. "We want to know how the servants managed."

Anna chose the Palace Staterooms and the Untold Stories exhibition and Eseld and Judith joined her. I had allowed two hours for this stop. I bought the tickets, dispensed them and promised to meet them at the Water Terrace Café.

Once everyone had headed off on their tour, I bought a cup of coffee and returned to the van. I levered my seat back, placed the coffee in the holder beside me and pulled Lionel's blue book from my rucksack. Finally!

I smoothed the blue, thick cardboard cover. No serial number printed on it, so it was an observations-only book. Lionel's handwritten was small, ornate, with curls on some of the letters, but upright, so it was fairly easy to read.

I skimmed the first part where he had arrived at the Queen Bess, his description of Bob which he had already given me and came to his descriptions of the men who tramped through to a meeting once a week.

"No insignia on their clothes. No common tattoos. Maybe gormless." That was what he'd read out to me when I asked him about them.

He had some interesting comments about Shirley. "Ambitious. Wants to be a great chef. Resentful that the pandemic robbed her of her chance to shine in a city restaurant. Believe she was a sous chef and it is possible she would have risen to a great chef given the opportunity.

"She is the one who keeps the hotel running. Bob has to be told what to do. His brawn is useful. He runs the bar well, but isn't much help in the restaurant. Shirley has started a hand sanitizer business. She may be making more money on that than her breakfast service. And perhaps even more than on her hotel rooms. Spends a lot of time in the wine cellar which is where she concocts the hand sanitizer product. It leaves here in boxes which Bob loads into their van. She drives the van once a week to Bath, sells the sanitizers and brings back the hotel supplies. Efficient, but labor intensive for Shirley. She seems to be getting tired or frustrated. Even if she is making money from her sanitizers, she isn't satisfied. Her passion is to be a chef. She will look for an opportunity to work in a big hotel or take more cooking courses. The Queen Bess is only a stop gap for her. Excellent cook, so she needs to find a better place. Probably do better without Bob. His ambition seems to be here where Shirley works to support him.

"Her mother visits occasionally. Shirley is her only chick and she tries to dominate her. A bit of a Tartar, that woman."

Uncle Lionel definitely didn't approve of Bob. He had only a note about Richie. "Young. Still sees everything in relation to himself. Cheerful, but almost certainly not honest."

I sipped my coffee and thought about Lionel's observations. There was more. I just didn't have time to read it all now. So far, there was nothing worth an assault.

My group met me at the café, and we spent another half-hour there while they had tea and goodies. They were full of information about their tours and enjoyed exchanging tidbits of information. Matthew and Heather chuckled over Churchill's quips.

They quieted when we pulled away from the car park and most of them dozed during the hour-long trip back to Cirencester.

I hoped Mark could come back to the Queen Bess tonight. We needed to talk and to read Lionel's blue book, the entire book.

CHAPTER TEN

We arrived back at the Queen Bess around eight and had a quick meal at Jessie's Bistro. Most of the group had dozed on the way home so, although tired, were willing to walk to the Bistro—even Judith. I'd noticed Judith was more interested in the others in the group now, and they correspondingly were more interested in her. She was always well-prepared for whatever sites we visited. Everyone had the itinerary a month before departure, but Judith was one of the rare tourists who studied the information. She was the one who told Matthew and Heather there was a Cricket Museum in Stowe-on-the-Wold. I'd forgotten to mention it. They enjoyed the tour, but I heard them tell her they still didn't understand the game. Surprisingly, she did and explained it to them. I'd come to appreciate her.

We retired to the bar at the Queen Bess after the meal and were served by Dylan. Neither Shirley nor Bob were in sight. We sometimes had the attention of Julie, the part-time bar maid, but she wasn't here tonight either.

We had coffee and tea and most had a liqueur of brandy or Drambuie. Dylan offered us a house specialty brandy called Mériter Cognac from an elegant, curved bottle. It was a little tart for my taste. I like my after-dinner drink to be sweet.

At one point in almost every tour, a group becomes cohesive. It takes time, about a week, as if they have to jockey a little to find their places and learn to be open with one another. I never forced it. It either happened or it didn't, but usually after a week, the group began to feel relaxed.

Tonight was the moment that happened. I thought, looking around, how disparate they had been at the beginning, but how comfortable they seemed now. It might be the relief of having Lionel on his way to recovery or just the natural consequence of propensity.

Mr. Buchanan came in for an evening drink. I thought about the officer who was shadowing him. Was he outside keeping observation on the hotel? What have the police found out about Mr. Buchanan? He looked relaxed.

"You're welcome to join us," Matthew said. "Your farmer friend isn't with you?"

Mr. Buchanan brought his small glass of what looked like Drambuie with him and sat beside Matthew.

"No. He has some dairy cows as well as beef so he's tied to the milking."

Matthew introduced Mr. Buchanan.

"Alistair," he said and everyone offered their names.

Soon Matthew and Alistair were deeply entrenched in a conversation about cattle. I heard "1500 calves ready for transport to Portsmouth at once. A big transport headache."

I thought Mr. Buchanan, Alistair, was in for a bigger headache soon.

Matthew nodded and asked questions. He was happy.

The lounge was cozy tonight, homely with the soft amber lights of the side lamps reflected in the wood panelling. When Bob served, he was efficient if annoying, but without him here this evening, Dylan was struggling. He'd taken our orders and managed, after considerable delay, to get everyone the drink they preferred.

"No help in the kitchen tonight, Dylan?" Nancy asked him

"No. Bob has his meeting in the back and Shirley is making sanitizers in the wine cellar. She'll come up if I need her".

It seemed to me Shirley worked all the time.

"You're doing fine," Peggy said, giving the encouragement I'm sure she'd given her library patrons.

"Where's Mark?" Matthew asked as Dylan concentrated on putting some nuts and crisps on the tables.

"He's staying at the hospital with Lionel tonight. Lionel should be discharged tomorrow. "

"No after-affects then," Eseld said. She knew the doctors would keep him if there were any untoward symptoms.

"Not so far," I said, still worried about him.

"I expect symptoms would have manifested by now if there was anything drastically wrong."

"Yes. Yes. That makes sense." I believed her and was reassured. "I expect Mark will be back in the morning to collect his gear then liberate Lionel from the hospital."

"I heard Lionel was attacked. Young idiots around here do anything for a few dollars. I am happy to hear he's recovered." Alistair added his concerns.

"Thank you," I said. "We expect he'll be fine." We hadn't considered robbery. It seemed unlikely, although possible— except the only thing missing was Lionel's blue book. I suppose that made it robbery.

"Does anyone want anything more?" Dylan asked.

I looked around, but everyone was satisfied. They sipped their drinks and talked with one another. Judith, true to form, was explaining something about Cirencester to Anna. I reassured Dylan he could leave us, then listened to Judith.

"After the dissolution of the monasteries and with the reformation in the 1530s, the site was handed over to Richard Master in 1564. He was the physician to Queen Elizabeth I."

"That long ago!" Anna was suitably impressed.

I caught some bits of the conversations around me and had drifted into a kind of mellow relaxation. No one required anything of me at the moment. I should ring my sister tonight. She'd want to know Lionel was recovering, but other than that small task, I was free.

In about a half-hour, the Blighs went up to their room with Judith following shortly after and Alistair Buchanan following her. Heather, Matthew and the Nova Scotia ladies started a game of Mexican Train on one of the tables and the click of dominos pervaded with the occasional cry of protest, "You monkey. You shut me down." They were happily engaged. Nothing for me to do here.

Anna picked up her rucksack and headed for the stairs. She stopped for a moment. "I'm going to look at the results of Amy's analysis," she said to me. "She's sending them to me via email and we'll chat on the phone about them."

I roused and tried to look alert. "Should be interesting."

"Or not."

She was right. The specimens may tell us nothing at all.

I moved to the back of the lounge to the bar and asked Dylan for the bill.

He studied the till for a few moments, then printed out the ticket I needed. I checked it over and signed it.

"How are you doing here, Dylan? Is this the first time you've been on your own in the bar?"

"Right. Right. Did it show?"

"Not really," I lied. "You are doing well. I thought you'd just started here, though."

"I did. I've only been here a fortnight, but I'm not sure I can keep on."

He seemed nervous, but he could be habitually nervous. He wiped the counter obsessively, but many bar owners were doing that post Covid19. But he also shifted his weight from foot to foot. Perhaps something was worrying him. I gave him my attention.

"Why is that?"

"That Bob he's pressuring me to join his fitness group. Those weirdos pump iron at the gym on West Way and pop supplements and argue at meetings—all things I can't afford both in time or money."

"Bob is a fitness guru?"

Dylan snorted. "He thinks he is. Me, I'm taking second year sciences at the uni and have all that work and studying. I don't have time for that....stuff."

I appreciated him cleaning up his language for me. I'm sure it wasn't 'stuff' he was going to say. I leaned against the bar. "What's your ambition?" I remembered him telling Matthew he wanted to study medicine.

I found Dylan intriguing. He was a weedy looking soul, swaying a little like a reed in the wind. I could understand why Bob thought he needed a little more brawn.

"I'm going into medicine. I'll take two years on the Bath campus, then transfer to Oxford then three years after that. I have to have a strong base in science and a research approach to be accepted. I'm brilliant in chemistry, and they like that."

I considered Dylan. He may struggle to serve us our drinks, but he had ambitions to serve humanity.

"So, you're studying and doing this job?"

"That's right. And this job is more than advertised. They don't give me enough time to study and it's too far from home. I live in Chippingham with my parents and come to work on my bike."

I'd seen him arrive on his motorbike, a tattered-looking old Norton.

"It takes too much time to get here, then there is too much work. I've got a girlfriend. Noreen. She says I don't spend enough time with her. How can I? I work all the time."

"What did you think you *would* be doing here?"

"I thought I'd be sitting at the reception in the evenings and taking care of any calls. That would give me time to study. It's not happening. Noreen isn't happy either. I'll have to quit here."

He look physically weak, but I was discovering a steel-hard ambition in Dylan. Noreen didn't sound as though she shared those ambitions.

"Do you have any scholarships?"

"Two."

"Good for you."

He stood straighter and stopped his constant movement. "Don't tell Bob I'm going into medicine. He thinks all doctors are fakes."

"Does he think those protein supplements are going to let him live forever?"

"Yeah."

That Bob must get his medicine off the Internet from the producers of his protein supplements.

I knocked on the door of Eseld and Bran's room.

"Welcome," Bran said. "We were hoping you'd come tonight. Did you bring that blue book with you?"

"Mark told you I had it?"

"He did indeed, maid. He did indeed." Bran rubbed his hands together. "I can't wait to read it."

Eseld raised her eyebrows as if to show exasperation with Bran, but said, "I'm curious as well. Come in, my lover, and sit down a while."

Bran had fetched a ladder-backed chair from the nearby desk and we gathered round their small table.

I pulled the blue book from my rucksack and passed it to Bran. He sank back in his chair and began to read. I sat with Eseld and spoke softly. "I wonder if Bob is running some kind of drug distribution system from the back room there where he has his 'philosophy' meetings?"

"Did Lionel suggest that in his notes?" Eseld asked me.

"No. He talked about how those men in the back room were highly suspect and he was going to watch and see what he could learn. Perhaps he did learn."

"And was attacked for it?"

"Possibly," I said.

"Where would they keep the drugs?" Eseld looked at the practical questions.

"Maybe in the wine cellar?"

"Possibly," Eseld said. "Shirley concocts her hand sanitizers down there. Bob would have to avoid her, but Shirley is busy with the hotel, so there must be many hours when Bob could work in the cellar and she wouldn't necessarily know about it. He could stash drugs in corners and behind barrels. Shirley wouldn't likely move heavy barrels."

We were deep into a discussion of ways and means Bob could set up his distribution system when we heard a loud thump coming from the back of the hotel then a woman's cry of distress.

"The kitchen!" Bran said. He headed out the door with Eseld and me close behind him. We clattered down the stairs, through the hall and to the back of the hotel where the kitchen was located. I didn't see any sign of Dylan. He must have left for home.

We charged into the kitchen to see Shirley on the floor, huddled against the fridge and Bob bending over her.

"Well," Bran said in his deep booming voice. "What's to do?"

I don't know why that typical British police inquiry seems funny, but whenever I hear it I think I'm in a Gilbert and Sullivan farce.

"Bob," Bran repeated. "What's to do?"

Bob turned and glared at Bran. "A pan fell from the top of the fridge and nearly hit her. A heavy pan. It could have killed her."

"Are you hurt?" Bran moved closer to Shirley.

Bob answer. "I don't think so, but it scared her."

The pan was on the floor, a heavy, cast-iron, griddle pan. If it had hit her, she would have been in the hospital with Lionel, dealing with bleeding in her brain.

"Get a chair," Bob said. "She needs to sit down."

Eseld got the chair.

Bran moved closer. "What happened, Shirley?"

It looked as if Bob had attacked her. The way Shirley was cowering against the fridge was a reaction of fear.

"The pan f..f..fell," she stuttered.

Bob helped her up.

"I went to open the fridge and the pan fell. What was it doing up there?" She turned to Bob puzzled.

"I put it up there to get it out of the way."

"I don't want my pans out of the way." Shirley's voice was steadier now, quiet but insistent.

"I thought you didn't use it often and it was better up high."

If Bob hit her with that pan, she wouldn't be talking to us. She'd be out cold. Bran looked at the floor, I followed his gaze. There was a dent in the wood near the pan. Perhaps it had fallen.

"It didn't hit you, did it?" I asked.

"No," she said. "I'm okay. Just startled."

Upset. Maybe anxious. Was she ready to leave Bob? Did he object? Had they been fighting?

"Maybe you'd like to come to the lounge with Claire and me," Eseld said. "We'll get you a cup of tea and you can get your breath back."

"She's all right," Bob said. "I'll put the pan away and stay with her. Tea's a good idea then Shirl can go to bed."

"Good idea," Bran said. "Do you need a hand putting the kitchen to rights?"

Shirley protested. "No. No one in my kitchen. Thank you for coming, but guests shouldn't be in my kitchen." She sounded calmer.

It was her kitchen, after all. The health department would object to uncertified help in the kitchen. She said she'd just had a fright. She hadn't said Bob had attacked her. Nevertheless, I'd look for the women's shelter number and make sure she had it.

CHAPTER ELEVEN

We returned to our rooms trudging up the stairs and through the halls. Bran and Eseld pushed their door open. Bran stood in the doorway and turned to me.

"I'll read Lionel's blue book tonight and come to your room before breakfast to report. Will Mark be there?"

"I think so. You've arranged for one of his friends to arrive in the early morning, so Mark will turn over guard duty to him and come here to shower and change."

"We'll arrive with the larks then," he said and closed the door.

I slept deeply and only woke when I heard Mark's key in the lock. He gave me a quick kiss and headed for the shower. I was up and had the coffee in the French Press when he emerged.

"Is Lionel allowed out of the hospital today?" I asked as I poured him a cup and handed him the biscuits I'd stashed in my luggage.

"He is. And he's impatient to be going. I'll collect him after I've had a couple of hours sleep, get his prescriptions and drive him back to Ashton. Is there any food in the house?"

I don't usually leave much there when I depart for a fortnight tour. "I'll ring up Rose and get in milk, bread, eggs, cheese, some veggies and a couple of steaks. Will that do you for the first day?

"Coffee?"

"In the pantry. I just got a shipment." I ordered my coffee from Seattle and kept about a month's supply on my shelves. "I'll ring up

Rose to bring Gulliver home and ring Deirdre to tell her she won't need to dog sit."

"Right. Good," he said.

"Bran and Eseld…" I started to say when a knock sounded on the door.

"That's them now."

"Lionel? *Allycumpooster*?" Bran asked.

"Yes, everything's fine," Mark said. He was used to some Cornish words. "He's doing very well. I'm going to spring him from the hospital in a couple of hours."

"Have some coffee, or tea," I said as I plugged in the kettle.

"Tea, lover, if you'd be so good." Eseld said.

"Right you are." I took the cups she handed me.

"What are your plans for the day," Mark asked me.

"We're going to Bath. We should be gone the whole day visiting Jane Austen's house, the Roman Baths, Pulteney Bridge and the sites most tourists don't want to miss."

"We need to check out the Fashion Museum," Eseld said. "It's wonderful."

"I have it on my list." It was, indeed, wonderful. "You've been to Bath before, I'm sure."

"You needn't be too sure. We haven't traveled much, but yes, we've been to Bath and we're happy to go again."

"Are you sure Lionel is going to all right at home?" I asked Mark.

"No, I'm not sure," Mark said, demolishing a biscuit in two bites. "I'm a tad worried about taking him home. He is still a bit woozy."

"Can't ask him much about the attack then," Bran said.

"No. Not yet."

"Ask the district nurse to visit," Eseld said. "She can assess Lionel and let you know if she sees anything amiss."

"Oh!" I had a sudden inspiration. "Robert Andrews' girlfriend, Rosemary, is a district nurse. You might ring Robert and ask for her number." Robert was Gulliver's vet and a friend of mine.

"Always good to know someone," Eseld said.

I'd put tea into the pot and now poured in the boiling water. I set the teapot in front of Eseld and left her to serve it. People are fussy about how long their tea steeps.

Bran poured himself a cup, took a long drink of it, hot as it was, and sighed. "Now," he said. You will want to know what I found out in Lionel's book."

"He read into the night," Eseld said.

"Right worth doing, it was." He looked satisfied.

I wondered what was in that book in the parts I hadn't yet reached, and had been restraining my curiosity. What was so important that Lionel was attacked?

"Do tell us." I was almost beside myself with anticipation. What had Lionel known that made someone determined to kill him? What could he have possibly known?

Bran straightened and began giving his report, just as if he were still an inspector. "Lionel was suspicious of Bob and his cronies. He didn't believe the philosophy club anymore than we did. He decided to investigate those meetings taking place on these premises. He had a listening device."

I glanced at Mark. We'd both had those at one time.

Bran looked at Mark a little apologetically. "He wasn't working as a copper any more and he thought he needed more information to take to the local nick. They didn't know him there."

Mark nodded. There was a confederacy of colleagues in the police force. Within that, there were cliques.

Bran continued. "He planted it in the meeting room and listened to their conversations." While he was talking Bran had taken the blue book from his coat pocket and with his reading glasses on the end of his nose, peered at the book. He opened it to a marked page and read. "Bob and his friends have a Neo-Nazi group. They are full of the rhetoric of the ignorant, spouting forth how important they are and how unimportant everyone else is, especially people of color. Distasteful but not criminal unless they act." Bran looked up. "Lionel discovered they are going to act."

"Oh, my heavens," Eseld said. "Just what we need. A group of idiots causing havoc. What were they or are they going to do?"

"He's transcribed what he heard and put his comments beside their words. He didn't have much use for the ignorant yobs. Apparently, they were convinced they were the only ones who realized the world was being taken over by 'others' and that they were appointed by destiny to be warriors and attack." Bran smiled.

"That's not funny; it's downright frightening," Eseld said, reacting to Bran's smile. "That's what every tyrant believes and, as you right know, Bran my dear one, every criminal thinks the same."

"I know, I know, luv. It isn't Bob and his goons I think is funny. It's Lionel. His comment is 'a poorly educated lot with the problem-solving ability of a gnat.'"

"Sounds like Lionel," Mark said. "What else is in there?"

"He was going to collect specific information about their plans before he talked to the police. He isn't sure Bob could actually plan anything, but says, "I'd better find out more in case these louts are dangerous."

We were silent for a moment. Someone had turned out to be dangerous. Lionel been right about that.

"Do you think Shirley knows about these plans?" I asked.

"I don't think so," Bran said. "Lionel doesn't mention her except to say she was very busy. If what we saw tonight is any indication, she *might* suspect Bob is up to something but would be too afraid to say anything."

"Maybe she thinks he won't do anything," I said.

"Gis on! "Eseld said." He's either *dobeck* or *bylen*."

I looked at Mark.

"Stupid or wicked," he translated

"Or both," I said.

"True," Eseld said. "Or both."

"Did Lionel find any specific plans?" Mark asked Bran.

"Not that I found."

We sat in silence for a few moments. I was disappointed there wasn't more information.

"What do we do?" I finally asked.

Mark took a deep breath. He must be tired. He'd been up all night. "I'll talk to his Truro friend from the constabulary when I go to pick up Lionel. He might know something. Lionel might have talked to him."

"Lionel might have hidden his notes on the plans somewhere in this hotel," Eseld said. "He could be tricky like that. Not a trusting soul with strangers."

"I'll ask him," Mark agreed.

"Where's the receiver for the listening device," I asked.

"Good question. We'll have to look for it," Mark said.

"You have a nap," I said. "I'll give a quick look before I leave for the day and you can look when you wake up. I'll leave it on the dresser in our room if I find it."

"Do you know what to look for?" Bran asked.

"Yes," I said without explaining how a well-behaved tour guide knew about such things.

"If it's not in his room," Bran said, "that would mean Bob had found it. Would he be using it?"

"Could he be listening to our conversations?" I was horrified. That had happened to me once before, and it was unnerving.

"If Bob found the listening device he wouldn't necessarily know who had planted it," Bran said, "and, therefore, wouldn't know where to look for the receiver. He's not sophisticated. Lionel thought he was a small-time zealot, not part of an organized group with lots of back up."

I wondered if there *was* a sophisticated boss in the background manipulating Bob. Someone who would benefit if police and detectives were engrossed in hunting terrorists and would leave local crime alone.

"We don't know the others in his group, though," Mark said. "Someone might know about listening devices. They aren't complicated. And someone more intelligent might be using Bob and his group. It could be dangerous." I wasn't the only one who had thought of this.

"What we *can* do is get Lionel away from here. That's the first thing," Mark said. "I will stay with him. That leaves you three here with Bob."

"And the local constabulary," Eseld reminded him.

"I'll have a talk with Sergeant Thompson before I leave," Mark said. "I'll tell her what Lionel discovered."

Bran looked up sharply.

"I won't tell her how he found out." Mark understood Bran's caution.

"I'd like to remove that listening device," Bran said.

I could see he was worried that Lionel might be charged with unlawful use of that device. From what I knew about the law, it was unlikely, but Bran might think it reflected poorly on his friend. I'd search Lionel's room and the meeting room at the back of the hotel if I had to.

"How dangerous is Bob?" Mark asked. "Would he be planning a violent act? A riot, an explosion, an attack of the innocents in the streets?"

"Lionel didn't think so. He thought Bob liked to talk but not actually do much. He got slogans and ideas from the Internet, but Lionel didn't think he wanted to give up control of his group to anyone, so we can assume he hasn't a lot of resources." Bran must have studied every page of that blue book last night.

"Except for explosives," Mark said. "Who can get the makings for explosives?"

"Farmers can get explosives but they have to go through a lot of red tape," Bran said.

"Chemists can make them," I said thinking of Dylan. He said he was brilliant at chemistry.

"There are directions on the Internet on how to make explosives." Bran sounded disgusted.

"What are the most likely ingredients?" I knew nothing about making explosives. If I tried to find out on the Internet, the police would be at my door asking me why.

"Fertilizers." Bran was decisive. I wondered if he'd been on the track of someone making explosives in his work as an inspector. That was highly likely.

"Where would he store them?"

"Don't start nosing around," Bran said. "You'll tip him off."

Mark roused himself. "We'll just look for Lionel's copy of Bob's plans. It must be somewhere nearby. "

"And the listening device, or at least the receiver," Eseld said.

I left Mark to his nap and started toward the breakfast room to see if everyone was up and ready to go to Bath. I took the back stairs past the manager's quarters. I heard raised voices and stopped to listen. If Bob was attacking Shirley, I was going to call Thompson.

Bob's voice came through the door clearly. "I have to get back to the bar, Julie's giving me only fifteen minutes." Julie was a part-time bar maid. It sounded as though she was thoroughly up on the Work Standards.

"I want to talk to you." That was Shirley's voice, hard and shrill. "You *never* want to talk. I am so tired of this constant activity. You never take any time off to be with me. It's worse than being married."

"Hey, Shirley honey. We'll get some time once the tourist season is over. Maybe go to Morocco or someplace warm."

"Sounds good." Her voice softened. "Maybe I can take a course in Moroccan cooking while we're there?"

He laughed. "You and your courses. We can just relax."

"I need to get all the skills I can. I don't want to be at this hotel forever."

"This is a good gig, Shirley. I mean it pays the bills."

"Just. And I do all the work."

"Yeah you do. And you deserve a holiday. Next month. Everything will quieten down next month."

"You are in a dream world, Bob. Next month, the hotel is full." Her voice was closer to the door now, so I moved on.

Did he mean his terrorist activities would be over by next month?

I was pushing open the door of the breakfast room when Bob emerged from the kitchen.

The Nova Scotia ladies called me over to view the shambles of their Mexican Train game with the Montana couple. Tiles were strewn over the table and the four of them were laughing.

"I've never played this before and it's vicious," Peggy said. Her voice was light-hearted. I assumed she enjoyed the competition.

"We were going to continue the game we left last night, but there's no time this morning. We'd better put it away."

"Everything okay here?" Bob said as he walked past.

"Just fine," I said, not turning around.

I passed out the day's itinerary, then helped myself to a breakfast of omelette with chives and cheese. Delicious. The brioche was wonderful as well, quite as good as any I've had in Paris. Shirley was right to be ambitious about her cooking.

I had forty minutes before I had to leave for Bath. I nipped into my room to find Mark sound asleep. His pants were draped over the chair and his keys on the dresser. I pushed my finger through his keys looking for one similar to my room key. I found two. One would be to this room and one to Lionel's. I took them both.

The first one I tried fit Lionel's room. I slipped in and closed the door. If anyone asked. I was packing up Lionel's things for Mark to take home. I might do that if I had time. Bran thought Lionel had a copy of Bob's plans for insurrection or mischief. Dates, times and location would be vastly helpful.

First, I checked behind the toilet and under the lid in case he'd taped it there. I took the towels from the cupboard and looked through the shelves. I looked under the bed, under the mattress. I took the drawers out and checked behind them. I moved a chair to the window and reached above the curtains in case he'd pinned an envelope to the inside. Nothing. While I was standing there, I saw a delivery van back into the courtyard and open its doors. Shirley and Bob loaded cardboard cases into the van. That must be Shirley's hand sanitizers. She worked hard and from what I'd overheard the object of her hard work was to move to a bigger hotel where she could be a chef. Good for her. I hoped she'd manage that. Meanwhile, she would produce those bottles while people were still conscious of washing their hands and make some money toward her goals. I've never been that driven, but I understood others were.

I looked through Lionel's clothes and the pockets of his rucksack. I'd used up my time and seen nothing. I'd leave it for Mark. He'd give it another going over.

I returned to my room and replaced Mark's keys. I took time to text Deirdre. She'd be sleeping in as she didn't go into work today. *Mark is bringing Lionel to our house today. Mark will keep Gulliver. Thanks, but you won't need to fetch him.*

I grabbed my rucksack and mobile and fetched the van. I pulled up in front of the Queen Bess right on time.

CHAPTER TWELVE

I'd put a bag of goodies at every seat. My guests had a small bottle of water, some chocolate, brochures for the various sites we were going to visit and a couple of post cards of Bath. I didn't supply this every day but periodically throughout the tour.

Bath was thirty miles from Cirencester which was an hour's driving. I remembered driving in Washington State in America, where I would whip through thirty miles in thirty minutes. Here, the road slowed through villages, round-abouts and some narrow corners—so, one hour for thirty miles.

I drove south along what became the A429 through the beautiful Cotswold mix of farms and woodland. After crossing the M4 and still heading south, the land flattened somewhat and miles and miles of fields stretched on either side with woodland dispersed through it. It was beautiful in its own way, but I preferred the country around Cirencester. After Chippenham, I turned west and drove to Bath.

We were lucky with the weather. The sky was a deep blue, the temperature warm but not hot. The fields on either side were lush with crops. Because I was driving a van, my guests were high enough off the road so they could look over fences and hedgerows to view the countryside.

"This is going to be a full day," Judith commented from the left-hand front seat. "I would like to get a souvenir from a shop on the Pulteney Bridge. It's Georgian, you know."

She meant the bridge was Georgian. I did know.

"It was designed by Robert Adam in 1769," she said.

I glanced back. She wasn't using her notes. She had an amazing memory.

"It's beautiful," I offered.

"I want to buy something from one of the shops located on the bridge," she said again.

It was more a demand than a direction, but it would be easy to fulfill. I'd included The Pulteney Bridge on the tour today as it was a romantic, almost medieval-looking bridge, built for beauty as well as usefulness. Tourists took boat trips to view it from the water, but we only had a day in Bath with much to see and no time for a leisurely cruise on the Avon. I'd given them hop- on-hop-off bus tickets for Bath in their goodie bag today, so each person could choose what sites they wanted to see.

"Where are we going first?" Nancy asked from somewhere behind me.

"First, I will park, then we'll walk to the Roman Baths. Has anyone been there before?"

"Bran and I have," Eseld said, "but we are happy to go again. I think it was about thirty years ago."

"It hasn't changed," I said.

"Not in 2,000 years," Judith added.

We laughed. She was likely quite right.

"I'm keen to see the Baths," Anna said.

I expected her to pick up a sample from somewhere inside that site.

I parked two blocks from the Roman Baths and we walked to it.

"The plumbing still works," Bran observed. The men and Anna were examining the engineering.

"I've got an irrigation system that I have to fix all the time," Matthew said. "Two hundred acres under irrigation. I should have hired a Roman engineer."

I saw Anna reach out with a pair of tweezers and nip a sample from an old brick. I wouldn't expect much flora of antiquity as millions of people had come through here. She did take it from a crevasse between the bricks, so perhaps she had more chance of finding something—that famous byssum she was after, fallen from someone's toga two thousand years ago.

We left the Roman Baths and I drove them to view the Royal Crescent with it's sweep of townhouses in a semi-circle in, as the tourist brochure describes, "a breathtakingly uniform, palace-like façade".

"I'd like to see the plumbing in that sucker," Matthew said.

"Not as good as the Romans," Bran opined. "It's Georgian."

"If you are interested in knowing more," I said, "you can come back in the afternoon on the bus and investigate No.1 Royal Crescent. It's a show home of what it was like in Georgian times."

"Might do that," Bran said.

"Someone should write a Victorian novel set here," Nancy said. "I read that from the air the Circus and the Royal Crescent form a key design. It was a symbol of the Masons. There is lots of symbolism in the design. The architect Wood mixed them up. He thought Bath was an ancient druid site like Stonehenge. He created the circus with the same diameter as Stonehenge."

There are many theories about the design, and I wasn't about to spoil any discussion by discounting them.

"Peter Lovesey did," Anna said from further back in the van. "Set a book here, I mean. He set several in in this city."

"I see Bath more as the setting for the Regency period," Judith said. "The Jane Austen novels seem perfect for this place."

"Jane did live here but only for five years from 1801–1806," Peggy said. "You'd think she'd spent her whole life here from the way in which the city's tourist board appear to have adopted her."

There were many Jane Austen references. She wrote in the period when these buildings were contemporary, so perhaps it's only natural to see the whole area as her personal setting.

"Pickwick papers was set here. That, of course was later," I said, 1836 if I remembered correctly.

"Frances Burney. She's an early mystery writer," Eseld said.

1778, I thought.

"And, of course," Eseld went on, "there was an even more recent one by Hazel Holt. What was that one?"

Bran shook his head. He had no idea.

"*My Dear Charlotte.* A mystery written in the first decade of this century but set in Regency Bath," Peggy said.

I hadn't read that one. Charlotte was the name of Jane Austen's sister. I wondered if the novel was about Jane Austen.

"Hazel Holt wrote the Mrs. Mallory series, didn't she?" Nancy asked.

"Yes, and you still have the first of the series that I lent you."

"Remind me when we get home."

Nancy rolled her eyes.

I grinned to myself. I'd swear they were sisters.

We drove around the Circus which is similar to The Royal Crescent and by the same architect but a complete circle. It looked gracious, elegant and romantic and my guests got a quick view from the van. I parked at the Viaduct Car Park and led my group to The Jars Restaurant. I had planned an elaborate dinner for later, so picked The Jars for lunch with its variety of small Greek dishes. It was also near Pulteney Bridge over the Avon River, the Fashion Museum and Jane Austen's house.

"We *are* going to see Jane Austen's house, aren't we?" Judith wanted to make sure the itinerary matched her wishes.

The itinerary stated we would go there, but many tours listed sites on their itineraries and never went to the places they listed. She may have had some experience with that.

"Indeed," I assured her. "That tour is a short one. It isn't far from Jane Austen's house to Pulteney Bridge, so we can walk around those sites."

Heather and Matthew were planning to tour the Holburne Museum.

"We never, but never, go to art galleries," Heather said. "This trip is all about opening up our horizons and looking further than the Rocky Mountains."

"Good for you," I encouraged her.

"Otherwise," Mathew added, "Heather says we will become minds set in stone and uninteresting."

"The Holburne Museum is impressive," I said. "There are famous works hanging there by Gainsborough, Reynolds and Stubbs. There are lots of interesting porcelain, even furniture."

"Well, it won't kill me for one afternoon," Matthew said. He turned to his menu. Heather caught my eye and raised her eyebrows. I expected Matthew was in for a few more museums.

"You might have noticed how busy the city is," I said to everyone.

Bran and Eseld nodded, but the others had no comparison and may have thought the city was always this busy.

"It's the Bath Music Festival this week. There is a huge party tomorrow but plenty of activity today. Look for buskers on the street and concerts in local venues. I have them marked in the city map I put in your bags. Judith, the Pulteney Bridge is close. If you buy something you want me to store in the van, just text me, and I'll come and carry it to the van for you."

"I may do that." She looked pleased.

"There are many bookstores. They are also marked on your map, including Mr. B's which often has authors of note to speak. There are eateries. Sally Lunn's Buns is a must. They make a wonderful bun with cinnamon butter topping, and you can get tea there as well. It's near the Abbey and close by is a cellar museum." I looked up to catch Matthew blink and withdraw a little. Uh, oh. He hasn't even been in a museum yet and he's resisting.

"It dates from Roman times when I expect it was a pub."

Matthew looked a little more interested. I trusted everyone would sort themselves out and do what suited them.

"I'll remain in this area," I said, "in case you need me for anything. In fact, I'll see some of you because I plan to spend quite a bit of time in Mr. B's Reading Emporium."

I did meet Nancy and Peggy at the Reading Emporium. It's a delightful spot and I try to get to it as often as possible. It is, as expected, crowded with books from its floor to its twelve-foot ceiling. Cozy nooks invite readers to relax. If you want to discuss a book, one of the clerks will happily sit down with you for a natter. You might come across a book launch with the author in attendance, or a group meeting to discuss a book they are all reading. A children's story-teller seems to be part of the staff. It's lively but not raucous. There is enough of a subdued quality to the activities to allow readers to concentrate.

I found an empty chair in a nook there, pulled out my mobile and texted Mark.

"Where are you?" I asked.

He rang me immediately. "Home with Lionel."

"How is he?"

"Tired but okay. Rosemary is coming after work to sort us with the district nurse."

"Excellent. Did you get Gulliver?"

"Rose brought him and all his luggage."

"How is he?"

"Glad to be home if his tail-wagging and jumping is evidence. Lionel's taken to him and Gulliver shares the sofa with him."

"That's good." I smiled at the mental image of Gulliver curled up beside Lionel. That should help Lionel heal.

"There is soup in the freezer that Rose's mother gave me. It should be good. Also frozen bread from the same source."

"I can manage that."

Neither Mark nor I were good cooks, but I bought good quality food from many local sources, so we ate well. Rose's mother, Helen

Taylor, was happy to make and sell her soups and breads to a few customers.

"Any word on the murder of Richie Stonehouse?" I hadn't forgotten him. He lurked at the back of my mind.

"He was definitely moved from a cave or something like a cave to where he was found. Nothing on the knife. But the forensic entomologist, Dr. White's, report was interesting. Apparently, some of the spores found on Richie's clothing are particular."

"Particular?"

"I mean the combinate of spores would only be found in a few places or perhaps only one place. They just have to find that place."

Cirencester wasn't a big town, but it was big enough that searching caves would be a huge task and an expensive one in terms of paying the searchers. They'd wouldn't even start until they had more information.

"Needle in a haystack?"

"Quite."

"What about those plans of Bob's. Did Lionel say where he hid them?"

"He couldn't remember. He knew he was suspicious of something, but he doesn't remember what. Rosemary said his memory might come back or it might not."

"Don't lean on him." I didn't think it would help, and it might hurt Lionel.

"No. I won't. I told him it didn't matter."

I hoped Lionel was recovering, but felt better that he had left the Queen Bess Hotel and that Mark had a nurse to help him supervise Lionel's care.

I texted Deirdre as well and told her where I was and where Mark and Lionel were. She'd get back to me tonight. I texted Rose to thank her for her care of Gulliver. She sent me back a picture and said she missed him. I did as well. He was a darling.

That business done, I turned to the books around me and made some choices. I had about fourteen books stacked on the counter when Peggy and Nancy bustled up to me.

"I wish I could buy that many," Peggy said, "but I'd have to carry them."

I motioned to the clerk and read her name tag. "Emily here, will send them via post, won't you Emily?"

"Where should I send them, once you have some?" Emily, bespeckled and bejeweled with bling earrings and rings, smiled at Peggy.

"Nova Scotia, Canada,"

"Not a problem," Emily said.

"Is it expensive?"

"About the price of one book, so just get one less and you're even."

I rolled that around in my head for a moment. There wasn't a lot of logic in it, but Peggy brightened. "Good idea."

She reached beside me and took a basket, then turned and headed back to the bookshelves. I understood the need to have books. Any excuse to buy them was reasonable.

"Your friends?" Emily asked me as she started ringing up my purchases.

"My tourists. I run a tour company." I reached into my rucksack and found a business card.

"You recommended they come here?" Emily continued.

"I did and I do. I come here myself, as you see. It's a good fit for my tourists as they are all interested in mysteries, or their partners are." I thought of Bran and Matthew who were not fans.

I gave Emily my credit card, and she put my sale through.

"I gave you the staff discount," Emily said as she passed me the receipt.

"Thank you." I hadn't thought of asking for a discount. I was pleased enough to find some gems such as a Peter Lovesey I hadn't read and the latest Rhys Bowen. I hurried back to the van, deposited my books, then almost ran to Quiet Street. I might not have much time. It wasn't far but I was never sure when I sent my guests off on their own for a few hours whether they were going to ring me and ask for my help. I needed to get my shopping finished before I had to fetch someone.

I slipped into The Dressing Room, a lingerie shop for my occasional indulgences. The hush of that elegant shop relaxed me.

"Madam," an older clerk asked me, "can I help?"

"Yes." I looked at the luscious lingerie around me. "I'd like a nightgown."

"Something in black?" the woman asked.

I was delighted she hadn't said, "Something in flannel?"

"Definitely, something in black," I said.

Twenty minutes later I was back at the van, poorer by what in my youth was a month's rent. I was the first one at the van, but they arrived shortly after in ones and twos.

Anna had been clothes shopping and was loaded down with packages. I helped her pile them in the back noticing the name one. "That's a lovely shop."

"Super. I have to remind Peter that he missed me."

I pointed to my bag which I slipped into the back beside my books. "Same shop. Same motive?" Anna asked.

"Same motive," I agreed.

Nancy and Peggy had a few souvenirs but had sent their book purchases via post. Matthew and Heather had some bags from The Entertainer which was a toy store. Judith had a long roll which she said contained an antique map.

"Most entertaining place," she said. "The shop was full of antique maps."

"Which one did you buy?"

"It's only a copy," she said, dismissively, "but it's interesting. Of Bath in Roman times."

"You'll have to show it to us," I said. "I think the men will be interested as well."

She looked pleased. "I'll do that. Perhaps in the lounge when we get back to the Queen Bess."

I placed her map carefully at the edge of the boot. The cardboard roll would protect it but it still could get damaged.

"I dropped into the jewelry shop and bought myself a ring. The jeweler was most knowledgeable." She flashed a diamond and garnet ring. I looked at it closely.

"That's lovely, Judith."

She smiled. "I have a certificate of authentication on it."

She would. I expect she knew everything there was to know about it before she bought it.

"Good for you." She seemed to be careful about what she bought in terms of quality. I don't think she worried about price.

We settled into the van and I drove northeast. Just before Chippenham I took the B 4309 and headed north and slightly west to Castle Combe. I'd booked dinner at the Manor House.

"Tiddlywink," Nancy called from the back. "There's a sign for Tiddlywink. That's a town? "

"It is," I said.

"Well, I never," Eseld said. "I had no idea."

Most of the group had been dozing up to this point, but we were approaching Castle Combe and the comments from the two women caused everyone to stir, stretch and pay attention to the surroundings. They were all awake when I drove into the village.

"My God," Matthew said. "It's Brigadoon."

I laughed. I drove over the short stone bridge and immediately curved right into the village. It did look frozen in time, about the fifteenth century, and there were laws to keep it that way. Some houses were even older. The Roman bridge would have been built before the fifth century. I drove slowly, partly because it had started to rain, quite usual in Castle Combe, and partly so my guests could have a good look at the village.

"We don't have time to stop," I said, "because we have a dinner reservation a little further along, but it is quite lovely, isn't it?"

"Even in the rain," Nancy said. "It's… I guess the word is charming."

"However much that word is overused here," Peggy said.

"How would you describe it?" Nancy said with some heat.

I caught Peggy's grin in the rear-view mirror.

"Charming," she said.

Nancy half-laughed and half-snorted.

I stopped for a moment in Market Square as there was no one behind us. I heard cameras and mobiles ting and ping.

"Sorry," I said. as a car approached from my rear. "I have to move."

"It's cool. Thanks for taking us here," Anna said. "No one in Sacramento will believe a town like this exists. There are no wires anywhere."

"Everything is underground," Bran said. "Must be."

"Could be the telly comes in on the ether," Eseld said. "It's a magical place."

"No one is going to believe this," Anna repeated as she took pictures through the van window.

"They will if they watched *Downton Abbey*," Nancy said. "They filmed here."

"They filmed *The Murder of Roger Ackroyd* here as well," I said.

"Ah, Christie again," Heather said. "She's timeless."

"And they filmed Steven Spielberg's production of *War Horse* here." Eseld knew that.

"It *looks* like a film set," Matthew said.

"Have you been here before, Eseld," I asked.

"No, my lover. Never. It looks a little quiet for me."

I agreed. She would be happier in a larger village where there were more people.

"I promise you a fabulous meal," I said as I wheeled the van along the narrow roads. The rain had begun in earnest now, and I had to concentrate on my driving. It wasn't far, only about five minutes uphill on The Street.

I pulled into the Manor House car park and my group disembarked and dashed through the rain to the lobby of the restaurant, shaking their jackets and smoothing back their hair.

"The British Mystery Book Tour?" inquired a small man in the black trousers and white shirt beloved by waiters everywhere.

At my nod he gestured. "This way, please. "

"One moment," I said. "Could you direct us to the cloakroom first?"

"Certainly."

Everyone dispersed to refresh themselves and get as dry and tidy as possible. I followed the waiter to the table, approved the seating arrangements then joined the ladies.

When we returned, I looked around. I hadn't brought a tour to this restaurant before. The Cotswold stone walls gave that warm ambience typical of this area. The red damask curtains added the feel of elegance without formality. The plank tables were set with white china and, of course, silver or silver-plated service. The menu was impressive. Meals like this were certainly one of the perks of my job.

The short soaking we'd all received when leaving the van seemed to have chased away the torpor of the early evening and everyone examined their menu with interest. It was as if each person was reciting poetry when they mentioned a dish.

"Caramelized onion and braised ox shin, risotto, pickled shallots, aged parmesan," Judith said. "Sounds most interesting."

"Grilled Herefordshire rib eye steak, chips, Abernethy butter, vine tomatoes and parmesan salad," Matthew said. "That's for me."

"You eat steak everywhere we go," Heather complained.

"Got to see what the competition is up to," Matthew said cheerfully.

"You raise beef then?" Anna said.

"We do, but we are trying to see what other opportunities there are, what else we could do with our land. Beef isn't going to be on the menu forever."

"We think," Heather leaned forward to talk around Matthew, "that we can make a living on beef in our lifetime, but our kids won't be able to. So, we should start moving our business toward what can sustain them."

"Look at the menu here," Matthew said. "There aren't many beef choices."

That was true. I'd noticed there were fewer beef choices in many restaurants, and I'd noticed more of my guests looking for alternative options.

Others spoke about their choices. "'Pan fried fillet of Cornish hake, garden courgette, monks beard, herb beurre blanc?' I understand herbed white butter," Peggy said, "but what is monks beard? And," she added, "they are missing an apostrophe,"

I smiled. "Apostrophes are missing all over the world."

"So true," she said.

"Monks beard is something like shredded Swiss chard."

"That's sounds good," she said. "I'll compare the hake to Nova Scotia cod."

"Not that you can get cod any more," Nancy said. "Have to make do with sole."

"I have a strong memory of Nova Scotian cod," Peggy said firmly.

"Roast cauliflower steak, girolle mushrooms, caper and raisin puree," I said. "I might try that."

"Girolle mushrooms?" Anna asked.

"Chanterelles," I said. "At least, I think so." I glanced at the waiter who was hovering over Judith.

"Yes, madam," he said looking up at me then returning his attention to Judith.

"I'll have," Judith said. She took a breath as if to start on a speech. There was silence as we all waited to see what she was going to order.

"I'll have the caramelized onion as a starter, then the barbecued broccoli, garden mint and toasted hazelnuts as a salad. Then the buttermilk panna cotta, salad of English strawberries and after that a selection of British cheese. With tea, please."

I am constantly amazed at how much this tiny, elderly woman could eat.

"Certainly, madam," the waiter said as he rapidly finished writing. He collected the orders from around the table and brought the wine I'd ordered, a French champagne to start and both an Italian grenache and a New Zealand Sauvignon Blanc. Bran ordered ale and Matthew a lager. I'd also ordered two platters of appetizers and the house sour dough bread to ease the hunger pangs before the meal arrived.

Bran brought the conversation back to Matthew and Heather's concerns about the future of their ranch.

"What's your plan?" he asked.

"We'll be taking a farm tour after this one to look at what others are doing here," Matthew said. "We need to find out what choices we have. Our local ranchers aren't interested in changing, but change is coming quickly. That Lester Wright, the friend of Alistair Buchanan?" He checked to see we remembered him. Several people nodded. "He's got beef problems. He has more beef calves than he can get to market. It costs him to keep them even a few days past prime. I told him he should get out of beef. I mean look at this menu." Matthew flicked his hand on the menu he held. "He needs to diversify, get into regenerative farming. We had a good talk about it. It's a hard change to make."

"One of the reasons we're in England," Heather said, "is to relax. I mean, not only are we escaping from kids and chores, but we're experiencing a place that seems to have managed to remain a farming nation. Everything seems to stay the same here for centuries."

"Some things do," I said. Tourists generally see England as unchanging, but those of us who live here see a great deal of change. Observation cameras are on intersections in cities and towns so our every move is recorded. We have a health care system that seems to have lost its purpose, and education that still seems to be for the rich. Post-pandemic, life simply wasn't the same, although I agreed with Heather some things seemed frozen, especially places like Castle Combe. Change is a challenge. Heather and Matthew were facing that.

No one can anticipate all changes. I thought about Richie Stonehouse. He didn't expect to die. And Lionel. With all his experience, hadn't anticipated being attacked. His life would be changed by that. And perhaps Mark and I would need to change to accommodate Lionel.

In the meantime, the wine was wonderful, my roast cauliflower steak was being served and no one wanted anything more from me. The conversation remained general and everyone conversed easily.

It didn't last. Sergeant Thompson was waiting for me when we returned to the Queen Bess.

"Is Detective Inspector Evans here?" she asked me on the steps.

"No, but come in away. You could probably use a cuppa."

She followed me to my room. I plugged in the kettle and set out the cups and the biscuits. Sergeant Thompson absently reached for and ate three biscuits before I got tea in front of her.

"You're worried," I said as I sat across from her and sipped my tea.

"I am at that. I don't like the way this case is going. I was hoping to talk it over with D.I. Evans."

"He's taken leave to look after Lionel."

"I should have thought of that."

"Can I help?"

She looked directly at me. Her short blonde hair was plastered back flat against her head as if under orders not to move. She had a clear complexion and blue eyes like bullets. I straightened.

"Look, Maisie. I can be discreet. Talk away."

She sipped her tea, looked at me again, then made up her mind.

"I don't like this place. Shirley's mother's been a right eel, slipping around me like she had the freedom of the kingdom. No laws for our Lydia. She makes her own. I've almost got her a couple of times but she has lawyers as sharp as knives and she pays well."

"What does she do?"

"She manages a den of thieves, drug dealers and shoplifters. That's what she does."

I was stunned. Mrs. Harris? The Mrs. Harris of impeccable grooming, understated expensive clothes and fabulous shoes? I tried to reconcile Mrs. Lydia Harris, elegant matron, concerned mother of Shirley, to the picture of a crime boss. It seemed impossible, but Maisie Thompson was believable.

"Do you think Lydia's got anything to do with Richie Stonehouse's death and the attack on Lionel?"

"No. Not directly. She rarely does anything directly, but she'll be behind it somehow." I heard the bitter tone in Maisie's voice. "And I have a hard time thinking Shirley is innocent as a spring lamb. Mind you, her mother's always tried to keep her apart from her business. Bought a house in the best part of town so Shirley wouldn't associate with The Dells then sent her away to a good grammar school. Kept her out of The Dells. Trying to keep Shirley respectable. But I don't know. It's unlikely the acorn falls far from the tree. So, Shirley is a suspect too."

I must have looked sceptical because Maisie laughed.

"That's prejudice, I know. But instinct too. I checked Shirley's background on Holmes. She's clean, but so's her mother, and I *know* she's a wrong 'un."

"Not much to go on there."

"No." She looked discouraged and I didn't have anything to ally her concerns, so I entertained her with the story of Anna taking sample's everywhere she went.

Maisie came alive. Her eyes sparkled and she laughed. "Now there's an interesting woman. I wish I had constables with her curiosity."

"If she finds anything she'll bring it to the station."

"Not tomorrow," she said almost absently. "I have to go to court tomorrow to try to tack some annoying car thieves to the jail wall."

"We won't be here either. We're going to Oxford."

She stood, and I escorted her to the door.

"You know what discourages me," she said as she paused at the top of the outside stairs.

I waited.

"I'll look to retire in twenty years and that smug, self-satisfied Lydia will still be living off the profits of her drug sales, and I still won't have touched her."

"A policeman's lot..." I said.

"Is a sorry lot," she agreed.

CHAPTER THIRTEEN

I locked the door behind her and returned to my bedroom, tidied up the crockery and got ready for bed. I was worried about Lionel, but it was useless to waste time in anxiety because Mark was with him and would look after him. I lay back on my bed and stared at the ceiling. I followed the vines on the elegant cornice around the room, noting the tiny bunches of plaster grapes. Then, looked at the small chandelier. I stared at it for a few minutes before I saw the camera.

I shot up in bed. It *was* a camera, small, almost hidden by the gilded metal flowers.

Bob must have put it there. That Nazi creep. Add voyeurism to his toxic-man image. I threw a sweater over my pyjamas, slipped out of the hotel to my van and found the duct tape I kept in my emergency supplies. When I lived in America, my friends used duct tape for everything.

Back in my room, I cut off a six-inch strip of tape, pulled a chair under the chandelier and covered the eye of the camera with the tape.

I looked around the rest of the room. No more cameras in this room, but I was sure I was going to find another somewhere. I cut off another strip of tape and moved to the bathroom. There it was, in the corner, positioned to film the shower—and anyone in the shower. Eew! This was disgusting. More than disgusting. Intrusive. Criminal.

I pulled a chair into the bathroom and taped off the camera.

I checked the time: ten-thirty. Not too late.

I texted Anna.

Check your room for observation cameras. I'll be there in ten minutes with tape.

The answer was quick, *Will do.*

I knocked on Bran and Eseld's door.

They were still dressed.

"There were observation cameras in my room," I told him. "One in the bedroom and one in the bathroom. Would you check to see if you have any?"

"I did check," Bran said." I always do. No cameras, no mics."

"Oh God. Mics! I didn't look for them."

"Would you like me to check for you?"

"Yes, please. Then come to Anna's room. I'll take my tape there." I was grateful Bran had been a police inspector and unflappable. Imagine checking your room routinely for cameras and mics? I might do that myself from now on.

Obviously Maisie hadn't checked. If those cameras had recorded our conversation, Bob would know about the blue book, about Maisie's suspicions of Shirley. She would definitely regret talking to me.

We went directly to Anna. Bran removed the cameras from her room. "These are not set to record. They're not sophisticated. He would have to set these before you arrived or get into your room when you weren't here and set them manually. More expensive ones can be operated remotely. Not these, though."

"Are there any mics," I asked.

Bran spend a few minutes checking the bedroom and bathroom. "No," he said.

We moved to my room. Anna and I sat on the bed while Bran removed the cameras. He toggled a switch. "These were live."

"Eww." I said. I felt as if I needed a shower. "It must be Bob, the creep." I took a breath and asked the important question. "Were they set to record?"

"No."

I felt the relief down to my toes. My conversation with Maisie would have been seen but not heard.

"Shouldn't we leave them in place and get the police?" Maisie would be home by now, but there would be a duty constable at the station.

"You taped over them. If they were active and he was watching, then he knows you found them. He would be shocked and appalled when the police came. He wouldn't know how they got there. He would be very cooperative."

"It's gross!" I felt as if I'd been exposed to a lower form of life.

This was so frustrating. Creatures like Bob should be caught and prevented from ever doing it again. But Bran was right. Even if we got someone from the station to come over, we wouldn't be able to prove Bob put the cameras in place. I couldn't *know* he'd put them there.

"What will we do with these?"

"I'll take them to my room tonight then over to the station in the morning." Bran said. "I'll bring them to Sergeant Thompson. She'd appreciate that especially if I ask her to do naught about it, and I give her a statement."

"She's in court tomorrow. You 'll have to leave them for her."

We accompanied Bran back to his room and told Eseld what we had found. I told them about Maisie's visit.

"What about the others in the group?" Eseld asked. "What about checking their rooms?"

"I hate to disturb them now," I said. It was eleven and the Nova Scotia ladies, at least, would be asleep. "I'll check their rooms in the morning. I'll do the same for Heather and Matthew's room. If there aren't any cameras or mics, I won't tell them. It would disturb their holiday. I am so sorry, Anna."

"Not your fault. Nice to know my cameras weren't activated. Why was yours, I wonder?"

"He knew which room Claire would be in," Bran said. "She wasn't likely to tell him your names before you got here, so he didn't know where you would be assigned. He might have put those cameras in your room after you arrived and was disturbed before he could set them."

"And still, we only *suppose* it was Bob," Anna said.

"Yes." Bran gestured to the chair and sat on the bed. He invited Eseld to sit beside him. "I have something on my mind, I was going to talk about with you."

"Would you like me to leave?" Anna asked.

Bran looked at her. "No. You have a first-class brain. You might be helpful."

Anna sat.

"The blue book we gave to Sergeant Thompson," Bran said. "The one that had Lionel's observations in it?"

We nodded.

"It was complete."

I waited.

"It was complete," he said again. "There were no blank pages at the end. So, I'm wondering if he started another book which we haven't found."

"I hadn't thought of that." I hadn't even considered there might be a second book. "It wasn't in Lionel's room. Mark did a thorough search. He found one book up the chimney, but there wasn't anything important in it."

"Oh," Bran said. "I thought there was a second book. Too bad it wasn't useful."

"Can we *assume* there was no book after that one?" Anna said. Anna was quick. She had grasped the importance of the books without asking any questions.

We were quiet, considering that idea.

"Perhaps not," I said.

"Do you think Lionel hid another?" Eseld asked.

"He might have," Bran said.

"If he hid it and it isn't in his room, or, I expect in his luggage…?" Anna said and looked at me.

"I packed his belongings. It wasn't with his luggage".

"So," Anna continued, "where did he go where he could hide it and yet have it available to him but not to everyone else?"

We were all quiet for a moment.

"A bird blind," Eseld said.

"Ah!" Bran looked at her. "That's proper brilliant. Of course."

"Which one?" I wasn't sure that brought us any closer to finding it. There were many bird blinds around Cirencester, small huts with one side boarded half-way so bird watchers could sit in comfort and watch birds without being spotted. I didn't know where they all were.

"Bran?" I asked. He would be the most likely to know which ones he and Lionel frequented.

"At breakfast tomorrow," Bran said, "Eseld and I will talk about birding and announce we are going to have a quick search for a yellow wagtail. We'll ask anyone who likes to come along. That would be you, Anna, unless you have plans."

"Nothing I can't change," Anna said. Her eyes sparkled with excitement. I expect, like me, she was hoping to find something to incriminate Bob.

"Take your blue bird book, Bran," Eseld said. "And let everyone see it is full of notes about birds. Then if you find Lionel's personal observation book, it will look like your bird book."

"Clever, my hen, bleddy clever."

She smiled and bowed.

"We may have to go several mornings in a row because we may not get the right one on our first try. Now, everyone out because we need our sleep. We will see you at breakfast."

We agreed on the time, and Anna and I left.

I walked her to her room. "I am so sorry, Anna."

"Bob and his perversions are distasteful. You feel worse than I do, but the rest of the problem is intriguing. I don't think I'm in danger, except from racist comments from the resident Nazi, but I like a puzzle, and this is puzzling."

"You haven't heard anything back from Dr. White?" I asked. That was her professional puzzle. It would be disappointing if she heard nothing.

"No, but I'm working away on it."

I raised my eyebrows. She was working on a murder case without sanction from the local police. That could be trouble.

Anna looked around. "I'll tell you tomorrow."

She was right. It was not a good idea to talk about her plans in the hallway.

I was still unsettled. Putting cameras in a guest room was nasty, gross, repugnant. If it wasn't so late, I'd call Deirdre and ask her if there was any way I could punish Bob. I was feeling vengeful; I'd feel much better if I could cause him some harm. I could rate the hotel as below average and that would affect his business, but it would affect Shirley's business as well, and I had no quarrel with her. I'll tell her what he's been up to. That might be the best revenge.

I'd text Mark, but there was no point in texting him this late either. It would just upset his sleep and he couldn't leave Lionel to do anything about it. I'd text him in the morning. My nerves were jangling, and I knew I wouldn't sleep.

I put on a sweater against the chill of the May evening and slipped out to the garden. It was a peaceful spot at the side of the house, with a few chairs. I chose one under the weeping cherry tree where I could sit without being spotted from the house. I was glad I was partially hidden when I heard someone come from the house and drop something in the dust bin.

Bob spoke. "I'm going up to London for a couple of days, leaving in two days."

"What for?" That was Shirley. "You're not going to buy more exercise equipment, are you?"

"No. No. Just looking in on an advertising seminar. We have to get this making more money."

"That's true enough. I can't make millions with muffins and hand sanitizers."

They both laughed. What was funny about that?

"Are you still cleaning the cellar?"

"All is neat. A tidy place to bottle the sanitizers."

They laughed again and close the door.

I stayed under the cherry tree and thought about what I'd heard. It seemed casual, a calm discussion of their business. My neck tingled, and I felt alert. What is going on in that cellar?

At breakfast the next morning, Bran and Eseld were full of information about birds. I could hear them wittering away about the yellow wagtail before I was fully in the room.

Shirley had outdone herself with omelettes which she was cooking at a small table near the kitchen. You gave her your order—cheese, shrimp, ham, plain, or herb—and she cooked it for you. Judith had given as usual a precise order and had sat with her pot of tea, fresh scones and omelette in a table by herself.

Nancy and Peggy were enjoying their omelettes, while Matthew and Heather were waiting their turn to give Shirley their order. I picked up a couple of boiled eggs and some scones as well as a strong cup of coffee and joined Eseld and Bran. I didn't want to stand in line. Eseld had dry cereal with fruit and Bran a cheese omelette.

"Eseld and I are going to go for an hour's bird watching," Bran announced.

"You will only have an hour," I warned them, "because we are scheduled for our trip to Oxford, leaving at ten."

"I like a short walk in the morning," Bran said.

"Are you part of a conservation group?" Heather asked Bran.

Eseld replied. "We are. Birds are coming back in Britain, but it takes a lot of education and effort."

Matthew joined the conversation. "Farmers made a big mistake in my area one year and sprayed crops with pesticide. The birds disappeared. The farmers and ranchers learned their lesson and now, after five years, birds are coming back."

"Education might have prevented that," Eseld said.

Heather agreed. "We make a donation to the conservation fund every year. Conscience money," she said, a little embarrassed. "We did spray one year."

"But you learned from that," Bran encouraged her.

Anna added her opinion. "It was probably the effect on the insect life as a result of the spraying that sent the birds away. You killed the insects they depended on."

Heather looked at her. "That makes sense."

"You might have had a lower crop of, say alfalfa, that year because the bees weren't there to pollinate it."

Heather looked at Matthew. "We suspected there must be some connection. The bees are back."

"Good." Anna smiled at her.

"Come with us, Claire. We can show you some of the local birds. Even at this hour, we'll see some," Eseld said as if she'd just thought of it.

"Would anyone like to join us?" Bran asked.

"Are you going far," Heather asked.

""Not far, perhaps to the river or we might go on to the other side of the town."

"Are you walking?"

"Aye."

"I'll stay here, thanks anyway. I've never been to Oxford, so I'll read up on it and be better informed. If I miss anything, Judith can fill me in." I looked at her sharply but she wasn't the least bit sarcastic. Judith stared at her for a moment then smiled.

"I'd be happy to," she said.

Nancy and Peggy exchanged a look. "We'll stay behind as well. It takes us too long to get ready. Perhaps another time."

I doubted they would get up early to go bird watching, but travel was all about new experiences, so perhaps they might.

The four of us finished our breakfast quickly, gathered our cameras, notebooks and rucksacks and headed out the door. I hadn't seen Bob at all this morning which considering how I'd like to smack him one was probably a good thing.

Bran led us along the path we'd taken to the River Churn and turned off before the bridge. This time we went to the left where we found a bird blind.

"This is the one we use the most," Bran said. "It has a couple of chairs, and since we can see the river, we spot a lot of waterfowl."

"It's bare," Eseld said looking around

She was right. It was a simple construction of two by fours and boarding with no insulation or added covering. There were no lights, no wires.

Anna surveyed the interior. "The only place to hide anything in here is taped under the chairs."

We turned over the chairs. Nothing. I looked at the rafters, just a few thin trusses. No hiding places there.

"What about outside?" Eseld said.

We trooped outside and looked over the structure. We each took one side of the blind and examined it. I was in the back where some hazel bushes crowded the boards. I fought my way through them and felt along the overlapping cladding. At the bottom, I felt smooth plastic material. I dropped to my knees, cranked my head sideways and stared at the spot. I could see a small piece of plastic at the edge of the cladding. I pulled on it gently. Slowly, I inched out a plastic bag. Once it was fully released from its hiding place, I opened the bag. Eureka!

"I found it," I yelled.

They were all around me in seconds.

"Ah," Bran breathed. "Gedon, me lover"

"Thank you." I *had* done a remarkable job.

"Are you going to give this to Sergeant Thompson?" I hated to see it go out of my sight before I read it.

"Not quite yet," Bran said. "I need to read it first, and I expect you," he turned to Anna, "and you" he looked at me, "would like a gecko at it."

"I would," Anna said.

"Indeed," I said. "I can't resist it."

"I'll get it to you as soon as I can." Bran stowed the book in his rucksack and glanced at his watch.

"That was quick. I have time to get those cameras to Sergeant Thompson and join you at the van. Ten you said?"

"Ten."

"I'll go with Bran," Eseld said. "It will look more natural to the others if he and I come back together."

"Anna and I will return now," I said. It would give me time to text Mark.

"If you don't mind," Anna said. "I'll go with Bran. I need to leave some samples for Dr. White."

I glanced at her. What samples? What was she up to?

CHAPTER FOURTEEN

I didn't get a chance to find out what samples Anna had collected as I had only a few moments to ring Mark.

He swore. "Cameras? That's criminal."

"It is but Bran says, since we took them down from where they were hung, Sergeant Thompson is unlikely to pursue it."

Mark was quiet for a moment. "That's true enough."

"But we're reading Lionel's second blue observations book.

"Brilliant. Tell me about that."

I took five minutes to tell him about it. "I haven't read it all."

"You need to get it to Thompson."

"Bran will do that." I didn't tell him *when* Bran would do it. "How is Lionel?"

"Better every day. He's Gulliver's new best friend. They're both enjoying the sunny garden."

"Has he remembered anything? "

"Not about the attack or a few days before the attack. Everything else is good."

"How are you doing?" Mark wasn't used to staying home for long.

"I miss you. Really. Let's plan our own holiday."

"I will need a few days at home, but after that, yes, good idea."

"Lionel shouldn't be on his own." He sighed. "I guess we'll have to put it off for a while."

I laughed. "We are far too responsible a couple."

"True, but I've been accused of worse things."

Both of us took our responsibilities seriously. We liked the feeling of being productive and contributing to the welfare of others, but perhaps we were *too* responsible. We needed relaxation and frivolous living some of the time.

Bran and Eseld were at the van when I arrived at ten. Everyone loaded in as soon as I opened the door. Judith, as usual, had several papers in her hand and was studying them. Matthew and Heather looked rested and happy. I'm glad I hadn't disturbed them last night. I was going to have to find time to search their rooms for cameras.

Nancy and Peggy were sorting out their belongings and checking through the itinerary I'd passed under their doors last night.

"I've never been to Oxford," Nancy announced." I've wanted to go there since I read *Gaudy Night*."

"That was a Dorothy Sayers novel, publishing in 1935," Peggy said.

"Shrewsbury College at Oxford to be precise," Judith added.

"There are many mysteries set in Oxford," I interjected before Judith, Peggy and Nancy could get into a competition. "I listed some in the itinerary."

"Oh look, *Landscape with Dead Dons* by Robert Robinson. I remember that one," Peggy said. "It was funny, actually."

"Some of them are," I agreed.

"Simon Tolkien set a trilogy in Oxford in the time of the Second World War or just after," Judith said.

"Any relation to JRR Tolkien?" Matthew asked.

"Great grandson. He was a barrister."

Heather was enthusiastic. "I remember reading *Gaudy Night*. I've always wanted to visit Oxford. We will be going to the campus, won't we?"

I smiled thinking that, while English was our shared language, it was not universally understood. "We will be seeing the colleges, yes. But they aren't in one place. The colleges of Oxford are all over the city."

"Ah." Heather absorbed this information. I hoped she wouldn't be disappointed.

"We will see the Bodleian Library and Oxford Castle and Prison. Then afternoon tea at the Quod, which is near to Christ Church Cathedral with its medieval spires."

"Isn't Oxford the city of 'dreaming spires'," Anna said.

"It is. It is a little like a fairyland city on a lovely day."

"Which we have today," Eseld said from the back.

It *was* a lovely day. I was driving along the A40 through flat, agricultural lands. As we went south on the B4044 we skirted the hills and woodland with farms on either side.

"Good looking farm land," Matthew commented.

It did look productive with large fields and acres of planted crops. After the communities of Deans Court, Botley and Seacourt (no sea anywhere near here), we drove past more farms then across the Thames and into Oxford.

Parking is a problem in Oxford. The city is typically medieval in that the winding, narrow streets are built for foot traffic. I parked as close as I could to the Royal Mail building. We could walk from there.

Our first stop was the castle and prison. I had tickets, and we were quickly admitted.

"I am sorry," I said," but we only have this day in Oxford and there is far too much to see here in one day. I plan to take an hour here, then give you a choice of how to spend your time until four p.m. when I have booked us into the Quod for an English afternoon tea, resplendent with scones and watercress and cucumber sandwiches. After that, you can pick a site your want to see and take in as much as possible. I'm sorry there is so little time."

"Understandable," Anna said.

"Nancy and I studied the itinerary and the choices on the way here," Peggy said. "We'd like to punt. It seems to me the quintessential thing to do in Oxford or Cambridge."

"It is," I said, "and you have a beautiful day for it. I suggest you punt on the Cherwell River which isn't far from where we will meet for tea. The river makes a loop and it's tranquil."

"Lovely. Can you mark it on my map?"

"Certainly." I did so.

"Will we have any trouble renting a punt?"

"You can easily rent a punt and someone to punt it."

"Oh, good," Nancy said, "although I was looking forward to the challenge."

"What bookstore do you recommend?" Anna asked.

"Blackwell's. It's near the Bodleian Library which you can tour if you like. It has several floors of books and attentive staff."

"Ah," Anna said. "That is what I'd like to do."

"Matthew and I are going to wander and try see as many of those colleges you talked about. We might punt as well." Heather looked around for Matthew who had gone ahead to examine the tours available.

"Matthew," I called.

He raised his head and ambled back to us.

"I pre-arranged the tour of the castle and prison. And here's our guide." I welcomed a small, older man, dressed in grey trousers, called grey flannels no matter what material was used, and a blue blazer over a bright white shirt and red tie.

"Martin," he said. "Welcome, everyone."

I stepped back and let Martin ask my group where they were from and what interested them. I knew he would take them to eighteenth-century debtor's prison and the D wing and give everyone a chance to climb St. George's Tower where they would get a marvelous view of Oxford, then down to the 900-year-old crypt.

I left them and headed for Blackwell's Bookstore, but not before I'd managed to get Lionel's blue book from Bran and stow it in my rucksack. He *was* going to take it to Sergeant Thompson, just not right away.

I was free now until four p.m. I'd listed many sites of interest on the daily itinerary. There was Magdalen College where Lewis Carroll taught English literature for thirty years and The Alice Shop nearby on St. Aldates Street. Carroll mentioned this in his Alice's Adventures. I'm not sure Matthew, Heather or Anna had been brought up on *Alice's Adventures in Wonderland*, but Nancy, Peggy, Eseld and Bran likely had been.

I walked quickly to Broad Street and Blackwell's Bookstore. I was near Balliol College and not far form the Bodleian Library, both sites of mystery novels, but I managed to contain my adulation and hustled into the book store to find a secluded nook. I took a moment to admire the glorious, soaring ceiling before I huddled in the comfortable chair, retrieved the blue book and began reading.

I put my alarm to buzz on my mobile, so I wouldn't read for more than two hours. It took only an hour to read as Lionel had not written for more than a week before he was attacked. But it was instructive.

The philosophy club was a Nazi group. They had serious aims of destruction. Lionel suspected they were stocking the composite materials needed to make explosives in the shed at the hotel. The goal for their violence was an anti-Nazi rally that was going to take place in…I checked the date…four days from now. This was hot information. Bran had better hand this into Sergeant Thompson today. He may have called her. I'd better check.

Lionel had noted Bob's obsessive-compulsive devotion to his exercise regime, his need to exercise in the same way on a strict time schedule, no matter what else was happening in the hotel. Shirley did most of the work and supervised the other workers. Bob ran his life around his bar tending, his exercise regime, his vitamin and protein supplements and possibly hormonal supplements with his once-a-week meeting in the cellar.

In the cellar? I hadn't even thought of that.

Lionel had seen deliveries made to the shed in the garden with what looked like feed. When he investigated, he found it was fertilizer. He was almost caught by Richie who had also come to investigate the shed. Lionel had watched Richie come and go into different rooms in the hotel. He wondered what Richie was looking for. Lionel had thought the cellar had been worth investigating, but had not yet had a chance to do so. He noted Richie had been in the cellar, but Richie could have been getting wine or the hand sanitizers that Shirley made and sold. Perhaps he had listened to a meeting of Bob's group. He might have known of the plans of the Nazi group to disrupt the rally. Perhaps he tried to blackmail Bob? He had too much knowledge, and so he died. It was a theory and it fit the facts.

Lionel ended with a note that he would consult with the local sergeant before Bob discovered he knew his plans.

I assumed he was attacked before he could do that. I felt as if I was holding a live grenade. Bran needed to put this book in the hands of Sergeant Thompson as soon as possible.

I headed for the exit —for the first time without new books— when I saw Anna waiting her turn at the counter. She had four books. I waved and indicated I'd wait for her at the door. We still had about forty minutes before we needed to be at the van.

"Would you like to sit in the park for a few minutes?"

She looked around and spotted the inviting garden close by. "Sure."

I hustled her to a park bench in the neat garden and lawn near Trinity College. "Anna, tell me about the samples you've been collecting."

She looked at me in silence for a moment. I might have offended her with that peremptory order.

"Please." I rephrased my demand into a request. "Tell me what you are doing to help solve Lionel's attack and Richie Stonehouse's murder. I have new information and I'd like to share."

"Ah, that's different."

She sat straighter. "I've been collecting samples from sites at the hotel. If Richie was killed at the hotel and later moved which is probable, then there will be one site and one site only that will have the matching profile of pollen, grasses and spores that correspond to those found on Richie's body."

I digested that. "So, you are picking up samples."

"That's right."

"Do you analyze them?"

"Only rudimentarily. I send them to Amy White. She has the necessary equipment."

A visiting American professor collected the samples and passed them to a paid consultant of the British police. That was amazingly complex and inefficient. "Why doesn't she pick up the samples?"

"She will if anything matches, but she hasn't the time, and the department hasn't the budget to send someone to do so. They'd need a search warrant to collect the samples."

"And you don't?"

She was patient with me. Obviously, scientists figure out how to work within the system to get the best results, even when that system was cumbersome. "I would need permission if anything I did was going to be used in evidence. But Amy can't use my samples for the prosecution. If there's a match, she'll get a search warrant and 'discover' the sample herself. That could get used as evidence. In the meantime, I'm enjoying myself."

I thought about that. "Anna. Richie died, and Lionel was left for dead. Be careful."

"Ah, good point. I will."

"From what sites have you taken samples?"

She leaned back, closed her eyes and enjoyed the sun. "Let's see. The bar, the yard outside, in the shed."

I felt a chill run up my arms. "In the shed? Did anyone see you?"

She straightened and opened her eyes. "No. I don't think so, unless they were looking out one of the windows of the hotel."

I closed my eyes briefly. "I fervently hope no one was looking."

"There's something in the shed?" She leaned forward. "I don't think Richie was killed there. The spore combination isn't right."

I experienced some of the helpless feeling Mark must have when I ventured into areas he considered dangerous. I hoped Bob hadn't seen her around the shed.

"Let me know if Dr. White gets a match," I said.

"If I can," Anna promised, or half-promised. "What did you discover?"

I'd agreed to share information. "I read the second blue book. I would like to lend it to you so you can read it as well, but Bran is going to need to take it to Sergeant Thompson tonight."

"What did Lionel say?"

"Quite a lot." I sighed and stared at the immaculate green lawn in front of me. I wondered how the groundskeepers kept it so tidy when there were so many students in the city who must walk around it or over it every day.

"And?" Anna said.

"First of all, Bob and his group are Nazis."

"Not surprising." Anna shrugged. "They hate the 'other' as they define 'other'. Irrational and therefore dangerous."

"They're planning on setting off an explosion in London in four days."

She blinked. "Our little Bob, of the creep variety? He's planning this?"

"He and his group of goons."

"Oh." Anna looked at the peaceful Oxford scene in front of her. A don hurried across the lawn with gown flapping as dons had done for centuries, giving the impression of a crow.

"I feel as if we shouldn't be sitting here, enjoying the sun," Anna said.

"Yes, as if we're not doing enough. Bran will give the blue book to the sergeant when we get back. What else can we do?"

"I think we need advice. Why don't you give that handsome inspector of yours a call?"

That was sensible.

"We're wasting minutes. Four days isn't much time to avert such an act."

She was right. "I'll ring Mark now."

He answered immediately, likely hoping for some diversion. I imagined he was committed to looking after Lionel but frustrated at not being able to look into the attack on Lionel and his refugees. I told him what I'd read in the blue book.

"Repeat that?" he said.

"Bob and his crew are going to plant a bomb in London in four days."

"You need to get that book to Thompson," he said. "Immediately."

"I know but she's in Cirencester and we're in Oxford."

"Get Bran to take it to the local nick and have them rush it over to Thompson. I'll ring there and tell them to expect it. That should expedite the process."

That was brilliant. "Wonderful. I'm glad you're a copper."

"It has some perks," Mark said.

The local constabulary would pay attention to Mark as a Detective Inspector of the Major Crimes Investigations Team.

"I'm meeting Bran in," I checked the time on my mobile, "ten minutes."

"Good. Talk to you later. I'll make a few calls."

I clicked off and stood.

It took us about ten minutes to walk from Broad Street to High Street and the Quod Restaurant.

Bran and Eseld were there. Anna sat and was quickly scanning the blue book as I explained Mark's directions to Bran.

"Right you are," he said. "I wish I'd had a chance to read it, but I'll go immediately." He held out his hand. Anna reluctantly passed him the book.

CHAPTER FIFTEEN

Bran stood ready to leave immediately.

"Do you know where the station is?" I asked.

He shook his head. "I was going to ask at the desk."

I conjured up Google. "On the A420 past Christ Church and Alice's Shop, on the east side of the road. It's the Thames Valley Police. It looks to be about a five-minute walk."

"I'll probably be there for an hour."

"I will come and get you if you need me to," I said. 'Just text me."

"I'll order you a pastry to-go, if you don't get back in time for tea," Eseld said.

He gave a lingering look at the tea table. I imagine he missed many teas in his career.

I was sorry this was interfering with his holiday, but I was glad he was with us and could deal with the police. They'd pay more attention to him than they would to me.

Heather and Mathew arrived. Heather enthused over the view she'd seen from the top of St. Mary's. It is spectacular. The church is medieval with the usual delicate spire and what looks like lacework in stone on the façade.

"You could see all over Oxford from the top," Heather told us. "There are so many parks, trees, old stones. It's beautiful."

It was. I remembered I was a tour guide and tried to get into the spirit of discovering Oxford.

Nancy and Peggy bustled in behind them. "We found the Oxford University Press Bookstore," Peggy said. "It was as if I was visiting an old friend. Really. I had no idea I would be so affected."

Nancy smiled at her friend. "You were a little awestruck."

"I was." Peggy settled into a comfortable chair with an *oof* of satisfaction. I had reserved a round table that seated us all in the main room. There was a more private back room, but it was a little claustrophobic and decorated with more pink than was reasonable.

The tea was sumptuous and, as promised, we started with a glass of Henry Favre champagne and moved on to the crustless finger sandwiches: watercress and cucumber, and deviled egg. There were crumpets, scones and Devonshire cream with raspberry jam and what they called 'little cakes' and puddings. After the champagne the waiter took orders for tea and coffee. There were four tea pots on the table with different kinds of tea.

"This is so not Montana," Matthew said. He grinned at me. "The Ranchers' Association would never believe it."

"Don't tell them," his wife advised.

Bran had been quick at the station and joined us when the cakes were being served. I'd spoken to a waiter, and he presented Bran with a plate of sandwiches and a selection of pudding and cakes. Bran rapidly ate what was in front of him and caught up to us with his tea.

Eseld send me a look of gratitude. It felt a little odd to receive it. She was the one who usually provided Bran with sustenance. She appreciated that I had filled in for her this time. I suppose my attitude to my guests was nurturing. I felt it my job to see they were happy. Perhaps that was how she viewed her job as his wife as well.

I gave the group another hour to wander over Oxford, and asked them to meet me at the van about six.

They were all there but Judith who had gone off on her own.

"She was going to the Bodleian Library," Heather said.

"She won't be able to get into the reading area," I said. "You have to have a research reason."

"If you'd like to put money on it," Matthew said, "I bet she has some kind of letter that got her in."

Judith arrived at that point accompanied by a don with the usual flapping gown who was speaking earnestly to her. Judith pressed a business card into his hand.

"My thanks," she said and shook his hand.

"My pleasure," the don said. "Do call me."

We waited in silence as Judith climbed into the van.

"I am sorry to keep you." She looked at her watch. "I am a few minutes late. I apologize, but the professor was fascinating."

"You got into the Bodleian?" I was dumbfounded.

"I have been studying...," she broke off. "I'm sure you don't want to hear about my studies. Needless to say, all went smoothly. It is a fascinating edifice."

"It is indeed," I murmured and started the van.

I drove to Cirencester and announced as I pulled up to the Queen Bess, "Dinner is an independent choice tonight. You will see the restaurants and bars listed on the itinerary for today. There are quite a few to choose from, so I hope you enjoy your evening." *In other words, I am not taking you anywhere tonight.*

They thanked me as they moved to the door and disembarked. Anna was last. I touched her arm. "Would you like to meet in my room in about a half-hour?"

"Sure thing."

After I'd parked the van in the car park and walked back to the Queen Bess, I knocked on Bran and Eseld's door. "Can you come to my room in about fifteen minutes?"

"We will," Eseld said.

I dropped my rucksack on the table in my room, glanced at the chandelier and checked the shower to be sure there were no cameras.

I took a bottle of prosecco from the small fridge and put four glasses from the counter on the table just as a knock sounded on the door.

Anna arrived with Bran and Eseld behind her. Bran carried a bottle of beer and Eseld a bottle of red wine.

"Welcome," I said.

When everyone had their favorite drink, Eseld and Bran settled onto the chairs and Anna and I sat on the bed.

"What did the police say?" I asked Bran.

"Your Mark had rung up, so they were ready to accept the book as important evidence. They sent a constable to Cirencester with orders to give it to Sergeant Thompson."

"She should have it now," I said.

"She should," Bran agreed.

"You took the cameras to her this morning," I said.

"I did that," Bran said. "Her court case was cancelled so she was there. She was interested, but there wasn't much she could do. With the new information about the plan to plant a bomb in London, she will be much more aggressive."

Bran had just finished speaking when we heard a commotion in the hall.

Shirley's voice was shrill. "A search warrant?"

Bran opened the door so we could hear more clearly.

"For what? What has that idiot been doing?"

We heard a murmur from Sergeant Thompson as she and two officers crowded into the hallway near the front door. We peered over the railing and watched.

"I can't have this disruption. People will leave. We will get black listed."

"I suggest, Madam, that you lower your voice so your guests are not disturbed."

"Shirley. Lower your voice."

That was her mother, Lydia Harris. She was standing behind Shirley, one hand on Shirley's shoulder.

"But, Mum."

"Just take a deep breath and let the officers do their work." She patted her daughter's back and nodded at the officers as if giving permission for the search.

I saw Shirley's shoulders heave. I felt sorry for her. Bob was pulling her into a mess.

Sergeant Thompson did have to disturb the guests. She and her constables searched every room. The hotel wasn't a big one, and we could track their progress throughout. When they were finished with the guest rooms, they went through the swinging doors to the kitchen. I peered out the windows and saw them in the shed.

Anna left us at one point and followed Sergeant Thompson outside. I could see them leaning close and speaking to one another. Anna passed something to Thompson. It looked like her sample bottles. Anna returned to us.

"What did you tell her, and what did you give her?"

Anna settled back on my bed and resumed drinking her wine. "I advised her to search the cellar and take samples of the floor, especially in the corners."

"The cellar? The tidy cellar? If Shirley cleaned it, would it still have the spores and weeds and such things?"

"Oh, yes," Anna said. "No one ever cleans completely."

I wondered what they'd find.

Bob arrived as Sergeant Thompson emerged from the cellar and met her at the door. She had two of Anna's sample bottles in her hand. We were still near the railings, watching and listening.

Bob looked at her. "What's up. Whatcha doing here?"

"We'd like you to accompany us to the station," Thompson said quietly.

"I'm not going anywhere with you."

"Indeed, you are." She motioned to the two constables who moved up on either side.

"What's all this about?"

"It's about some plans you and your friends have made that are destined to be interrupted."

Bob stood frozen for a few seconds.

Sergeant Thompson spoke to the constables. "Take him to nick and charge him with planning terrorist activities. Run him through the usual paperwork, fingerprints and contain him."

"I want a solicitor."

"You can ring one in the morning."

"I'm entitled to one now."

"This is Britain, and it isn't a telly show," Sergeant Thompson said. She nodded to the constables and they shoved Bob to the door.

"I'll get someone for you," Shirley called to him.

"You'd better."

That was a faster response to Lionel's blue book than I'd imagined.

We reconvened in Bran and Eseld's room and talked about Bob as we finished the wine.

"He's not being arrested," Anna said. "Just held for questioning. They won't lay charges, at least, if the justice system is anything like ours in California, until they have Dr. White's analysis."

Since the justice system in the States was based on the British system, it shouldn't be too much different, unless it was modified out of its prior existence.

"Securing the line of evidence," I murmured.

"That's right," Anna said. "Sergeant Thompson can swear she took the samples and gave them to Amy White who will swear they are the samples she analyzed. All secure and legal."

"How long will it take her to analyze them?"

"She has more equipment at her lab than I do here, so she should have the results in the morning—if she has to work all night."

I thought about how that evidence would be used. "That may tie Richie's death to the cellar if the spores in the cellar match the ones on Richie's clothes."

"Yes, that's right."

"But it won't pin the murder on Bob, will it?" I asked Bran.

"No, it won't secure his prosecution, but it will allow Thompson to keep him incarcerated, at least over night."

"And," I offered optimistically, "it might make Bob think twice about his terrorist activities if he knows the police are watching him."

"Possibly," Bran said.

"I wouldn't hold out much hope of that," Eseld said. "Zealots love to be martyrs."

We were interrupted by a knock on the door. Eseld was closest and opened it.

"Hello, all," Nancy said. "We're heading out to The Fleece for dinner. Would you like to come?"

We looked at each other.

"Lovely idea," I said.

"Great," Anna said. "Give me five minutes."

"Meet you all in the foyer."

"Bran and I will stay here," Eseld said. "We'll order pizza in and relax. You go off."

"Are you sure?" I asked.

"Yes. Yes. We can use an early night."

"We thought we'd ask Judith," Peggy said peering at us over Nancy's shoulder.

Nancy rolled her eyes. I could tell it had been Peggy's idea. They went off to knock on Judith's door.

Anna and I hurried to fetch our rucksacks, and met the others in the foyer.

"Matthew and Heather have already left," Nancy informed us. "They must have opted for a romantic evening without us."

"Who can blame them?" Peggy said.

"I just remembered I have to check a reservation. Go ahead without me. I'll be ten minutes."

They left and I darted to the kitchen and called Shirley.

"What now!" She came from her office, her mother still with her.

"I am sorry for your trouble, but I need to check all the rooms. May I have your pass key?'

Shirley sent a glance to her mother but turned to get the key.

"Now what's all this about, dear," her mother said. She sounded kind and concerned.

"It's about Bob planting cameras in our rooms. We've discovered four of them and removed them, but I need to check the rooms without alerting my guests.

Lydia Harris looked shocked. Then she looked angry. "That stupid git."

Shirley handed me the key and turned to her mother.

I heard Mrs. Harris say, "I've every good reason to leave that useless jubber in the nick."

"Mother!"

Now that I knew what I was looking for, it took me all of ten minutes to check the five rooms. No cameras. I left the key on the hall table and scooted to the restaurant.

It took ten minutes to walk to The Fleece, but they were just settling in with their menus at a large, round table. A waiter was hovering.

"Oh, look who's here." I thought Peggy was speaking to me, but looked up and saw Heather and Matthew hesitating in the doorway. When Heather spotted us, she smiled. "Can we join you?" she asked as they got closer.

"Certainly," Nancy said. "I thought you were going to gaze at stars in each other's eyes tonight."

"We can still do that. It's not late."

Matthew smiled and pulled out a chair for his wife. "I like the food here," he said.

"There's steak," his wife agreed with an affectionate look. I doubted she'd budge Matthew from his meat diet.

I ordered a bottle of Sauvignon Blanc, Oyster Bay, New Zealand. Judith ordered another bottle of the same. Matthew ordered a lager and Heather, after consulting with Nancy and Peggy, a bottle of red. Then, we concentrated on the fabulous food.

The 'roasted beetroot pear and walnut salad' intrigued me… no comma. Was it 'roasted beetroot pear' or 'roasted beetroot, pear and walnut'? I expected it was the latter. I didn't want a hearty meal and reluctantly passed on the pork chop, venison haunch and creamy chicken and gammon pot pie.

"Want to share the fishmonger's platter?" Anna asked me.

"That and the beetroot salad will do me very well," I said.

The waiter stood beside Judith. I waited to see what she was going to order and how long that ordering was going to take. She inquired what the fish of the day was.

"Hake, madam."

"I will have the fish of the day with the vegetables and salad."

That was all she said. There was a slight silence as we absorbed her change in manner. No cautions about dairy products, no queries about where the fish had come from or the method of its catch. She passed the waiter her menu, and he moved on to Nancy and Peggy. I didn't dare catch Anna's eye and concentrated on sipping my excellent wine.

The desserts were wonderful. I had a light one--lemon, lime and pineapple posset. 'Jude's ice cream' was a feature. There was an apostrophe in the menu here I was happy to see. Nancy went for a rich chocolate cheesecake and Peggy for the warm chocolate brownie. There were adjectives all over this menu. Matthew had sticky toffee pudding and Heather asked for an extra spoon to help him with it. Judith had asked for the ice cream and was taking small portions on a spoon, making it last until we were all finished. The waiter served tea all around, except for Heather and Matthew who took coffee, and we returned to the hotel.

Sergeant Thompson was waiting for me in the foyer.

"Sergeant," I acknowledged.

"Ms Barclay. Can I have a word?"

"Certainly. In my room?"

"That would be convenient."

She followed me up the stairs to my room. I shut the door and indicated the chair. I sat on the other side of the small table.

"How can I help?"

"I can keep Robert Simpson overnight, but, without more evidence, I'll have to let him out in the morning. Dr. White is processing the samples I collected. If they match the pollen and spore mixture found on Richard Stonehouse' shirt, I will have enough to keep him for a few days or until a solicitor arrives to ask for bail. Although, even if they do match, a good solicitor or barrister will have him out because, while I might be able to prove Stonehouse died there, I wouldn't be able to prove Robert Simpson killed him."

I processed her reasoning. I had thought Bob would be away until my guests and I were gone, but it looked as though he might be back tomorrow. That was disturbing.

"I see. What can I do?"

"I'm looking for any idea that might point me in the right direction. Can you think of anything you've seen or heard that might help? My name's Maisie, by the way."

"Mine's Claire," I said absently, thinking about her question. *Or heard?* I thought back to the conversation I'd overheard in the garden.

"It wasn't much," I said.

"Anything," Maisie said with feeling.

"I overheard Bob and Shirley talking when I was in the garden. They were laughing about Shirley's hand sanitizers. What they said didn't seem funny to me, but it might be an inside joke. Why would they laugh about hand sanitizers? I think Shirley makes money on them."

Maisie was quiet for a moment. "What is hand sanitizer made of?"

"Alcohol," I said. "That's what is effective against the Covid19 virus."

We looked at each other.

"Illegal spirits?" I suggested.

Maisie shook her head. "Not the same kind of alcohol. If she tried making drinkable alcohol out of the stuff she uses for sanitizers, she'd blind her customers or kill them."

I didn't know much about the production of spirits. "But the sanitizer alcohol would mask the production of the drinkable kind, wouldn't it?"

"It would." Maisie was thinking about it. "I wonder if Mummy's business is drifting into Shirley's. I wonder if Lydia, Bob or Shirley, or all three are distributing drugs."

"Her mother?" I thought of the respectable-looking Lydia Harris with her expensive suit, glowing pearls and kind concern.

"She grew up in The Dells. Drug-dealing is a common occupation there and Lydia Harris is smarter than most. She stays out of jail."

"What about Shirley's father?"

"In prison. Lydia testified against him. I always thought she'd set him up. Wanted to get rid of him, but didn't want to execute him herself."

Execute him? Lydia Harris was that ruthless? I blinked. It was quite a bit to absorb. "So you're saying that Shirley might be distributing more than hand sanitizers."

"She might, but her mother wouldn't like it. She wants Shirley to succeed in legitimate business. And what Lydia doesn't like, she usually manages to eliminate."

"Shirley also said she'd tidied up the cellar. I wondered at that because she's busy right now. Why would she 'tidy the cellar' at this time?"

"She won't be able to tidy away the pollen and spore evidence or even traces of blood." Maisie shook her head. "I'd love to get the two of them on some charge, but there wasn't anything suspicious there. I didn't see anything but the hand sanitizers when I was down there, and she has a permit for making them. I checked."

"Maybe there's a secret room?"

Maisie stared at me for a moment. "Perhaps. But an illegal still or even a stash of drugs is of less interest to me than the terrorist activities and the plan to bomb the rally in London."

"You found ingredients for explosives in the garden shed, didn't you?"

"We did. But we can't prove he was going to make explosives."

"He might still be going ahead with his plans." I felt the pressure of the rapidly vanishing time. "Could you listen in when they have a meeting?"

"With a listening device you mean?"

"Yes.

"We could, but those devices are tricky as evidence. Often, judges won't accept them so I can't rest my whole case on wire tapping, or listening devices of any kind." She paused. "I might do it anyway."

"You might find out when they are going to deliver the bomb. If they are traveling with it, you could stop the vehicle."

We were both silent. She was, no doubt, thinking, as I was, how dangerous it would be for the police to stop that van.

"We have three days," she said, "according the Sergeant Atkinson's notes."

It took me a second to realize she was talking about Lionel. "He was quite sure. Did you read the book?"

"I did, but quickly. How did he get the information?"

"He hid outside the cellar, near the window and heard most of what went on in their meeting. At least, that's what I understood from his notes." I wasn't exactly lying. Well, yes I was, but I didn't want to admit Lionel had planted a listening device.

She considered where Lionel might have hidden and how he had heard the men talking. "He must have been seen, or left footprints of something. He wasn't attacked for no reason at all. He could have been seen. That's the most likely reason."

"A listening device would have been safer." I muttered. They were an invasion of privacy and illegal or somewhat illegal as Maisie had said, but they could certainly pick up conversations from far away so that a person could hear the conversation without being near the speakers.

Maisie looked at me with some curiosity.

"No. No," I said." "I don't have one, but I took one from one of my guests once so I know how they work, and that they *do* work."

"There must be a more reliable way to hear their plans," Maisie said.

"Too bad you can't rely on those bats' ears." I began to sound as if I were whining. If Maisie couldn't use them or wouldn't use them, there was nothing I could do about it. She was an experienced officer and had her reasons.

"I have to find a legal way to stop them. Dr. White's evidence will help, but until they make that bomb, I can't arrest them." She was still determined to nail Bob with his crimes and, more importantly, prevent a disaster.

"Assuming Lionel's date is correct, you can get ready and use your search warrant the morning they are going to strike."

"That's the back-up plan, but it still puts my officers in danger. I don't see any other way. Do you?"

"I don't, but you should ring Mark. He might have more ideas."

"I've talked to my supervisor and I will ring Detective Inspector Evans. But I'm supposed to let Scotland Yard know though official channels if there is a terrorist threat. I can't request a particular officer."

"That will complicate matters."

"It can, but I have to do it, and I will do it. Probably tonight. That doesn't mean they'll act. I've already put in a call that hasn't been returned."

We were quiet. Bureaucracy was a handicap to action.

I talked to Mark after Maisie left.

"That's a dangerous situation," Mark said.

"I realize that. I'm worried about my guests. Anna in particular. If Bob is back tomorrow, he can really threaten her. He hates people of color; he's making a bloody bomb; he's got a temper and loses it whenever he wants to; he has a gang of like-minded idiots surrounding him" I heard my voice rising. I took two deep, calming breaths. "I can really pick a guest house."

"It's not your fault," Mark said. "Look. I'll see if Rose can come and stay with Lionel while I drive over."

"Would you? Wonderful!" I hadn't realized how alone and incompetent I'd felt until he said he'd come. I hadn't even realized I wanted him to come. "How is Lionel?"

"Fine. Doing well. Just not up to making his own meals and walking Gulliver. I'll ring up Rose in the morning. If she agrees, then I'll drive up and be there in the afternoon."

I felt my shoulders relax.

"I'll feel better if you are with me."

"Good to know."

"I love you and that makes me feel better, but you are a detective whose job it is to catch murderers. That combination is irresistible."

"Again, good to know. I'll see you tomorrow, *fy nghariad*. Dream of me."

I smiled as I disconnected the mobile. *My darling.* My Welsh was improving. I'd try to dream of Mark. Those dreams would certainly be more satisfying than dreaming of Bob and his plans for destruction.

CHAPTER SIXTEEN

Bob was not back by breakfast the next morning, and no one was helping Dylan. He hustled in and out of the kitchen, arranging the cutlery on the tables, making multiple trips to the kitchen for items he'd forgotten. He looked harassed. He was more proficient with the orders and the delivery of them when he had the tables organized, but he still had to concentrate hard on his tasks and didn't have the smooth patter of an experienced waiter.

"By yourself, Dylan?" It seemed a lot to ask of a new employee.

"Yeah. Yeah. Shirley's in the kitchen."

I left him to his troubles and passed out the itinerary to my group. I planned to visit the nearby parks and woodland today as a change from museums and city life. There was a Wildlife Preserve not far from here and another Cotswold village nearby to impress my tourists.

I had extra binoculars and two bird books, but several of the guests had apps on their mobiles which explained the birds even better than an identity book. Those apps had the bird's song with the description of the plumage. Sometimes you never saw a bird, just heard it. I advised everyone to bring a full water bottle and had snacks and sweets in the individual bags I'd left on their seats.

Mark had texted he was heading my way. The drive would be an hour-and-a-half, not allowing for stops at the local police station. He'd have to get Rose settled before he left and make sure Lionel was up and ready for her. There was no hurry for him to come to me as I would be out until mid-afternoon, but he would want to meet with Sergeant Thompson.

I drove the group around the Bathurst Estate. It was huge, 15,000 acres with The Broad Avenue sweeping five miles from the grand manor house to Sapperton lined by 200-year-old horse chestnut trees; but I didn't stop. I just wanted them to see the extent of it.

"Lots of bird life in there," Bran commented.

"It's interesting how many mysteries have birds in them," Judith said. "That writer Steve Burrows," she continued. "His protagonist is a birder."

"That's set in Norfolk," Nancy said. "And the writer is a Canadian."

"Fancy that," Eseld said.

"There are lots of mystery that feature birds. Chris Goff, *A Rant of Ravens*," Peggy offered from her extensive knowledge. I expect she was attempting to soften Nancy's rather sharp comment.

"Birds are interesting, even to mystery writers," I agreed, working with Peggy to smooth any ruffled feelings.

"This place is as big as our ranch," Matthew said, "but it's more like a garden. Ours is more wild-like."

"We have lovely pastures," Heather protested, "full of wild flowers."

"We do. And farm buildings, corrals and fences we keep in repair, but somehow when you compare them, this looks more, I don't know, tidy somehow."

"Maybe it's all that bright green," Heather said. "Our pastures are a different color green. They must have different grasses here. This seems to be emerald green everywhere. More like a lawn."

"That's it," Matthew said. "That's it. It looks like there's lawn everywhere."

"We will be coming into more woodland in a few minutes," I said, activating the mic. "Sapperton is a lovely little village. It was the center of the arts and crafts movement in the nineteenth century. You'll see some fine examples of the architecture in the houses, particularly around St. Kenelm Church. Ernest Gimson was a furniture designer and also an architect who lived here in the early twentieth century and brought his style to the area. It included the use of English hardwoods and had some distinctive characteristics of inlay and stringing. They established the arts and crafts design in furniture and not only designed furniture but had a workshop and produced it here."

"It's a small village," Bran observed.

"You haven't been here before?" I asked.

"No," Eseld answered for him. "There is a lot of Britain we haven't seen."

"This country is so beautiful it's hard to remember that centuries ago it was a thriving manufacturing and industrial center. There is a canal tunnel than starts here at Sapperton. It is part of the Severn-Thames canal system. The tunnel was completed on April 20th, 1789 and was the longest in Britain at that time."

"It was for cargo boats?" Matthew asked.

"Yes. It was mostly for barges that conveyed goods for many years, although the canal was plagued by leakage and the constant need for repairs. The railroad replaced it in the nineteenth century. Lorries take most of the goods back and forth to the cities now."

"All that work and it's not used today?" Bran asked.

"There has been a huge effort to restore it, and there are now pleasure boats on parts of the canal."

I pulled over into the layby. "We'll have a short stop here so you can stroll through the village. Twenty minutes?" I parked outside The Bell Pub. They could buy snacks there, if they liked, and use the cloak room.

I collected them at ten-thirty and we drove on to Daneway where they had another look at the canal.

"This is where Ernest Gimson lived," I said. "As did Norman Jewson, the writer of *By Chance I did Rove*."

"I've never heard of him," Peggy said, as if admitting to a default in character. She did know most of the writers I'd mentioned so far.

"He was a minor writer but well-known in the Cotswolds. He was writing in the 1950s. He wasn't a mystery writer."

"Oh, that's why I didn't know him." Peggy excused herself.

"It doesn't look as though anyone has done anything here since," Heather said.

I looked at the village for a second as if I was a foreigner. It did look sleepy. Villages looks are deceptive, though. Sleepy-looking villages can harbor all the general problems people face and sometimes they hold great wickedness. I wondered who was hiding from authorities, who was coasting along trying to be inconspicuous and who was creating amazing art and literature behind the walls of their individual homes.

I left the van in at the Daneway Pub. I checked that everyone had water and sunscreen. The weather was overcast, but that didn't mean the UV rays wouldn't manage to burn delicate skin. We crossed the road and joined the path beside the canal. In minutes, we had come to the beautiful Siccarridge Woods. Birches, beech and ash created a canopy over our heads, and hazel and viburnum, the wayfaring tree, scattered around us in the undergrowth. I knew this was a managed forest with only some ancient oak, but it was beautiful and rich in bird life. When we stopped,. I heard a thrush.

"I see you have binoculars," Heather said. "What are you looking for?"

"I have another pair, if you'd like to join me." I shrugged my rucksack from my shoulders, fished into it, found the bins and passed them to her.

"What are *we* looking for?" she amended.

"Nightingales, turtle doves, goldcrest, and my favorite song thrush."

"Any animals here?" Nancy asked.

"Dormice," I said. "They're protected."

"Really? Those cute little Beatrix Potter mice?"

"That's right."

Everyone seemed to enjoy striding off into the woods. Anna had her mobile in her hand, no doubt, clicking open her bird app. I knew the trails well, and they were marked. After an hour wandering through the trees, we were back at the Daneway Pub where I'd arranged lunch.

We hurried from the van into the pub. The wind had picked up and there was a chill in the air that hadn't been there earlier. I hoped it wouldn't rain. I'd planned another small hike in the Sapperton Valley Nature Reserve which would be a struggle in the wet. I'd have to substitute something else. I thought about it as I escorted my group inside.

The eighteenth-century pub was warm and the Inglenook fireplace inviting even when there was no fire.

"Cask ale sounds so English I'm going to try it," Matthew said.

Heather beamed at him. I expect she had a difficult time persuading him to come on this trip and was delighted he was willing to try something new.

"The food has certainly improved in pubs like this," Judith said. "When I traveled in the sixties and seventies you got fish and chips and mushy peas everywhere. Not delectable choices like these."

I'd heard stories of the bland English food of the past, but my experience, which has been extensive, is that the food is uniformly good in pubs.

Several of the group had soup and crusty bread. It was that kind of day.

When we departed I had them wait in the pub while I brought the van to the door. The rain was pelting down. They dashed into the van and settled in their seats.

"A change of plans," I said through the mic as I drove. "We'll scrub the walk through the Sapperton Valley Nature Reserve, and

I'll drive you on to Gloucester. We can view the cathedral and the National Waterways Museum. Would that suit you?

"How long is the drive?" Nancy asked.

"Just a half-hour."

"Sounds good," Peggy said. "Touring inside in this weather is my choice."

There was murmured assent, so I headed north-west for Gloucester.

They thoroughly enjoyed the Waterways Museum and the guide was particularly enthusiastic. We were a little longer than I'd planned and didn't get on the road home until about two-thirty. I'd texted Mark before we left so he wouldn't worry. I took the A17 as it is a little faster than other routes. Almost everyone dozed as I drove. The swish of the water under the tires and the monotonous clicking of the windshield wipers soothed them.

They stumbled out of the van when I pulled up in front of The Queen Bess. It was still relentlessly raining. I parked in the car park and headed back to the hotel. I flipped up the hood on my rain jacket and, trudging through the rain, considered the plans for the evening.

I'd booked seats at St. John Baptist Church for the evening concert. A Welsh men's choir were guest artists. I couldn't be sure my guests would enjoy it, but it was on the itinerary and no one had complained. We would dine after the one-and-half-hour event. Until then, the rest of the afternoon was free. I expected most of the group would stay inside, read and doze. Perhaps with the exception of Anna. She had efficient raingear— pants and anorak with waterproof boots—and was happy to explore on her own. She donned her rucksack and waved to me as she left the hotel. The door to the owner's private residence near the stairs was open, and I saw Bob in the hallway with an exercise weight in his hand. He had been released from custody then, and was back at his obsessive exercising. Drat!

I pushed open the door of my room and found Mark.

"Wait until I get this wet anorak off," I said, "or I'll soak you." It didn't take me long to throw the jacket over chair and greet him properly.

He had been in the middle of getting tea for us with the plates and biscuits on the small table and the kettle boiling. He attended to it while I sat and watched him. It was lovely having him with me, and I liked him to fuss like this. In the small space of the bedroom, it was bit like having a stocky, dark bear shuffling around.

He placed the pot of tea on the table and sat across from me. He reached over and picked up my hand. "I missed you at home," he said. "Lionel was good company but I missed you. It seemed like the walls were moaning for you."

I smiled at him, just enjoying him and his lovely attention. We'd spent so much time together during the pandemic we'd more or less ironed out all those early relationship bumps and surprises. I knew he snored. He knew I hated messy counters. He'd come to terms with my wealth. I'd come to terms with his erratic hours. We would hit more problems as life had a way of dumping surprises on the innocent, but at the moment, we were coasting along smoothly. I tried not to look too far ahead.

"Lionel?" I asked.

"Amazing old gaffer. He's up trying to cook for me now."

"Can he cook?"

"He's good on cheese sandwiches."

I shook my head. "Rose will see he has soup and a good dinner."

"He doesn't mind eating if Rose is cooking, but he doesn't think a man should serve him."

"Ah, well, as you say, he's an old gaffer."

"But sharp."

We were silent for a moment. I thought of how close we'd come to losing Lionel. We would lose him one day, but not yet.

"Tell me," I said as I sipped the tea—Yorkshire tea, I noticed, peppery but not overloaded with scent or spice. "What is Bob doing back here? I thought Thompson was going to keep him."

"She can't. Shirley had a solicitor in there this morning with a demand for release. Thompson had to release him. There wasn't enough evidence."

"The sergeant won't use bat ears to listen to the meetings."

"No, she can't use the evidence she collects that way unless she gets all kinds of permissions which would take too long. She can use them to keep herself informed, but she needs to get evidence she can present to the Crown prosecutor. Oddly enough, she can use a camera, mounted outside the property on a county pole. She's got a camera that records audio, and she's ramped it up."

"So, a video camera that listens?"

"That's right."

"Let's hope it picks up something. I hate just depending on luck here."

"We have two more days."

We looked at each other. That wasn't long.

"Where are you tomorrow?" he asked.

"Stonehenge. It's their last day. Would you like to join us?"

"I think I'd better stay here and watch Bob."

"A good idea. The day after tomorrow I'm taking everyone back to Heathrow, even the Montana couple as they are meeting their next tour there. I hope Heathrow isn't Bob's target."

"According to Lionel's information, the target is the anti Nazi rally in central London."

That was some fifteen miles from Heathrow. I reflected on my attitude. I was dedicated to protecting my group. That didn't mean I was insensitive to the targeted rally in London, just that I didn't have direct responsibility for them. Mark had much more.

We wandered down to the lounge about six and found most of the group having a pre-concert drink. We'd just joined Anna and

Judith at a table and given our order to Dylan—sherry for Judith and me, lager for Mark and Anna—when we heard yelling from the kitchen.

Dylan rolled his eyes.

"Are you looking for another job, Dylan?" I asked.

"With all my heart," Dylan said.

"Good luck."

I thought about Dylan. I might be able to help him financially. Helping others was the perk of having a substantial legacy from my stepfather. My portfolio had survived the plunging recession of the pandemic years. Luckily, I didn't need to use the money when the stock market dropped suddenly. When it recovered, my money recovered as well. What a burden Dylan was taking on —a life of education for many years. If he lived in Scotland, his tuition would be paid up to post-graduate years. If he lived in Norway or Germany, all his education would be free—but not here. I'd at least get his address before I left and consider what I could do.

Bob strode into the bar carrying plates of food. There was an uncomfortable silence for a moment, so we all heard Bob say to Dylan, "I don't want to serve that savage."

I froze. I felt Anna stiffen.

Before I could react, Judith stood. We were totally still, watching her. "I'll thank you to remember," she said looking directly at Bob, "that my friend Anna's people had a sophisticated language and culture when your ancestors were painting themselves blue. Behave yourself, and serve pleasantly and without bias. You will also apologize, or I will take this further."

I will report you was hanging in the air.

Bob straightened and stared at her. He held her gaze for a moment, then looked down. "Sorry," he mumbled without looking at Anna. He may have remembered he'd just left the police station and Judith might send him back there. He set the plates on a spare table and left. Dylan brought them quickly to our table.

A few minutes later, Shirley arrived at our table with a plate of deep-fried shrimp.

"My apologies," she said. "I heard Bob was rude. It's the stress. He needs everything to be regular: exercise, work, meals. He gets irritable when he's life is disrupted."

We looked at the shrimp. This was her way of apologizing. I was tired of her running after Bob and trying to clean up the messes he made. I would not be bringing guests here again, shrimp or no shrimp.

After she returned to the kitchen, I studied Anna. "How are you feeling?"

"Absolutely astounded at Judith," she said, smiling. "She's a veritable dragon."

Judith just blinked and smiled. Anna turned to me. "And angry," she said, her voice low. "I'm hoping my samples can put a noose around Nazi Bob's neck." She smiled.

The contrast between what she said and her smile shocked me a little, but I understood. I'd be furious at being treated the way Bob was treating her, and I was upset on her behalf.

"Sorry to shoot down your fantasy," I said in a low voice, "but we don't hang villains any more. I hope we do find the murderer and I expect it is Bob. It's unnerving, spooky even, to have him serving us. I know the police need more evidence."

"Whatever punishment you have here, I'd love to land Bob in it." She helped herself to shrimp and crunched down hard as if Bob's neck were between her teeth.

The concert was impressive, almost overwhelming as those Welsh men could really project their voices. They were just as wonderful in the soft airs as they were in the boisterous coalminers' songs. Mark, who sang baritone in a men's choir in Alton, smiled throughout and I, who sang alto in our village choir, gave myself up to the beauty of it.

It was still raining heavily, so I drove everyone to dinner after the concert, then back to the hotel. It was the kind of rain that overflowed streams and gave the Cotswolds its reputation for moisture. A soaker, Matthew called it.

"Tomorrow is our last full day of the tour," I reminded them as we arrived back at The Queen Bess. "We're off to Stonehenge at nine, and the next morning, I will take you to Heathrow."

"It's gone very quickly," Nancy said. "Peggy and I had better check to see we have all the books and souvenirs we want."

Mark and I retired to bed. I told him about my plans for Dylan.

"You can't…" Then he stopped. It no doubt occurred to him that yes, I could.

He tried again. "He really isn't our business. He'll make it on his own with the help of his parents."

"I believe he could, but if I help him, it will be more possible for him to succeed. And I disagree. Everyone is our business. You of all people are in the field where everyone's welfare is your business."

He stared at me. "You got me there."

I grinned. I didn't often counter his arguments so neatly.

My good feeling didn't last long. With the knowledge that Mark and I had of the planned bombing in London and the irrational racist hate Bob had shown Anna. I felt as though I was sleeping in a war zone. How could Bob direct such fanatical hate toward someone because of her skin color. It must be a great failing of psychic health to allow that kind of feeling to fester. Centuries ago the English thought the Irish were a different race. Humans just construct boundaries and put whole groups of people outside those boundaries. It was bizarre. Once convinced they held a superior position, cruel and irrational actions seemed reasonable. I chased ideas about prejudice around in my head for an hour. I finally faced the fact I was upset by Bob's verbal attack on Anna and angry I hadn't done anything about it.

CHAPTER SEVENTEEN

I left The Queen Bess in the morning with a day's touring in front of me and no racist attacks, police or terrorist problems in the offing.

Mark stayed in Cirencester. "I want to be on hand if anything develops. I know I'm not officially involved, but I have a strong interest and Thompson seems happy to include me."

Stonehenge wasn't far from Cirencester, a little over an hour. I'd included material in their tourist bag this morning on the history and the speculative rational behind the construction of Stonehenge. Most people on a tour had some understanding of the ancient Neolithic times and realized Stonehenge had likely been a way in which the Neolithic people calculated time. The sun hit a certain stone at dawn on the summer solstice and another stone at sunset on the winter solstice, allowing the ancients to plan their planting, harvesting and feasting around these dates. There were dozens of mystical theories as well.

"I understand," Judith said, referring to her notes, "sixty-three people, men, women and children, were buried here in about 3,000 BC. The stones to mark their graves were hauled from Wales."

"They did find those bones," I agreed. "The stones did originate in Wales."

"Those people must have been mighty important," Matthew said, "to have them haul stones from Wales. I mean the stones are huge, aren't they?"

"They are," Bran agreed.

"So, it must have taken many, many men to heave them, using logs to roll them."

"And they'd have to cut the logs and carry them with them."

"Must have taken years," Matthew said.

"It might have been a marvelous center for music," Eseld said. "The acoustics are wonderful, I've been told. Perhaps they held concerts there."

"Perhaps," I said. It was an intriguing idea. I imagined Neolithic men, women and children singing for the edification of those hundreds or thousands who gathered at the Solstice, sitting in the fields around the giant stones. I wondered if the Welsh taught them to sing.

"I don't see why it couldn't have been a center of commerce," Heather said. "People could gather here and have a huge market."

"That's your business degree showing," Matthew said. "You know the world can't get by without a market place."

"No doubt they needed one," Heather said. "I suppose they could combine religious or mystical experiences with other goals. I bet they traded while they were here."

"You're probably right," I said, never having considered that.

Judith had been more or less ignored during these speculations, so I wasn't surprised when, after I'd parked the van, she told me she couldn't possibly walk all the way around Stonehenge and would need a wheelchair. I agreed she would need it. I passed out the site tickets to everyone, set them off on the long walk to the stones and went into the facilities building to rent a wheelchair. Judith was happy to have me push her to the site. The path was reasonably level and she was light, so it wasn't a hardship. The benefit for me was she was full of information about Stonehenge and I learned even more than I already knew about it.

We tried to recollect any mysteries set here but neither of us could do so. There were many non-fiction books around the origins, the possible use and importance of the site but authors seemed to shy away from setting their novels here. Perhaps, the site itself was intimidating, and they felt overawed by it. There were many authors who set their plots around the Wiltshire countryside but ignored Stonehenge.

"Perhaps we simply haven't discovered those novels yet," Judith suggested.

Perhaps, although I had made a diligent search for them.

"Or, someone has yet to write the mystery we want," she added.

"I like that thought," I said.

We joined Nancy and Peggy to gaze at the huge stones.

"How in the world did they drag those?" Nancy said.

"Amazing," Peggy said.

"The site itself could be more impressive," Judith complained. "It's fenced off, I suppose, to keep the graffiti artists from desecrating it, and it has paved paths. It looks more like a theme park than a sacred site."

I agreed with her on that. It looked almost too civilized, like a constructed setting for a film.

After our tour, I drove everyone to Avebury to the Waggon and Horses located on the outskirts of the village. The stone-built pub built looked as though it housed fairies with its thatched roof or roofs, as there were several different ones covering different parts of the building. One of them looked like an oast house roof, conical, like a cap sitting on the top of a tower. I wondered if they had dried hops here in the past. The pub was surrounded by countryside. Coaches had probably stopped here centuries earlier.

The menu was wonderful. I took a picture of it and texted it to Mark.

"Look at the beer menu," Matthew said. "Bishop's Tipple, Swordfish, Wadsworth Game of Stones. How do you choose?"

Bran peered at the menu through his half glasses. "There is a description beneath each. Why don't you order a couple to compare them? You could get three in a flight," he said reading from the menu.

There were several mouth-watering descriptions of vegetarian and vegan meals. I chose the butterbean, chestnut, parsnip and shallot casserole with lemon and thyme polenta, but I was the only one who chose vegetarian. Matthew, predictably had the sirloin steak, Heather the chicken, Judith had the soup of the day then ordered the chocolate and coconut tart with vanilla ice-cream for afters. I had my eye on the white chocolate tiramisu cheesecake with coffee ice-cream, but I wasn't sure I'd have room for it.

"This is a beautiful building," Nancy said after she had given her order to the waiter. "How old is it?"

"It was built in 1669 with Sarsen stone which they think came from the Avebury Circle close by." I'd researched it.

"It's gorgeous," Peggy enthused. "The oldest building I know of in Nova Scotia was built in 1699, so not long after this one."

"That seems a kind of connection," Nancy said.

Peggy smiled. "Yes, I feel that."

Several of the group had joined the men with their beer order but Ann, Judith and I enjoyed a gorgeous sparkling white, Ridgeview Cavendish Brut 2014 from Sussex. I knew the Romans had grown wine in England so long ago, but I hadn't tried many of the new wines coming from southern England. This one was brisk and refreshing.

We spent almost two hours at lunch and everyone was mellow when we finally boarded my van and headed to the Alexander Keiller Museum. It is situated in the center of the Avebury Circle and easy for everyone to access views of the stones and the West Kennet Avenue, the parallel rows of stones that outlined the one-and-a-half-mile road to The Sanctuary of Avebury. Avebury is more accessible and impressive than Stonehenge, almost as if the stones and the patterns they formed were a living village.

It had stopped raining, so I handed out the tickets I had pre-bought for them and remained outside on a bench enjoying the view. That is where Mark found me.

"What are you doing here?" I looked at him in surprise.

"I need a break, just a short one. I'm not getting anywhere and Bob spends all his time in his gym, so observation is useless right now."

I smiled and moved over so he could sit beside me. "What did you do all morning?"

"One of the things I did was try to talk to Dylan about sorting out his job and maybe his girlfriend."

"Noreen."

"Yes, Noreen. I took Dylan out for lunch, bought him a hamburger, actually two hamburgers—that kid can eat. Then I listened to his plans and suggested gently that he ditch Noreen."

"Oops. How did he take that?" People rarely want advice on their love life.

Mark let out a deep breath. "Well, I didn't put it that bluntly. I told him I'd had a couple of affairs just after my divorce and found that when it wasn't right, it was best to part. When the girl doesn't believe in the same things you do, it doesn't work."

"The same things. Like justice? Honesty? Integrity?"

"Something like that. I hope I didn't sound like a prat."

I smiled. I really loved this man. "You tried. He might remember what you said when it's important."

"To be fair. I don't know Noreen. She might be good for him, but she sounds like a right cow."

"You didn't say that?" I was startled.

"No, of course not." He grinned. "Just implied it."

I shook my head. He talked to Dylan because he thought he could support me that way. If Dylan resented it, he could avoid Mark.

"How's Lionel"

"Rose says he's doing fine, eating her cooking, so they are both satisfied."

"I'm sorry you missed lunch here. It was spectacular."

"It's a wonder you aren't twelve stone."

"Genetics rather than discipline," I said. I'd always been grateful I didn't put on weight the way some people did and could eat as much as I liked. "How is the inquiry going?"

"Maisie has a budget for three days. Scotland Yard has arrived—a detective called Richardson who is frustrated by the rules of Gloucester police."

"Maisie's refusal to use a listening device?"

"Right."

I remembered Mark's friend Phillip who worked for Scotland Yard had used bats ears. I couldn't imagine Maisie Thomson being so rule-bound she wouldn't make use of them.

"Maisie still won't listen?"

"I expect she's planted some, although not admitting to it, but there is nothing of note to hear. Bob's lifting weights and running in place in his gym; Shirley's in the cellar working on her sanitizer business."

"Or her still?"

He stared at me. "Do you think she has a still?"

"Maisie couldn't find it."

"It would be hard to hide."

"True."

He was quiet for a moment, then said, "The report from Dr. Clarke's colleague came in. The pollen and spore mix is exactly the same as on Richie's shirt."

"What does that mean?" I wondered what kind of evidence it was. What did it prove?

"You can only say that he lay in the cellar at some point. They also found blood traces there which matched Richie's' blood, so he lay in the cellar bleeding. That's evidence he was killed or injured there. Or hid there while he was bleeding. Still no enough evidence to charge Bob."

It made sense to think whoever had killed Richie knew about the cellar. That meant Bob and Shirley, at least. Perhaps Dylan and anyone else who had worked there in the past, or even worked there for the previous owners. Or the present owner, Shirley's mother.

"Does anyone care about Richie? I mean, did he have any family?"

"There's usually someone. In this case, he has a mother, father and sister. They have been worried about him for a couple of years. They live in the Dells, but somehow they've managed to lead a respectable life—except for Richie who didn't want to be part of the family's fish and chip shop."

I took a moment to feel sorry for those relatives. It must have been difficult to hear he died so young, then difficult to discover the police didn't have a suspect for his death. I remembered a song by Finn Napier of Scotland about the heartbreak parents felt over their son's behavior. Desmond. The name of the boy in that song was Desmond. I heard that lament in my mind.

"So the spores and grasses tell us he was killed in the cellar?"

"We or rather your friend Anna and Dr. White found the exact same combination in the cellar and on Richie's clothes. That combination didn't match the area where he was found, so it's highly probable he was killed in the cellar."

"Maisie will be happy with that."

"Thompson's murder investigation is getting subsumed into the Yard's plan to interrupt a terrorist bomb plot. It's complicated."

"Where are you in this?"

"Nowhere. I am related to one of the victims, so I can't be involved." His voice was flat. He was still upset by being regulated out of the investigation.

I had momentarily forgotten Lionel had also been attacked. "So, you aren't involved."

"Not officially. I am also getting right anxious about this terrorist plot. We don't have much time."

Two days--the plan for the terrorist attack was for two days hence.

"I drove over to see you as we haven't had much time together, but I also wanted to pick your brains. Can you think of anything that might help discover when and how this attack is going to happen? That's the most important file at the moment. It's one file the Yard will accept my help on, if I find out anything."

I was quiet for a moment, thinking of Bob and his usual routine, his attitude and his xenophobic ideology.

"I'd watch Bob. He must be going to meet with his group soon. I think you need to stay close to him in the hotel."

Mark agreed. "I thought perhaps something might go down tonight. At least a planning meeting. I think he's just marking time this afternoon."

"That sounds logical."

He left me before my group decanted from the museum. They wandered around the fields and paths looking at the stones and the landscape around us, and chatted about it all on the way home.

"What an experience," Matthew said. "How old is everything here?"

"Can't be much more ancient than 5,000 years BC," Heather said. "There isn't evidence of people before that."

"Oh, yes, there is," Nancy corrected her. "We have evidence in Labrador of people living there 10,000 years ago, the Beothuk people."

Peggy added her opinion. "New evidence is suggesting the Indigenous people in other parts of Canada were there even longer."

"Really? I'd better do some studying. Maybe we have ancient peoples in Montana. I'll have to read up on our history." She was quiet for a moment then added. "History that doesn't start at the Mayflower."

We were back at The Queen Bess about seven in the evening. Everyone was free until the next morning. I hadn't organized anything so they could wander around Cirencester on their own, pick up last-minute souvenirs, visit local sites they had missed and get themselves ready for the trip home.

Anna came to my room. Mark was in the bar trying to make a beer last as long as possible, waiting for the arrival of the Nazi group. I hoped Thompson had sent another detective to be with him.

"I feel as if something is going to happen," Anna said. "I know someone killed Richie in the cellar. That should make everyone here uncomfortable, but I seem to be the only one who is tense. Most people are ignoring it."

"Not all of them have your information," I said. "You understand the importance of the pollen and spores; they don't. You also have been the subject of Bob's Nazi hatred of anyone who doesn't look like him. So, it feels oppressive. I'm sorry this has happened on your trip."

"The sample taking and research I've enjoyed. But it's frustrating not to have my own lab and the recognition of the authorities that I know what I'm talking about."

"And Bob is a pain."

"And Bob is a pain," she agreed. "I have to tell you there are Bobs everywhere. "

"I'm sorry."

"Not your fault. Want to go to dinner?"

"Sure. Mark won't leave the hotel, so let's just nip up to Jessie's Bistro and have a meal."

That's what we did. I enjoyed her conversation. She talked about karate competitions. She had a brown belt and practised regularly. That might contribute to her confidence.

After the meal, Anna joined the others who were going to a pub where there was live music. It was a Celtic music evening so

it suited everyone. I left them to it and walked back to The Queen
Bess. I had yet to finish my paper work so it was done by tomorrow.

The lights from the pub area of the hotel lit the edge of the
garden. Tonight, with the rain finally stopped, the garden looked
almost mysterious in the moonlight with glittering drops on the
trees and the smell of grass. It was inviting. I wandered over to the
patio and appreciated the bluebells at the foot of the elm trees and
the tulips, almost black in this light but still lovely.

It was peaceful.

CHAPTER EIGHTEEN

From the garden, I could see Mark sitting in the bar area through the leaded panes of the bay window. The amber lights of the lamps bathed him in a glow. Very romantic. I should join him. Then I saw the backs of several men at the bar. Bob's crew. I stood in the darkness under the elm tree watching them. They were all tall, broad-shouldered and tough-looking with dark clothes and dark jackets.

Wasn't Maisie going to send anyone to help Mark keep track of those yobs? I squinted, trying to see if there was anyone else in the lounge. If there was, he or she was out of my range of vision.

The mist swirled in and settled over the garden, obscuring my view a little. It started to rain. That got rid of the mist. Now, I could see the men from the bar just as they were leaving the lounge. I stayed where I was, but they didn't appear at the front door. They must have gone to the back or to the cellar.

I wished I had a listening device. I hoped Mark did.

I paced back and forth under the tree where it was relatively dry. I saw a light at a low window at the back of the hotel. The cellar? Probably. I should slip to the side of that window and listen.

Remember, Claire, Lionel was attacked. Richie died. Do not be foolish. Don't get too close.

Mark would be following them, wouldn't he? I needed to find somewhere I could listen to whatever was going on in the cellar. There was no one in the garden. Those men could not see or hear me from the cellar. In any case, I would be quiet. I didn't know if Mark had bats' ears. Perhaps. He might be listening. Should I wait and get information from Mark? Or should I try to get the information myself? *Face it, Claire, you're too impatient to wait to get your information from Mark. And what if he didn't get any?* If there was a terrorist plot, I wanted to know about it.

I crept up beside the low window. I could hear a rumble of voices, but I couldn't distinguish any words.

I examined the wall around me. A few paces away was an old coal chute. Years ago coal would have been dumped down this chute and delivered to the many fireplaces that heated the hotel. Now, it was used to deliver goods. I felt along the outside of the chute and pushed at the swinging door that hung covering the slide to the cellar. I could hear a little better, but still not clearly.

Beside the coal chute was a water faucet and beside the water faucet, a hose. I slowly picked up the hose, uncurled it and fed it under the hanging door and down the slide. I hoped the chute was in an unobtrusive place in the cellar where no one would notice the hose coming into the room.

Periodically, I put the end of the hose to my ear until I could hear clearly.

I heard someone say "...lorry."

I concentrated.

"Listen up, Bryson. We'll deliver the lorry to you. It's stolen, with new plates, so you won't want to have it long. I'm handy here, so I'll load it." It sounded as though Bob was giving orders. He must be in change.

"Aaron, you're our explosive expert. You go with me to fix the detonator. This cannot go bollocks. I'm counting on you."

There was a murmur of reassurance.

The voice continued. "I'll exchange places with Bryson at this intersection."

I repeated the names of the streets to myself: Trafalgar Square and Duncannon.

"Remember that's a one-way."

"It's a good spot." That was a deeper voice. "We can take out people going to Charing Cross station as well as the protestors."

"Yes, that's why I chose it," Bob said. "Bryson will drive the lorry as close to the march as he can get. Just slide up, quiet-like, Bryson, like you were looking for a delivery address. Aaron, you'll fix the accelerate, plant it near the crowd. Then both leave fast."

"We'll catch a bus heading out and be away when the bomb goes off."

"You need to be quick," Bob said.

"We will be. We'll clean up Britain for those who deserve her."

That was sickening. Explosives were horrendous. I took a deep breath.

"What about your alibi?" That was the deep voice again.

"I'll attend that seminar I'm using as an excuse to go to London. I'll stop on the way and sign into the seminar like a good boy. But I'll set everything up. I'll drive to Blythe's garage and you and Aaron will take the bomb, load it into the hot van. The number plates will be good. So no one will pick you up because of the plates. Blythe is one of us. He won't ask any questions, and he'll forget the van was ever there. I'll go back to the seminar. I'll talk to people immediately, so I can say I've been there all the time. I'll find out what they talked about in the session that I missed and get the details of what went on. That'll be my alibi. No one will be able to prove I wasn't there. Too many people millin' around there to keep track of one."

He sounded smug as if he was so much cleverer than anyone else. He might be smarter than his friends, but not as clever as he thought. I wished I could see them. *Don't even think about it, Claire.* There was no way I could get a look at them. The information I'd already heard could get me killed.

"Do you think that old man really was spying on us?" That was the deep voice again. I hadn't heard the other man say anything.

"Definitely. We need to find that blue book."

"It wasn't in his room?" the deep voice asked

"No. I searched it."

"Maybe he gave it to someone," the voice said.

"Maybe his nephew, but he's a cop. I don't like that."

I didn't know how long they would stay talking and I did not want to be caught in the garden listening. I left the hose where it was. They hadn't seen it when I lowered it, but they might if I tried to pull it back.

I moved slowly toward the front of the hotel, glanced into the bar but Mark was gone. I heard heavy footsteps coming down the hall from the back of the house. The meeting was over. That was close. I looked back as I started up the stairs and was horrified to see my wet footprints an obvious trail from the front door.

Bob was suddenly in front of me. "You were outside?"

I looked around the foyer. There was no one. Bob was dangerous. I thought fast. "Don't tell my group. I was sneaking a cigarette. "

He frowned. "You should give that up. It'll kill you."

I nodded solemnly. "I was doing fine but that Mrs. Vancouver gets my anxiety level up."

His lips tightened. He hadn't enjoyed being chastised by Judith. "What a bitch."

"Yeah. But her money's good."

"The hospitality industry. Who'd want it? We put up with weirdos."

I considered him the worst weirdo I'd met in many a year, so couldn't agree more. "Some days it's just a bit much."

"Lay off those cigarettes and vaping isn't any better."

"So they say. Good night."

"Good night. "

I turned the key and slipped into my room.

I locked the door, turned my back against it and sank against the wood. Shit!

I breathed deeply for a few seconds. Now I had this information, what should I do with it? Mark. I needed to talk to him. I was afraid to venture out into the hall. Bob might want to question me more closely. I texted Mark and gave him a synopsis of what I'd heard.

He texted back immediately. "Stay in your room. Stay on the line, I'll use another mobile to send officers to you."

Oh good. From where? Hampshire? Bath? "What are the chances of getting help?"

"In theory, The Major Investigations Team can use anyone."

"Let's hope." I wasn't sure of that. It seemed to me every time Mark tried to be efficient and coordinate the police forces, some kind of paperwork intervened.

The hotel was quiet, but when I listened hard, I could hear creaks and groans. Just old timbers settling, I was sure. Bob had believed me. He couldn't have known I'd overheard him. I felt cold then nauseous.

"Are you still in your room?" I read the text.

"Yes."

"Don't call anyone. Just stay put."

"Right you are."

I thought about who might be members of Bob's cult. Local rugby players? Local gym members? Imports from London committed to their crazy ideology? What did they think they would accomplish? Getting a leader who looked like them?

There was a great deal in the world I didn't understand: meanness, snobbery, racism, terrorism. I know all these subjects are nuanced; I just don't understand why anyone would see them as positive aims.

I heard footsteps on the stairs then silence as they stopped outside my door. No one called out to me. I kept my eyes on the door knob. No one tried it. I heard the footsteps go away then a few minutes later, I heard Eseld scream.

I ignored Mark's direction to stay in my room, grabbed a can of hair spray and my mobile, unlocked my door and ran into the hall. The Bligh's door was slightly ajar.

I darted across the hall, flung wide the door and snapped the light switch. Three goons were in the room. Bran was against the wall with Bob holding him by the throat. By the look of it, he had already hit Bran and had his fist drawn back to hit him again.

"Stop!" I screamed. "The police are on their way!" I held up my mobile, snapping pictures, the mobile flashed over and over as I held the camera button down.

Everyone in front of me froze. Bob, Bran, Eseld standing on the bed with the lamp in her hand, ready to bash the nearest yob. A tall, broad-shouldered, dark man near the bed had a small, wicked-looking knife, concentrating on Eseld. The knife distracted me. There was no way I could disarm him. A shorter but muscle-bound, blond man was behind Bob, ready to weigh in on Bran. Three of them. Three vicious, driven zealots who might want to be martyrs. They were all staring at me. The one with the knife turned and moved toward me. I heard the sirens the same instant the men did. I was standing in front of the door. They were going to push past me to get out and wouldn't care if they killed me in the process. The dark-headed one with the knife took one step toward me. Eseld brought the lamp down on his head. He staggered but didn't drop the knife.

Bob chopped Bran on the neck; he dropped unconscious, and Bob whirled around. I dashed for the hall, ran toward the stairs and darted into the alcove at the top where the statue stood and slipped behind it. I heard the police rush through the front door and mill around the lobby.

"Where is she?" That was Bob. He'd gone past me and down the stairs. Did he think he could claim he was helping me?

"Where are those perps?" That was the police.

Mark didn't bother explaining Bob's status to the officers. He gave orders. "Hancock. Take this man in. Careful, he's dangerous. Two of you up the stairs."

I didn't dare call out for fear Bob's goons were nearby. As soon as Mark got to the top of the stairs, I called. "This way. "

I came from behind the statue to find two guns pointed at me. I didn't think the British police had guns. I must be behind the times. "Claire," I said quickly with my hands in the air. "I called this in."

Mark said. "Hold it!"

They started to holster their guns, but I stopped them.

"Keep them out. You are going to need them."

I pointed down the hall. They moved silently now. I gestured toward the open door. Only Eseld and Bran were in the room.

"Which way?" I said to Eseld.

She pointed to the left.

"The back stairs," I said. "Two of them." I clicked up their pictures on my mobile and showed them to the officers. They stared at the men. Those mobiles take shots with fantastic detail. You could even see the tattoos on their arms.

"Send those to me," Mark said

"I will."

They moved quickly down the hall. One was speaking into his mobile, rallying the troops. I went over to Eseld who had Bran cradled in her arms. He looked gray. But I could see his chest rise and fall. I swallowed. "Ambulance?"

"Yes," she said tersely.

I rang 999.

I found some ice in the mini-fridge, wrapped it in a towel and handed it to Eseld. She gently placed it on Bran's jaw, where Bob had hit him.

He opened his eyes, glanced around, looked straight at Eseld and smiled.

She started to cry quietly, tears streaming down her face. "Hello, old man. The ambulance is coming."

"I think I'll be all right."

"Probably," his wife said.

He saw me then.

"They thought I had Lionel's journal. They thought he had put something important about them in it."

"Did you?"

"No. I gave it to Thompson, remember?"

"Oh yes. Right." I was rattled. He was the one with the head injury yet he was more coherent than I was.

We were quiet for a moment. I was feeling a tremendous relief I hadn't led them from the coal chute to Bran. The relief was short-lived.

"They thought I'd been listening outside their meeting. Saw some tracks I guess. A hose? I didn't get it all."

"Don't worry about it," I said. "I know what they were talking about." I *had* led them to Bran. How had those female spies in the Second World War managed to be so competent. I couldn't even manage to eavesdrop without causing trouble.

The ambulance arrived then along with Shirley who was distraught.

"Mr. Bligh, I am so sorry. Someone attacked you. In my hotel? I will hire security. I am so sorry."

"Not your fault," Bran managed to whisper.

"That's enough," the medic said. "Who is the wife of the patient?"

"I be her," said Eseld.

"You can ride with him to the hospital."

"Is he okay?" I asked. "I'm the tour guide I'm responsible." In more ways than one.

"No, he is not okay, but he is not in danger of dying. Vitals are fine."

Vital signs: blood pressure, respirations and heart rate.

"Still, he's old. A night in the hospital wouldn't hurt," the medic concluded.

"Which hospital?" I hoped they were taking him to the local one.

"There's only one. The Cirencester off 429."

"I'll be there in an hour."

Eseld followed the gurney. "Bring my sweater, Branock's glasses, his wallet and mobile," she called back to me over her shoulder.

"I will."

I hadn't forgotten there were two armed and dangerous men on the loose, but I needed to make sure Bran got away. As soon as the medical crew maneuvered the gurney through the front door and into the waiting ambulance, I turned toward the back garden. The police had had the sense to block the car park with their own vehicles. Three of them. That meant there were likely six officers around somewhere.

The attack on Bran had derailed the terrorist plans--at least, I hoped so. The police could hold them on assault charges while they searched for explosives and the stolen van Bob had mentioned. There might be enough charges to keep them apart and incarcerated. I wondered if the others in the group would continue planning destruction without Bob.

I'd promised to send the pictures of Bob and his band of weirdos. I sent them to Mark. As if I had conjured him, Mark appeared in front of me.

CHAPTER NINETEEN

Mark stood in the door, blocking my view. I looked past him and saw he had added his car to the blockade.

"What's happening?" I asked him.

"They ran towards the back garden. Is there an exit there?"

"I think so. A gate."

Mark turned and sent a constable who had appeared behind him, around the block to the back gate.

"Come in that way, but don't let anyone out," Mark instructed him.

"Yes sir," he said and was gone.

I heard a shout from the back garden. Mark looked to the side of the building.

"It's quicker to go through the house," I said, whirled and dashed for the kitchen with Mark at my heels. We passed the lounge which was empty and tore through to the kitchen. Nancy, the Montana couple and Anna were gathered around the back window peering out. Peggy was sitting in a chair crying. I had no time for her now. We raced down the short hall towards the back garden. I reached for the back door.

Mark put his hand over mind. "Get behind me."

I moved behind him. He was the trained officer, after all. He wasn't reaching for a weapon. He didn't have a weapon. He opened the door. I looked past him.

If it wasn't so serious, it would be funny. The blond assailant was on the ground with his hands cuffed behind him, an officer standing nearby. There was a rake on the ground lying across the path. Either he'd tripped on it, or the officer had used it to trip him.

The dark-haired man was trying to scale the brick wall. He had managed to get almost to the top but, as we watched, an officer knocked his foothold away with his truncheon and the man slid down the wall. Two officers pounced on him. He fought, but the two officers subdued him. I was glad Bob had already been apprehended. I just had that thought when I was seized from behind, a strong arm encircling my chest, pinning my arms and immobilizing me. I gasped and felt a prick at my throat.

Mark turned quickly and froze.

"Not a twitch of your hand, pig, or I'll slit her throat." How *could* that be Bob?

Mark nodded.

"You told one cop to take me in. One isn't enough. No one's taking me anywhere. I'm in charge here. So, listen hard, copper. I'm going to back into the hall here then into the garage. My car is ready; she's going with me. You stay here. If you let the others know and they come, she dies. Are we clear?"

"Clear," Mark said. His eyes held mine, checking to see if I was going to faint.

I thought about it. I could fake a faint, but I thought Bob would stab me and run. That would delay Mark as he'd make sure I was okay. *Think Claire, what else can you do?* If he was going to put me in the car and drive off, I'd have some opportunities to get away. Maybe just go out the passenger side door when he was getting in. He might kill me before he got in the car. He only needed me to get *to* the car. I might not get *into* it. He might leave me dying on the floor to delay pursuit.

We moved awkwardly backwards. The connecting door to the garage was only a few feet away. The group who had been peering out of the window were nowhere in sight.

From behind Bob, I heard Shirley.

"Bob," Shirley said. "Stop right there."

"Go back, Shirl. Don't try to stop me. Do you want to put me in jail? I only have to get to the garage. I'll leave this bitch there."

"Do not take another step," Shirley said. "I am standing behind you, and I also have a knife. I will shove it through your stupid heart if you so much as move. Drop your knife."

"Don't be crazy. Ow."

"I won't have to stab you, Bob. I'm between you and the car. You're going to move right into the knife."

There was silence. Mark stood immobile, watching and listening. I felt the pressure on my neck lessen. Then I heard the knife drop.

In seconds, Mark shot his fist over my shoulder and slammed it into Bob's jaw. Bob sagged. Mark grabbed me and shoved me behind him. I turned and saw Bob slumped on the ground.

"Put that knife away," Mark said to Shirley. I saw the knife shake as she slowly lowered it.

"Is he dead?" she said.

"No, just knocked out." Mark turned Bob over, snapped a pair of handcuffs on his wrists. "Larson, get here with more cuffs."

The small, wiry officer appeared with handcuffs dangling from his fingers. "You called?"

Mark smiled and grabbed the cuffs. He snapped them on Bob's feet. "This one needs an ambulance. How did he get away from you?"

"Not me," Larson said. "I turned him over to Barrow. Bob, here, tripped Barrow and ran."

Mark shook his head.

"That's all? Three?" Larson asked.

"That's all," Mark said with satisfaction. "We'll get them off for evading arrest to start, carrying a weapon, assault, and threatening assault."

"We'll lodge all three chummies comfy in the cells." Larsen said.

Mark turned his back on Shirley. "Thanks," he said to the constable.

I touched Shirley on the shoulder and herded her toward the kitchen. I knew Mark wanted her out of the way so she wouldn't be questioned by the other officers. The guests had vacated the kitchen.

"Where are they?" I asked.

"I told them to go into the lounge and help themselves to a drink," Shirley said. "They aren't supposed to be in my kitchen."

It was a little odd to insist on the Department of Health rules at this time, but people feel more secure when they follow rules, especially in difficult times.

"Put the knife back," I advised. "And say nothing about it. Mark is not going to mention it".

Shirley thrust the knife into the wooden block on the counter. We moved into the lounge where she was surrounded by the rest of my tour.

"What happened?" Anna said. "What was that all about?"

I sat Shirley down in a chair, and brought her a brandy. "Judith, can you make her a cup of tea at the bar."

"I certainly can," Judith said, rising from her chair.

"I'll help you." Heather followed Judith.

I realized my hands were shaking. I in turn followed Judith to the bar and helped myself to a brandy.

In a few minutes, Judith served Shirley her tea and the guests sat around her listening to my explanation of Bob's perfidy. I sipped the brandy and felt marginally better as I told them what had occurred in the back hall.

Cst. Larson arrived when I was half-way through. "No one is planning on leaving, are they?"

We assured him we were all staying put. He left us.

In telling the story, I left out the knife and said Shirley had persuaded him to drop his knife.

Peggy petted Shirley and Nancy stroked her hand. "So hard for you," she said.

Shirley had tears in her eyes, but she didn't cry.

"I think Bob must be mentally ill," she said.

I didn't think he was mentally ill in terms of not understanding what he was doing, and I was sure he would be deemed fit for trial, but it might be easier for Shirley to find him mentally ill than to realize he was bigoted, self-serving, grandiose and narcissistic. I was angry and tried not to let Shirley see it.

"I've been thinking I'd have to leave him. It just wasn't working out."

I'd say that was an understatement. How could it, when one half of the partnership was committed to mayhem? Shirley was the victim here, but Maisie Thompson told me Lydia Harris had manipulated her husband into jail. Just for a moment, I wondered if Shirley had done that to Bob.

Just outside the door, I heard Mark address an officer who must have been standing behind him. "Spin the hotel, top to bottom." Mark then entered the lounge and spoke to Shirley. "We're going to search the hotel, particularly your office and bedroom."

She stared at him. "The office and bedroom?"

"That's right."

Shirley must have understood the police wouldn't need a warrant as there was enough indication of criminal activity to make that irrelevant. "The computer near the window is Bob's," she said.

"Good to know."

Perhaps the police would leave Shirley her computer. I'd hate to be parted from mine, and I expect all the spread sheets for the hotel were on Shirley's.

I felt instantly tired. Reaction I suppose to having a knife at my throat. My shoulders were still tense. My hands had stopped shaking, but I would like the time and privacy to have a good cry. *It's over, Claire. No sense getting hysterical now.* I drained the last of the brandy and felt it warm my chest. My shoulders eased.

It was going to be a long night. Mark or one of the officers would have to interview all the guests, including Bran and Eseld who were at the hospital. Mark returned as I was trying to think of how to avoid having my guests stay up late. Some of them had a long flight the next day.

"Sorry for inconveniencing everyone," Mark said, "but I will need to talk to each of you."

"Can you start with Judith, then Peggy, Nancy, Heather and Matthew, then Anna?"

The guests looked at me. I was presenting them to Mark in order of age.

"I can," he agreed. "I'll take each of you in turn in the kitchen."

I saw Shirley wince. Health regulations again.

"Would the breakfast room do?" I asked Mark.

"Of course."

Shirley sent me a grateful look.

"I'd advise everyone to go to his or her room after the interview as Shirley will want to clean up and set her kitchen in order—and we have a long day tomorrow," I said.

"Of course," they murmured agreement. They were a cooperative group. Not even Judith objected.

Shirley left us and disappeared into the private part of the hotel. Mark didn't take long with each interview, and it was about an hour later he came for Anna.

I'd made tea at the bar, and Anna and I had a big pot of it in front of us. I still had to get Bran and Eseld's belongings to the hospital, but I couldn't leave the hotel until I'd given my statement.

"Mark, I need to get a bag of supplies to the hospital. Can you send someone with them?"

"You get them ready, and I'll arrange that."

I dashed up to the Bligh's room, grabbed Eseld's straw bag and loaded it with her sweater, Bran's glasses, his wallet and mobile as requested. I handed it to Mark on my return, and he walked to the front door and passed it to a waiting constable.

I was seated and drinking my now lukewarm tea when Mark came back into the lounge.

"Sit down, love," I said. "Anna is a police consultant; you can talk easily."

"Yes, I remember that." He sank into the chair and reached for my hand. "Are you all right?"

"Just about." I didn't want to think about those few moments of terror. They were over. "Just about," I repeated. He stroked my arm, then looked at the teapot.

"That tea looks good." He looked tired.

I disengaged my hand, fetched another cup and poured it for him.

"Ah," he sighed with satisfaction. "That is just what I need."

I was not *that* relaxed. "What is happening?"

"The three who caused all the damage here tonight are off to the nick. We're searching the hotel."

"Are you finding anything?"

He sipped tea again while we waited. "Explosives in the shed, made up neatly into two bombs."

"That's enough?"

"No, not quite enough. We're looking for evidence, perhaps on the computer emails, that they were planning to bomb Trafalgar Square. We have Bob and two of his friends for attempted grievous bodily harm among other charges."

"Because he held a knife to my throat." I swallowed a couple of times. I had a working throat. I should be grateful. "You'll have my statement of what I overheard."

"That'll help."

Anna leaned forward. "I suggest you search that basement thoroughly."

"What do you expect me to find in the cellar?" Mark asked.

"Some reason for Richie Stonehouse to die."

Mark was quiet for a moment, then stood and hurried to the back hall. We could hear him speaking.

"Skipper, give that cellar a good look," he said. "Tap walls, shove cupboards aside, check dimensions to see if there is anything that doesn't look normal."

"Will do," we heard.

Mark came back for his tea.

"Who is Skipper?"

"Sergeant Thompson. You met her."

"I thought her name was Maisie."

"It is. But she's a sergeant."

Anna interrupted. "Are all sergeants called Skipper?"

"Usually."

I hadn't known that. Mark didn't call Andy Forsyth skipper. There must be unwritten, arcane rules about it.

"Did you leave a poor note-taking constable in the breakfast room without tea?" I asked.

"No, I sent him to help Maisie before I came in here. I said I'd ring him when I was ready for your interviews."

He didn't call him. Just as he finished his second cup of tea, Sergeant Maisie Thompson marched in, flushed with satisfaction. "Found it!"

"What?" Mark got to his feet.

"A hidden room. Looks like a still."

We followed her to the cellar like foxes after a scent.

CHAPTER TWENTY

We couldn't see much as there were at least four police officers in front of us. I managed a quick peek and saw a deep room going back into dark corners. A table sat against a wall with big cauldrons on it and tubes connected to smaller shiny containers. The Macbeth witches would feel right at home in there.

"Cognac," Mark said. "Someone's been making cognac here." He was reading a label on the table.

"That's high-octane liquor," one of the constables said.

"Expensive," said another.

I studied the label. "It looks like Kelt cognac," I said. "A sophisticated brand. The shape of the bottle here is the same as the Kelt brand and the colors on the label are also the same."

"Thank you, that's useful." Mark turned to Anna and me "I'm sorry, I'd like you both to return to the lounge or to your rooms. We don't want any evidence compromised."

Anna and I looked at one another.

"Damn," she said quietly.

"Oh." Mark reconsidered. "You can stay—a professional consultant."

She brightened.

That meant I was the one who had to leave. I resented that but knew it was the correct decision. Mark might have to testify in court about how he gathered evidence. My presence would be hard to explain. I returned to the lounge and gathered up the teapot and cups, washed them in the bar sink and put them back on the shelves. I was a professional tour guide, not a professional detective.

I heard constabulary footsteps tromping down the hall and a knock on the door of the private rooms.

"Yes?" Shirley answered the door. I stood still and listened.

"You will need to come with me, madam." That was Sergeant Masie Thompson.

"Me? Whatever for?"

"We've discovered a still in your cellar and we need you to come to the station and explain it."

There was a brief silence, then, "Tonight?"

"Yes, madam."

"A still? I don't understand. What was Bob doing?"

It wouldn't be Bob who was operating the still. It didn't seem to be something Bob would do. He was more the smash and destroy type. Shirley, on the other hand, was the businesswoman and a creative cook. I could see her creating brandy. I heard another set of heavy feet approaching Shirley's door.

"I'm coming," Shirley said with some irritation. "I have to be back to get breakfast for the guests."

"Please come now, madam." Maisie was polite but insistent.

"Let me get my handbag."

"I'll come in with you while you do that."

They weren't going to let her out of their sight now. It was unlikely she'd be back for breakfast.

There wasn't time to take my statement. I'd give it to Maise over my mobile in the morning. She could send it to Ashton-on-Tinch and I could sign it there. I had other concerns right now. I sat at a table in the lounge and thought.

Shirley might be innocent, but the police were not going to let her back to the hotel until they'd taken her fingerprints and checked the still for a match. Her mother would be there as soon as possible with a high-priced solicitor. That would take at least a day.

Shirley would be held at the station until the solicitor arrived. I had the immediate problem of what to feed my guests for breakfast. Eseld might be back and she'd want something hot.

Dylan would help, but I hadn't seen any evidence he could cook. He could start the coffee and put out the fruit and dry cereal. I pulled my mobile from my purse and checked on restaurants near the hotel. I found one about a block away. I rang and prayed there would be someone there. Luckily, there was.

I told the snappy man at the other end of the call the proprietor of this hotel had been called away suddenly, and could he supply breakfast for eight? We talked about boiled eggs and Danish pastries as well as the local ham and bacon. He promised to have everything here by eight the next morning.

I went to bed. Mark arrived about four in the morning.

"Did you keep Shirley?"

"We did, my love. We did. What a night!" His voice oozed satisfaction.

Good, I didn't want Shirley in the hotel while I had guests here. "You're going to search again. What are you looking for?"

"Fingerprints. DNA. If Shirley is innocent, there will none of her fingerprints on any bottles. If we find fingerprints on even one cognac bottle, then she can't deny she knew about it. That might be enough to nail her. I'm sure that's her still."

"I agree," I murmured drifting back to sleep. "Doesn't seem Bob's thing."

"I got some momentum on my refugee case." Mark was wide awake and talkative. I fought sleep.

"You did?"

"You gave me an idea."

"I did?" I murmured, struggling to understand what he was saying.

"You told me about Buchanan transporting farm workers to Wright. I put a shadow on Buchanan and Wright. The tail on Buchanan's lorries has information. We should nab them both."

"That's good," I managed.

"It might be just the crack in the organization I need. But the paperwork is going to take weeks before it's sorted."

The notion of paperwork sent me sliding down into sleep.

I was up early to load the van with my luggage, take it to the petrol station, fill up the tank and return to the hotel by seven. I rang Maisie who was at her desk at the nick. She recorded my statement over the phone and she agreed to send it to the Aston-on-Tinch station. Now, I just had to deal with breakfast.

Dylan arrived and fluttered around like a lost gull.

I told him about Shirley. Even if Shirley was guilty of tax evasion, running an illegal still and perhaps other offences like murder, I still owed her for my guests' stay in her hotel. "Can you take my credit card?" I asked Dylan.

"I can."

I settled the bill. Dylan concentrated and printed out a receipt for me.

"Now, breakfast," I said. "I hired a local restaurant to bring the hot food at eight. Can you start the coffee urn?"

"I can do that. I'll set the tables and put out the napkins. I usually do that anyway."

"What about the warming table?"

"I can get that started. I only have to flick a switch." He looked around the breakfast room. "What charges are they holding Shirley for and where's Bob?"

"They're charging her with various crimes including running a still. Bob's also at the nick, for assault, I think." Dylan didn't need to know all the details.

"Lovely," Dylan said. "What a pair of bosses. After I do the dishes, I'm off to look for another job. Good thing I got paid yesterday."

That reminded me I was going to talk to him about money. If he was off to another job, this might be my only chance.

"Listen, Dylan. You need to give me your address and mobile number." Off and on in the past few days, I'd been thinking about how hard Dylan had to work to stay in school and how discouraging that could be. "I'll get my solicitor to contact you and pay for your tuition to university."

His jaw dropped, and he stared at me. "Why would you do that?"

"Because I can and because you have been trying hard to support your ambitions. It's just tuition. You'll have to find the money for books, food, and all other expenses."

"Gel on! Tuition? That's proper wild."

"Are you serious about a becoming a doctor?"

"I am."

"Then, I'm going to help you."

He looked stunned but wrote down his address and mobile number on a blank receipt. I tucked it into my purse and put that in my rucksack. I'd look after it when I got home.

Anna came into the room, a little early for the eight o'clock meal.

"Any hope of having a look at the cellar?" she asked me.

"We won't be able to go in. The police will have it taped off, but we can look over the tape." I also was curious about that still.

Dylan left his duties and followed us. I didn't blame him. Curiosity is a driving force. He gave me one sidelong look, no doubt wondering if I really was going to pay his tuition. I was. I would give instructions to my solicitor when I got back to Ashton-on-Tinch.

The door to the hidden cellar had been part of a shelving unit. The whole unit moved to reveal the room behind. The police had left the door open, and we could see a little way into the room. I saw the table I'd seen last night with the cauldron on it and tubing connecting it to pear-shaped metal containers on the floor.

Dylan whistled. "Some set up."

I studied the tubes and tanks. "She was making hand sanitizers, but she was making brandy as well. Look at those labels. They look like the expensive Kelt brand."

Dylan studied the room, the containers of alcohol and the still. "She can't make drinkable alcohol from the isopropyl alcohol she uses to make the sanitizers." He gestured to the white plastic gallon jars on the floor. "That's C_2H_5OH. Poisonous. That," he gestured toward the small copper still, "is ethyl alcohol C_3H_7OH. She'd make that from yeast and sugar."

I hadn't known that but I imagined every chemistry student knew it.

"They smell the same?" I asked him.

"Pretty close."

Anna was giving this business some thought. "So, Shirley was making brandy, selling it in London, and Bob was delivering it in the van. Maybe selling it to gangsters who had pretentions to grandeur."

I thought it was a highly imaginative scheme. "You mean displaying expensive brandy at their gang meetings?"

"Just the upper echelon of the gangs."

"It's like that in California?"

"So I hear."

I considered the process of producing and marketing illegal brandy. "She was selling it illegally, so you wouldn't see it in legal outlets. The Kelt company wouldn't complain because they'd not catch a glimpse of it."

"Pretty ingenious," Dylan said.

I remembered Shirley telling me about her life goals. "She wanted to fund her own bakery, a *boulangerie*. The pandemic stopped her plans."

"Along with the plans of millions of others," Anna said.

"Yes, but she probably thought she was a special case, and owed a special privilege to fulfill that ambition any way she could." Her mother might have encouraged that idea. Many criminals thought they had a special dispensation from the gods to create their own world. Many politicians, as well.

"I'd better get back to the breakfast," Dylan said and left us. Anna and I continued to stare at the hidden room.

"Mark asked me for sample tubes yesterday and took samples for Amy," Anna said. "He's trying to link Shirley with Richie Stonehouse's death. He might manage it. It would be great to find a piece of Shirley's hair on Richie's vest or some of her DNA somewhere. Hair isn't always the best source, but it's possible."

"That would be a break," I said. "Mark would like to solve that case. Do you think it was Shirley who killed Richie?" I thought Bob had done the deed, but I liked Shirley and I didn't like Bob. That would influence my thinking.

"I think Shirley is a logical suspect. Amy is going to keep me informed. I assume Mark will keep you informed."

"He might." I hoped he would. If he didn't, I'll ring Anna for an update. "You didn't get away from your work on this holiday." I worried about that.

"I had a great time. It felt wonderful. I didn't have to cook, look after a fourteen-year-old who knows everything, or listen to my hubby complaining about his co-workers. I don't mind all that most of the time. They listen to me, after all, but it was lovely to get away from it. This was an interesting case for me. I enjoyed myself."

I hugged her. "I'm glad I met you."

In the morning, Mark breezed through the breakfast buffet, stuffed a couple of hard-boiled eggs and a pastry into his pocket and filled his thermo-cup with coffee. I followed him to the foyer for a quick kiss and goodbye just in time to meet Eseld as she arrived by taxi. She'd left Bran in the hospital visiting with another retired officer. The doctors wanted to keep him another day to check his heart and make sure he was stable.

"I need to stay close by," Eseld said, waving to Mark as he walked quickly down the steps,

I opened my mobile and clicked on the B & B's on that side of town and showed her the choices. She picked one and I registered her, putting the cost on my credit card. She hadn't gotten her money's worth from my tour, and I owed her.

"I'll say my goodbyes to everyone," Eseld said. "In spite of it all, Claire lover, I enjoyed my tour with you. Very stimulating."

I looked at her. Was she sarcastic?

She smiled. "No, really. It was right interesting. As long as Bran recovers, I'll have good memories. Most of them. I still get right mazed when remember those thugs crashing into our room and attacking Bran."

Better angry than fearful. "He's going to be all right?"

"So the doctors say. All the constabulary in the west seem to be ringing in to make sure of it."

I knew how closely knit the constabulary was. Mark was a part of it. I envied them. They were like an extended family, in time including wives and girlfriends or husbands and boyfriends. I'd seen Lionel treat Eseld as if she was an officer. I thought about the detectives, sergeants and constables I'd met in Cornwall last year and the ones I'd met in Yorkshire. They treated me as if I was a confederate because of my relationship to Mark, or more accurately, some of them did.

Anna came up and gave Eseld a hug. Matthew and Heather asked about Bran. Nancy and Peggy, after hauling their suitcases to the foyer, fluttered around Eseld.

"What actually happened to Bran? We saw what happened to Claire in the yard, but we don't know what happened to Bran before that. We were so busy giving statements to the police about what we'd seen from the window last night, we didn't have a chance to get your story." Nancy said.

Eseld went into story mode as the Cornish are likely to do at any moment.

"We were sitting there, two pensioners having evening tea, as respectable and dull as Darby and Joan, a bit of music on the telly, and a lamp on low light when the door burst open and Bob and two ruffians burst in and grabbed Bran. It happened so fast I couldn't move.

"They hit him, and I screamed. Seconds later Claire flipped the overhead light and everyone stopped and stared at her." She turned to me. "You knew there was danger, didn't you?"

"The scream was a good indicator."

She nodded satisfied. "Yes, I can do a proper scream when called upon. You knew there was danger and you came anyway. You have courage, lover, and a strong sense of duty. It can trip you right into danger."

"We were in danger together." I protested.

"That we were, lass." She recounted the rest of that wild incident.

"That was an escape," Nancy said. "Are you all right?"

"I am and now I'm wondering what happened to the *bleddy tuss*?"

"Bob?" I said, correctly identifying the *bleddy tuss*. "He's in jail pending more charges. Shirley is also in jail for running an illegal still and selling illicit brandy."

"Oh my," Eseld said. "She might be Cornish."

I laughed. "Back in the nineteenth century, maybe, when smuggling booze was a Cornish occupation. She'll likely have to face charges now. In the meantime, we're trying to leave before she's released. Breakfast first," I said firmly and led everyone to the breakfast room where Dylan had laid out the fodder.

Sergeant Thompson arrived with Cst. Larson in tow and asked everyone to read and sign their statements, except mine which wasn't ready. They did that, and we finished our breakfast. I provided the officers with coffee and pastries.

"Thanks for your help," Masie said to me. "It was a nice haul."

"Glad to be able to do a bit," I said. It was a relief to get Bob and his dangerous cohorts safely incarcerated. I felt sorry for Shirley.

"D.I. Evans says you have a knack for precipitating an arrest."

I stared at her for a moment. I didn't have a knack for anything but landing myself and my guests in trouble. Her comment bothered me, though. Tourists may not want to book with a tour that involved guests in criminal activity, however innocently.

"I don't understand Shirley," I said. "She was making money here, at least enough to keep her and Bob. Why did she risk so much to make more.?"

"The illegal liquor earned much more than the hotel. We had a quick look at her books. She kept good records on her computer."

"Even so," I said.

"Bob was making much more than her distributing drugs along with the liquor."

"Crikey! You found that? Who would have thought of it?" It made sense, though. He could use Shirley's delivery van for his own side hustle. If Lydia was supplying the drugs, he might not even have to set the business up. Lydia could have done that.

Masie had thought of that. "When a man has a connection to Lydia Harris, I always think of drugs. She was using Bob. That woman has business everywhere."

"Can you prove it?"

"Of course not. We can prove Bob was distributing drugs because there were traces of the drugs in the van, but we can't prove Lydia supplied them. We never can. And we can't prove Shirley knew about it. Her mother is always careful of Shirley. We can't even prove Lydia was setting Bob up so he'd be caught and incarcerated, freeing her precious daughter from an abusive partner."

That was a new idea. Lydia was not a benevolent mother-in-law.

Maisie stood and shook her shoulders as if shrugging off the problems of Shirley Harris and her nefarious activities. "You'll sign your statement when your local nick gets it?'

I promised I'd do it that, and she left.

CHAPTER TWENTY-ONE

I saw Eseld off in a taxi to her new B & B and helped everyone else load their luggage into the van. We drove along the M4 to Heathrow. It was less interesting than the back roads, but much quicker. When we were nearing the airport, I activated the mic.

"It was such a pleasure having you with me for this tour," I said. "I hope, in spite of the troubles, you enjoyed yourselves."

I was assured from the seats behind me that they had.

"I'm a little worried there will be publicity about Bob and Shirley's arrest and the thwarting of the terrorist attack, but I don't think any press will pursue you."

There was silence for a moment then Judith said. "I suppose you're worried people will hear about it and won't want to book a tour with you."

"Exactly," I said with some relief at being able to discuss it.

"None of this is your fault," Judith said. "I admire the way you work hard for your guests. I, for one, will report what an excellent time I had and how attentive you were. I don't see any need to discuss the peccadillos of criminals who, were, after all, tangential to our trip."

In my rear-view mirror, I saw her gaze around the van with a commanding air.

"Good point," Matthew said. "I had a good time. No need to talk about the rats in the ship."

There were murmurs of assent.

"Thank you," I said.

I deposited them at Heathrow, helped with their luggage and made sure Heather and Matthew found their next tour, an in-depth look at farms. I gave everyone, especially Judith and Anna, a huge hug. I exchanged the nine-seat Mercedes Sprinter for my own van and drove back to Cirencester.

Mark was on the trail of the Buchanon/Wright trafficking problem and wanted to stay in the area, so I booked a room for us at The Fleece. It was comfortable without being ostentatious, and it was in the heart of Cirencester, handy to Eseld and the police station. I drove to the parking spot at the same garage I'd used for the past two weeks. I paid for two days and headed to The Fleece. I was looking forward to a long nap.

I texted Mark the name of our new accommodation. He sent me a happy face, so I expect his sleuthing was going well for him—not so good for Buchanon and Wright. I left Deirdre a message asking if she could keep Gulliver another day.

It was Sunday and, aside from the bells from the cathedral, it was quiet. I had just hit that lovely floating sensation I get before sleep when my mobile rang. I struggled awake and checked the ID: Deirdre. It cut off. If she was calling to tell me she couldn't keep Gulliver, I'd have to go and collect him. I might have to ask the hotel if I could keep him here. Bother!

I sat up straight, blinked a couple of times then hit the speed dial to Deirdre.

She answered immediately. "What's going on?"

That's my sister. No "Hello. How are you?" Just a demand to be informed. I realized I hadn't told her about the events of last night.

I started on a recap of events. I'd managed a few sentences before she interrupted.

"Don't bother. I'm in Stowe-on-the-Wold and can be with you in a half hour, and I'll hear it all then."

"Pardon?" I wasn't sure I'd heard her correctly.

"I had to interview a potential witness for a murder trial, so I'm working this weekend. I've interviewed the annoying, useless idiot. Michael's got the kids and the dogs, so I'm free."

"Do you want me to book you a room?"

"No, I'll stay for dinner with you and Mark, but I'll head home about nine. Traffic will be better then."

"Great. Call me when you arrive, and I'll come down to the lobby."

There went my nap. If Mark and I were going to talk about the case with Deidre over dinner, we'd need privacy. I rang down to the lobby and booked the private dining room. I was lucky the room was free, as someone had just cancelled.

"How many are you expecting, Ms. Barclay?"

I'd feel a fool saying "three" so I said "six.""

After I finished the call, I thought about the dinner. Maybe I could make it six. I'd invite Eseld, and Bran if he'd been discharged… and Masie. I rang the police station and got through to her. "If I give you supper, would you like to come to The Fleece? I've booked a private room. Mark will be there and my sister who is a barrister."

"Can I talk in front of her? What about confidentiality?"

"Give her a pound to retain her, and she'll keep your confidence because then you'll be her client."

Maisie laughed. "I could do with a good mulling over. I'm not happy with our friend Shirley and her mother."

"See you about six."

I wondered about her choice of culprits. She was worried about Shirley and Lydia, not Bob. I texted Mark the plans for dinner. I got another happy face. That made four for dinner. Bran had to remain the hospital for another night, but Eseld sounded pleased to be asked.

"I'm that curious," she'd told me on the phone. "I wonder if our Maisie has anything to tell us."

"I've no idea." I hoped she had information because I was not happy with Bob or someone else getting away with murdering Richie. I know it isn't always possible to charge someone even when you strongly suspect them. The courts want evidence. I agree with the principle of conviction on evidence, but it's frustrating.

I pre-ordered a bottle of Canaletto Montepulciano d'Abruzzo and another of Côtes-du-Rhône, Villages La Ruchette Doree as well as the focaccia, olives and the little pork pies which should assuage hunger while my guests made their choices. Deidre texted when she was in the lobby, and I scooted down to meet her.

"Tea in my room?" I asked.

"Sounds good."

"I can get you crumpets, tea cakes or cake of the day which today is carrot cake." I'd looked at that menu when I ordered dinner.

"You make the tea," she said and entered my room, heading for the bathroom. "Order me crumpets and carrot cake." Her voice was muffled by the closed door, but I heard her. I rang room service and started the tea.

"Will Yorkshire tea do you?" I called to her. She opened the door and smiled at me.

"Sounds lovely."

I returned her smile. She was a dear—sometimes annoying, sometimes dictatorial but always loving. I was lucky. We could have been distant as she was nine years younger and we had led different lives, but we'd had a loving mother and she taught us how to care for one another. I appreciated Deirdre. I sometimes had to remind myself of that because she could be irritating.

"So tell me about this latest murder." She accepted her tea and sipped. Her face smoothed and she sighed. "Blissful. I needed that."

Room service arrived. I signed for the delivery and set out two lots of crumpets and cake. Deirdre might eat it all if she was hungry. No doubt she had existed on tea all day.

I told her about Richie's murder, Anna's discoveries, the still, Bob and the Nazis, the thwarted terrorist plot, and my frustrations with the absence of justice for Richie.

By the time I finished talking, the crumpets and cake were crumbs and it was almost time to meet for dinner.

Deirdre hadn't spoken while I was talking, just nodded and made the usual encouraging comments.

"What do you think?" I prodded.

"I'm thinking," she said "It's a lot to process. Do I take it that you're satisfied that Bob is getting his just desserts?"

I nodded.

"And Shirey is getting dinged for tax evasion?"

"I'm less happy with that because I think she's been a victim of Bob's and," I reflected, "a victim of her overbearing mother."

"Nothing you can do about her mother or Bob. And, if she didn't pay tax on that illicit cognac, she'll get no relief or understanding from the tax department. It's ruthless. So, nothing you can do there."

"I suppose."

"So the basic problem is: no one is going to take the blame for Richie's death."

"That's it. It's as though he didn't matter. I know he wasn't a likable character."

"Not respectable, you mean?"

"That too."

"Doesn't matter. Everyone's equal before the law and all that. At least, that's the theory."

Mark arrived. "Hi, Diedre. How are you?"

"Frustrated with a clueless witness. I've wasted a day, but it's improving if I can visit with you two." She gave Mark a quick hug and stood. "I'll use the bathroom to freshen up and make myself a little less business-like."

Occasionally, Deidre was tactful. I saw her back as she left us. She was wearing a black trouser suit. Beautifully cut to flatter her ample figure. I wondered what she could do to make it 'less business-like'.

Mark smiled, then reached for me and kissed me. Nice that.

I grabbed a soft blue shirt and white capris and changed while I talked to him.

"Tell me about the trafficking case."

"We intercepted the delivery of a truck-load of men, women and teens at Wright's yard. We had Buchanon under surveillance and picked him up at the same time. None of the workers had papers, poor sods."

We stared at each other. Nothing had changed since the last time he'd intercepted the trafficking except he understood the way it was done now. The migrants were going to be sent back to their home country or transported to a country where they needed low-paid-workers—the solution offered by the current government—as if they were animals like work horses. It was inhumane.

"I will check into what happens to them. Maybe, if the powers-that-be know the police are interested, they might come up with a better solution."

I didn't hold much hope out for that; I don't suppose Mark did either.

Deidre returned. I found my Lucia, gold-strapped wedge-heeled sandals and was ready. Mark took a moment to wash his face, hang his jacket on a chair and change to a causal open-necked shirt. Deidre had created a dressy outfit with the addition of a dramatic black, red and white scarf which she'd arranged with artistic skill in a soft drape around her neck. She looked elegant.

We entered the private dining room at five fifty-eight. Eseld was already there. I introduced her to Deidre, then moved to sit beside her.

"How's Bran?"

"Fair to middlin' but stable and perfectly fit to come home. The doctor just wanted one more night to be sure his heart didn't act up. I don't think it will," she said with the conviction of forty years of nursing behind her.

"That's a relief.

"It is that," she said and patted my hand.

Maisie arrived, still in uniform. I introduced her to Deidre.

"Are you the lass I'm to pay a pound to?"

Deirdre shot me an inquiring look. I nodded. She understood.

"I'd be happy to represent you, Sergeant," she said and held out her hand.

Maisie smiled and fished in her pockets for as spare pound. She passed the coin to Deidre who slipped it into her clutch purse. Deidre must have had that in her briefcase because I hadn't seen it when she arrived. It was another gorgeous accessory: Black leather with red and white leather accents. I admired her effortless elegance. I only managed that with shoes.

I herded everyone to the table. The waiters came with the starters and wine I'd ordered. In five minutes, everyone was eating and drinking.

I'd passed around the menus and discussed our choices. People would probably pay for their own main course but, if they didn't, I could easily do it thanks to my generous step-father and his legacy. I could likely pay for a meal like this every day of the year. I wouldn't because that would not be a good use of money, but I could. That gave me a sense that paying for such a meal a few times a year was positively frugal.

Mark ordered the eight-ounce filet and Maisie ordered the eight-ounce sirloin. I wondered if law defenders would all choose steak but Deirdre chose sweet-potato gnocchi. Eseld opted for the chicken with butterbeans and I asked for the hake with samphire, mussels and nori butter sauce. I poured more wine.

We chatted about the weather, the town of Cirencester and other inconsequential subjects. The waiter served our main courses and left us. We started to eat and silence prevailed until we had all managed about half of our meal.

"So, Sergeant," Mark said. "What do you have?"

We waited. This is why were gathered. What did Maisie know, and what could we do?

CHAPTER TWENTY-TWO

Maisie blew on her tea, then sipped before setting it down. It was as though she was setting her thoughts in order before talking to us.

"We have some charges moving along in an orderly fashion: the assault on Claire and the terrorist plot, but I can't see how we can prove who murdered Richie Stonehouse."

We waited.

"We have evidence of illegal drugs, including fentanyl in the van Bob used for deliveries. I expect Lydia was supplying Bob with the product, but I can't prove that either at the moment, and Bob's not talking. He expects Lydia to pay for the expensive barrister he asked for, so he needs to keep his mouth shut."

"Do you think Shirley knew about the drugs?" I asked.

Maisie took her time but finally answered. "She may have. But her mother has tried to protect her from knowing about her business Shirley's whole life. I don't think she'd tell her."

"Shirley's not stupid. She may have figured it out," I said.

"Possibly." Maisie agreed. "I can see Richie finding out because he helped load the van. He may have tried to blackmail Bob. I doubt he'd try that if he knew Lydia was the supplier. He grew up in The Dells. He wouldn't have crossed Lydia."

"But he wasn't the smartest crook on the street," Mark said.

"True. Still, he had cunning. He'd have avoided Lydia if he'd known about her."

"If he tried to blackmail Bob and Bob reported to Lydia, then it might be Lydia who ordered Richie's death." I said.

"Any other evidence on that homicide?" Mark asked.

Maisie smiled. "Yes, It just came in. A woman in the adjacent house was up late with her fractious babe and saw Bob loading Richie into the front seat of the van. She knew them both, having seen them coming and going in the yard many times. She thought Richie was drunk and didn't realize he might be dead until she read the local paper this week."

"That would have shaken her," Eseld commented.

"Hysterical," Maisie agreed. "Said she was going to pack up her daughter and go to Oxford to her mother's until the murder was solved. Might be a long stay. But I got her evidence down and recorded."

We all brightened at the thought of that evidence.

"You have that evidence secured?" Mark knew how often a case fell apart because the evidence had been lost.

"Nice and tight. She came in, gave a statement and identified Bob in a line-up. It's in the safe and all ready for court."

"Congratulations." Mark smiled at her.

"Best thing so far," Maisie answered.

"Could you persuade Bob that Lydia is going to abandon him?" I spoke slowly, thinking as I was speaking. "You could suggest she's not going to supply a lawyer because he's not a good-enough partner for her precious daughter. Maybe then he'd give more evidence."

"You know, lover," Eseld said. "That is a very good suggestion. No doubt that's something a controlling woman would do, and I bet her son-in-law knows it."

"Be careful," Deidre said. "You don't want the evidence thrown out because you deliberately gave him erroneous information."

"Oh, I won't lie to him," Masie assured her. "But it's a good idea, and I'll try it." She leaned forward. "We also have some samples our pathologist picked up: cat hair on Richie. No cat hair at his house. What do you make of that?"

We were quiet, considering it.

Mark spoke. "See if you can get car hair from Bob's clothes or Shirley's. There's no cat at the hotel, is there?" He looked at me.

"No. No cat" I said.

"See if Lydia's house has one," he continued. "When we were examining the cellar, Anna told me she could distinguish which cat an individual hair came from. If the cat hair on Richie is from Lydia's cat, that would be a connection."

"It wouldn't be conclusive evidence," Deidre said , "but it might add some weight."

"The trouble is, 'Maisie said, "even if I get a confession from Bob that Lydia ordered the killing, she will just deny it, and I won't be able to charge her."

"You definitely don't have enough to charge her right now," Diedre agreed.

We sat in silence for a few moments, then gathered our bags and left the restaurant. I put Eseld in a taxi and hugged Deidre, promising to see her soon. Then I joined Maisie and Mark on the pavement.

"We'll walk you to the station," Mark said "I could use a walk. Coming, Claire?"

A walk sounded good. I missed my walks with Gulliver. It was a fine night. Darkness was just starting to settle and the air felt slightly cool. Even though Cirencester is a market town, the nights were usually quiet without many vehicles and only a few people on the street. The amber glow from the stained-glass windows of St. John Baptist Church spilled over the roofs of the buildings beside it, leaving our side of the street in shadow.

A man coming toward us suddenly ran into an alley. Mark and Maisie were after him without even pausing to consult. It must be a Pavlovian response of trained police officers—someone running must be up to no good, and they needed to find out if that was the case. I could think of many reasons why a man would dart into an alley, none of them nefarious: he'd just remembered he was supposed to be somewhere; he'd got a text that his wife was in labour; or he was going to be sick and would rather do that in the alley than the high street.

I walked slowly entertained by my own imaginings. Why did I care so much about justice for Richie? *Because it's heartless to waste the life of a young man,* I answered myself. That might be why. It was tough to be young. I remembered how hard it was for me to find a job and support myself at seventeen. Life could be overwhelming. Often kids that age don't have the money, talent or judgement to deal with the choice they face. It would have mattered to me if someone had helped me. Richie was beyond my help now, but if we could find out who killed him, maybe they'd be stopped from repeating that violence with another young person. *Not likely, Claire. Maisie has tried.* The killer was probably one of that repellent trio of Shirley, Bob and Lydia, but they were well-protected by sharp lawyers. I approached the Queen Bess which was near the alley Mark and Maisie had disappeared into. I suppose they might have thought someone darting into that alley was connected to the problems there. The hotel was dark. There were no guests and Bob and Shirley were at the station. I was just at the alley entrance when I saw a woman tripping down the front steps of the Queen Bess..

"Lydia," I said and stopped.

It was Lydia Harris in her respectable matron disguise: long skirt, boots, tailored shirt, light sweater. "Who is that? Oh Claire. What are you doing here?" She spoke sharply but with her home country accent. It was as false as she was. She was playing the part of a respectable woman—a role she had no right to.

"It is Claire," I said. "how is Shirley?"

"She's in a filthy jail. It's a scandal. She's an innocent. She knows nothing. Nothing! I won't have it."

What was it Shirley didn't know? I was angry—furiously, wildly angry. Lydia had caused so much heartache with her drug business and her need to control everyone. What as she doing at the hotel this late? She was responsible for Richie's death; I was sure of it.

I didn't think. I just opened my mouth and ranted at her. "What were you doing in the hotel? Covering up evidence linking you to Richie's death? Picking up the knife you used? Or had your minions use? Spraying bleach everywhere to kill microbes to get rid of any trace you left?"

She stopped, stared at me and laughed. "What a good guess. How did you know?" She looked up and down the street. There was no one. Mark and Maisie were chasing someone in the alley and not in sight. She laughed again.

"You can tell me how you knew it was me. I will deny we had this conversation, so don't hold back."

"You're not that smart, Lydia. You left a trail behind you."

Her face changed. Her eyes narrowed, and her mouth thinned to a grim line. She grabbed my arm. "Hey, you foolish wench. What did I leave behind, hey? I be got the knife. What else is there? Tell me! Tell me!"

She shook my arm. I said nothing.

"You don't know nothin'" Her Gloucester accent rose as her temper rose. The society matron disappeared. This Lydia Harris was explosive.

I stood perfectly still. Now, she was angry; she was a murderer and she had a knife. She'd just told me that. *Think, Claire. Rein in your temper and think!*

"Everyone leaves some trace of themselves wherever they go. It's the principle of forensic science."

She shook my arm then stepped back. I breathed again.

"Is that all you got? They'll ne'er find enough to nail me."

"So you did it yourself? It wasn't Shirley?" I hadn't thought of *she'd* do it. Even Maisie hadn't thought of that.

She straightened and settled her shoulders. "Of course it wasn't Shirley. She could ne'er do it, not her, but I could. I don't so much these days, but the little prick got up my nose, so I ran him down at the hotel and killed him myself." She glared at me. "I haven't lost my skill. Now *you* don't have to worry, your posh head. There's no one to hear and you are married to a copper. I'm not stupid. To tell you true, I'm as mild as a hornet, but I won't kill you unless you nettle me more. I might order it done, but I won't dirty me hands. No, I am retired from that now."

"Except for Richie."

"Yes. Except for that dinio." Her accent had slipped from posh to local so quickly I felt as if I was talking to two different women. This one was rough and dangerous.

"That was cruel. He was just young and thoughtless. He didn't need to die."

"Ark at 'er!" Lydia said with great derision. "What do you know about running a business. Me, I'm gurt lush. In charge. I run a *big* business. Cross me and you're gone. For damn sure, you'd be jud if I wanted you jud."

I remembered Dylan using that word. It meant dead. I took a slow even breath. I needed to handle her carefully. Where were Mark and Maisie? They could be close by or a mile away.

Lydia wasn't finished with me. "You with your pitiful little tour business. You wouldn't understand the way a real business woman has to operate."

"You were making an example of him?" I was younger. Maybe I was faster. I could run. But she might throw a knife. She was probably good at it. If I kept her talking would Mark and Maisie have time to return?

"Of course. To be fair, the poor dinio didn't know I was supplying Bob, but he could have guessed. Terminally stupid, you know."

"And so you killed him." Behind her I could see Mark and behind him Maisie. They were close. I felt my shoulders relax, then

I stiffened. She was still dangerous. "With that same knife you're carrying?" Mark needed to know she was armed.

"Indeed. It was quite easy." Her accent had returned to her society matron role. It was disconcerting. Was she any less dangerous in this mode?

I saw Mark put his phone in his pocket, then, in a synchronized movement with Masie, he pounced. Mark grabbed Lydia's right arm and Maisie grabbed her left. In seconds, Lydia was clamped in constabulary arms. She struggled, kicking out with her feet, and shoving against Masie but that solid experienced officer stood like an oak, and Lydia finally gave up. She stared at me.

"You trapped me."

I shook my head.

She turned her head to Masie. "You set this up to trap me."

"You give me too much credit. I never thought of it. But it was brilliant. It was a treat to listen to you. Perhaps you don't think so," Masie said politely.

Mark spoke to her. "We've been here some time Mrs. Harris. You made the mistake of thinking Claire was alone. She wasn't. We enjoyed your conversation."

"Get your paws off me. Sod off! I can ruin you."

"Are you threatening me, madam?" Mark said.

"I'll deny it. I'll deny everything."

"Three witnesses and a recording. I don't believe you'll get out of this one." Mark smiled.

"Nice to finally have you at my place," Maisie said. "I've been hoping to offer you the hospitality of the nick for some time. We were on our way there. You can just come along quietly."

"Sod off! Why should I?"

"Because otherwise I'll call the police support unit and you'll get the full treatment with tasers and guns. Lots of drama. The press follows those units."

Lydia thought it over and began walking.

"I want my solicitor."

"You can call him or her in the morning."

"You're not getting bail, you know," Mark said. "You'll stay incarcerated as we heard you threaten Ms. Barclay so you are a public menace according to the law."

Lydia opened her mouth and then shut it with a snap. She never said another word all the way to the station.

I collapsed on a chair in the entry way while Mark and Maise buzzed past the plexiglass barrier and disappeared into the inner offices of the station.

Mark returned in about fifteen minutes.

"Maisie can handle it from here. " He grinned. "Finally! Maisie's over the moon." He hugged me "Good job, Claire. You kept her talking until she told you everything we needed to get her. How did you know we were there?"

"I didn't."

We were walking toward The Fleece by now and I had answered him in a low voice. He stopped, turned and took me by the shoulders. "You didn't know we were there and you baited her?"

I bit my lip and looked away. "I was angry."

"Christ Almighty!" He sounded as though he was praying. "Claire." I could see him swallow. "You didn't know we were there." He gathered me in and hugged me. "Ah, *bach*. You were having a temper tantrum with a cobra. She wouldn't care about you. She'd knife you just because you were arguing with her."

I realized that now. I snuggled against him and felt safe. I don't know why, but it was only then that I started to shake.

"Lets get you home." Mark hustled me down the street and up to our room.

"Bath," he commanded. "Now. A hot one. Got any bath salts?"

I pointed to the shelf.

He ran the water, poured in the salts, put the towel on a chair and undressed me.

"I can get in the bath by myself," I said.

"I'll make tea and lace it with brandy. Don't be long."

I had the bath, the tea and dropped into bed beside Mark getting as close as I could. The shaking had stopped, but I felt wooden.

"She's not getting out," Mark assured me quietly. "She won't be able to go after you or send anyone. She didn't trust anyone but herself, so she doesn't have a second in command. The gang will be splitting as fast as they can."

"They'll just go looking for another boss."

"Yes, but likely not here, and they won't care about Lydia."

I finally relaxed.

I headed home but Mark stayed another night to assist Maisie with tabulating her evidence. He called me mid-morning to tell me that Maisie got a no-bail order on Lydia because she had threatened to kill me. It was enough grounds to keep her in jail while the charges were issued and the conditions of her bail negotiated. I didn't need to look over my shoulder for Lydia or her minions.

CHAPTER TWENTY-THREE

I drove on to the village of Ashton-on-Tinch and to my home. The random flint in the limestone mortar glinted in the sun. The corners and window surrounds of brick gave a solid permanency to the house. It was symmetrical, as the Stonning's residence attached to the central wall was a reversal of mine, creating a balanced, gracious appearance. We had each painted our doors deep red, so the whole was pleasing. I hadn't owned it long, but I wanted to stay forever. I fitted the key into the lock; Gulliver announced me before I could open the door. He bounced into my arms. I dropped my rucksack and a package I was carrying and held him close.

"Hello, my sweetie. Did you miss me?" Of course he missed me. His whole body quivered with the excitement of reunion. Cavalier King Charles spaniels have a reputation for being regal and aloof. Gulliver wasn't having any of that. He was blatantly rapturous that I was home. I sat on the floor and talked to him.

"I'm here. It's okay. You were fine. I missed you, too." Dog owners are besotted. That's fine with me.

I heard movement in the back of the house. I stood, shoved my rucksack under the foyer table, left my jacket in the hall closet and moved to the kitchen.

Lionel was sitting at the table near the window with a cup of coffee in front of him. His face had some color and his eye were bright. I admired his wavy hair, still abundant, and white as a gull's wing. I hoped Mark had that hair-preserving gene.

"Aright, me lover?" he said.

"Yes," I answered him. "Everything is fine. How are you making out?"

I was so glad to see him bright and apparently healthy that I walked over and kissed his cheek—something I'd never done before. A little embarrassed, I crossed over to the hob and saw that there was a cup left in the coffee carafe. I poured some into a mug and sat at the table to visit with him.

"I'm in pretty good nick," he said. "Not cakey, anyhow."

Not confused, he meant.

"That's good. Did you hear from Mark?"

"I did that, lass. He reported like a good noy, telling me he copped that dobeck who brained me."

Noy that was nephew. *Dobeck*, stupid one. I wasn't sure I was good for much more Cornish.

"Lots has gone one. I'll fill you in on some. Mark will give you're the rest."

"That bright doctor from America picked up some cell samples from my head. Did she match them with Bob?"

I noticed his Cornish slipped into my kind of English when he talked about anything to do with policing.

"I expect she tried. She doesn't miss much."

"Aye, well, they'll get that chummy for attacking *you*, that's a certain thing."

"I believe so," I agreed. "Have Rose and Mark been taking care of you? You're looking a lot better."

"They have, lass. They're good people, but I'm well enough to go home now. I've been talking to my mates from Truro, and they're going to load me up with my bits and bobs and trundle me down to St. Mawes in the morning. I won't be driving yet. I might give that up altogether." He paused, then continued. "I can take my time about making that decision."

"Yes, settle in. See how you are. Then decide. You get good taxi service there, don't you?"

"Aye. It's not the getting around that's a problem, it's more the feeling of being independent that I might have to give up. I haven't been driving at night or long distances for some time now, but it's a big step from that to not driving at all. I'm a practical man, and it's surprised me how gawky I am about this."

"You'll make the right decision." I sympathized. I'd find it hard to give up my licence.

"I'll make it dreckly," he agreed, and we both laughed.

Dreckly meant at some vague time in the future.

"That superintendent of Mark's…" he said.

"Addison?"

"That's the one. She wants you to come by the station and sign your statement."

I had planned to do that. "With any luck, she'll be in Alton still, and I can get my statement from the constable."

"Might be a good idea to do it soon," Lionel said. "Keep her sweet."

I snorted. "Not possible."

Lionel smiled. It was lovely to see the light in his eyes. I hadn't realized how much I cared for him until I thought we'd lose him.

I enjoyed the walk to the station. Late daffodils still covered the ground beneath the trees, and the slight breeze tossed them in yellow bunches. It was if they were demanding my attention. I noticed lilacs in front of the bank were in full purple splendor. I'd have to check to see if the white ones Peter Brown had planted in my garden had blooms yet. The scent would be wonderful..

When I arrived at the station I found my luck was out; Addison was in.

"About time," she said as I walked into the station. I'd brought Gulliver with me and stopped to wipe his muddy paws before following Superintendent Addison past the plexiglass protective barrier and into an office.

She left me there while she went to a different office to pick up my statement. I watched her as she strode away from me. Competent, quick and intelligent. I admired her for what she'd achieved. She was a little older than I was, perhaps early fifties with dark hair, deep brown eyes and a trim figure. It wouldn't have been easy for her to achieve the rank of superintendent, particularly in her early years when prejudice against women, particularly handsome women, was rampant. From Mark's account, she was efficient, careful and accountable which made her a good boss. I didn't, however, like her.

She was meticulously dressed in her dark serge uniform suit, a trouser suit. No skirts for our Marjorie. Her black and white chequered tie was pristine, her suit without a bit of lint on it and her black oxfords polished until they glinted. She'd left her hat on the desk and the chequered band was also sparkling white and black. I leaned in to get a good look at the badge on the cap which was silver and black but had to abruptly straighten as she returned.

"Solving cases again?" she remarked, referring to the papers she set in front of me.

I shrugged and only said mildly. "I didn't solve this one."

"That's not what I hear. They're singing your praises from Penzance to London."

I shook my head. "I'm a tour guide."

"A rich tour guide."

Ah, here was the source of her antipathy towards me. She didn't like people with money.

"That's right," I said and was silent while I read the statement and signed my name. I looked up. "It is not a criminal offence to be rich."

She signed the statement after me as a witness. I could tell she wanted to say more but bit her lip and refrained.

Good. I didn't want to hear her opinion of me.

I walked home, feeling as if the problems of the Cotswolds were now behind me. I'd reported everything about Bob's attack on me and registered it with the constabulary in my statement. Done and dusted.

I saw Mark's car parked behind my van. Gulliver was already wiggling in anticipation of greeting him when I opened the front door.

Mark stood in the kitchen doorway as Gulliver launched himself toward him. He bent down, scooped him up in his arms, petted and praised Gulliver. Then he kissed me. "How'd it go with Addison?" he asked.

I shrugged. "She doesn't change much. Where's Lionel?"

"He's having a nap."

I was immediately concerned. "Is he okay?

"I think it's more he wanted to give us privacy than he was tired," Mark said.

"Oh." I was relieved. "How did it go in Cirencester?"

"It went a treat. Lydia will stay in jail until her lawyer deals with the crown prosecutor to arrange supervision and controls on her movements and behaviours. Maisie has Lydia's computer containing the names and addresses of her employees and is working with the Drug Action Team to round up the key players. They've made a couple of quick arrests and that should disperse the others out and away from Cirencester.

"Lydia made it easier for us to break up her organization than usual. Since she didn't trust anyone, all the authority rested with her. When she's out of commission, no one knows how to run the drug business. Maisie's is a happy sergeant."

"What about Bob?"

"Maisie leaned on Bob telling him that Lydia was in such trouble herself there would be no money for *his* lawyer. Scared him pale. Bob must know Lydia will save herself first and likely never give him a thought. We didn't get much out of him on Richie Stonehouse's murder. Bob says he didn't do it but wouldn't say who did. He admitted to moving the body."

The charges of illegally moving a body, assaulting Bran and me and the one for distributing drugs should keep him in jail for some time. The terrorist charge would extend his stay a long time.

"And Shirley?"

"Shirley is out on bail and can continue to run the hotel, although she can't use the hidden room behind the cellar."

Her mother must have hired a solicitor before she herself was picked up. Shirley would be protected as far as money could shelter her. I wondered if her mother would finance a bakery for Shirley from jail, or just use the money to try to keep herself out of jail. I didn't think money would be able to clear her of murder when she confessed to it, albeit in a fit of rage, but in front of two police officers. The Crown would probably appropriate Lydia's assets after a guilty verdict. There might not be any money left.

"As far as Shirley's future goes, the tax department is relentless, and they are after her for tax evasion. There is a lot of tax on alcohol, and she didn't pay any."

"The law is after her for tax evasion but not complacency in a murder?"

"We can prove tax evasion."

Shirley must have known her mother was responsible for Richie Stonehouse's death. She wasn't stupid. If she knew and did nothing about it, she was complicit. I was angry. "May the tax department land on her like an enraged elephant."

"Amen to that. Dr. White was in the cellar again replicating some of Dr. Clark's work. She seems to have enjoyed poking around, taking samples. If she can find evidence linking Shirley to Richie, she'll give it to us: Richie's hair on Shirley's clothes or on one of Shirley's knives. Lionel's too. She's checking out cat hair that they found on Richie's clothes, Bobs' clothes and traced it to

Lydia's cat. Not conclusive, but interesting. Dr. White's putting in extra time—her own time; she's not being paid—because Anna is interested and Dr. White is happy to work with her. She had nothing but praise for your Dr. Anna Clark."

"I suppose they rarely find a female colleague." Anna, also, had enjoyed her consultation with Dr. White. I switched the subject. "Lionel tells me he is leaving us tomorrow."

"I talked to his doctor," Mark said, "not that he can tell me much. Patient privacy and all that. I did tell him the plan for Lionel, and he didn't object, so I guess it will go ahead. A couple of the Cornwall coppers are coming tomorrow to help Lionel pack and take him home. One of them is going to stay with him overnight and make sure he can manage."

"That sounds reasonable," I said.

"A relief, really. I'd feel guilty if I left him on his own." Mark stood and rummaged around in the fridge. "Rose left us a stew. I'll heat it."

"Go ahead." I stayed where I was and relished the pampering. Mark poured me a cabernet sauvignon and one for himself and put the cast iron pot on the hob.

"Tell me about Shirley," I said. "Was she upset?"

"Didn't seem to be. She was cool, uninterested in Bob's problems but capable around her own. Her mother's solicitor applied for bail; that's why she's out."

She was going to be found guilty but probably wouldn't get a prison sentence. It would be hard for her to deny the brandy operations once forensic accounting investigated her. "She wanted to open her own bakery."

"A laudable goal, but her means to getting there were dubious and bound to fail."

"Bob is in jail now so perhaps she'll get her bakery when she doesn't have to support him." I felt as if she didn't *deserve* to achieve her dream. Richie never got to achieve his, whatever they were. "And Bob won't likely implicate Shirley in any of it or report her threatening him with a knife." What an uncomfortable marriage they must have had. So many secrets, self-interest and a mother who was a drug baron and who had no compunction about killing people who were in her way. With both Bob and her mother incarcerated, maybe Shirley had a chance to be a normal productive adult. Maybe it was too late. She had reached for a knife when she wanted to stop Bob. Most people don't do that.

"It turns out Bob can't remember the incident. Can't remember threatening you either. So he won't turn evidence."

"*Truly* can't remember?"

"Truly can't remember."

I thought about it. "He can't remember because you clocked him one."

People who have been concussed often can't remember the events just before the blow or just after. Bob probably *couldn't* remember.

"That's right. I didn't win anywhere on this one".

I disagreed. "I'm still alive."

He stared at me. "Well, that's a positive." Then he leaned down and kissed me.

Lionel came down for dinner and we discussed his plans.

"I'm that anxious to get home. Not that I don't appreciate you taking me in, me *noy*," he said to Mark, "but my garden will need tidying, and I need to get back to my darts club before my pub mates find a better player."

That sounded healthy to me. I hoped he'd manage it.

Mark had to work the next day and then had two days off. I was free of tourists until June.

"Shall we go somewhere?" I said. "A small trip?"

"We could go to Cornwall. Drop in on you, Lionel, to see if you need groceries or anything at all and then drive on," Mark said.

"A B & B near the sea?" I suggested.

"One that will take Gulliver and close to walking trails."

Mark liked walking by the sea. He said it helped him think.

The next morning, after Lionel's friends picked him up and we had packed him off with his medications, a few groceries and some of my special coffee, we retired to my study and had fun checking the B & Bs on line, finding exactly what we wanted with a beach nearby and fields where Gulliver could run

"We could take our bicycles, put Gulliver in my basket," I said, "and explore the countryside, eat at wayside pubs."

"A mini holiday," Mark said. "No murders. No traffickers. No Superintendents."

I grinned. "Just like normal people."

So that's what we did.

ABOUT THE AUTHOR

© Duke Morse

Emma Dakin lives in Gibsons on the Sunshine Coast of British Columbia. She writes fiction—traditional, *The British Book Tour Mysteries,* and historical mysteries, *Murder in Vancouver – 1886,*—and non-fiction. Her memoir *Always Pack a Candle: A Nurse in the Cariboo-Chilcotin* received the Lieutenant Governor's Community History Award. But she keeps returning to her favorite genre, traditional mysteries. She travels to Britain to villages, towns and cities she features in her books, meets people who live there and eats in the elegant restaurants—all in the name of research. Her love of the British countryside and villages and her addiction to reading traditional mysteries keep her writing about characters who live and work in those villages. She enjoys those characters and trusts you will as well.

Printed in the USA
CPSIA information can be obtained
at www.ICGtesting.com
LVHW031856060924
790342LV00016B/393